Larret Army

Larret Army

Rising Souls

Written by **Kenneth Shumaker**

With Inevitable Unicorn Press

Larret Army

ISBN: 978-1-988327-25-9

© 2018 by Kenneth Shumaker with

Inevitable Unicorn Press

Kenneth Shumaker

at

Rusty's Den

Box 3323

High Prairie, Alberta, Canada

T0G 1E0

www.kennethshumaker.ca

ken@inupress.ca

www.inupress.ca

inupress@inupress.ca

Larret Army

For my dearest forgiving soulmate, my wife, Donna.

Larret Army

Contents

Larret Army

We acknowledge the following for their contributions to this book:

Donna Shumaker, for developmental and copy-editing of the manuscript, and giving her two nickels worth.

Eric J Kregel, for beta-reading the revised first draft, as well as second edition draft and for giving awesome feedback.

InUPress, for the time and production in the content evaluation and for formatting the manuscript into a book.

Larret Army

Larret Army

Prologue: Tearmain's Visit

Winter 21 Pine

Outside Selenad's home in Shestan's capital city, the god's breath roars, pounding against the stone structures at over one-hundred kilometres an hour. Nothing shrouds the bright shining sphere's twinkling souls of the night sphere.

Many of his fellow Shes worship the Shestan hero. Tonight, we watch while the hero, Selenad, is praying.

The blood drips from the human's neck as Selenad slices the girl's throat open above an offering bowl to the god

Larret Army

Tearmain. The girl gurgles in pain, choking on her own waterfall of diminishing life. Selenad smiles, baring his teeth as the woman struggles. We scream as well, watching the final cut – the thirty-ninth cut – to her body. The Jalfem is young, seventeen human years old, and physically fit. She was kept as one of Selenad's domestic slaves – well fed and on light work duty to prevent injury and to be sure that she wasn't hungry.

We see the light go out in her eyes, and then Selenad chants the words that bring the new god to him.

. . . . .

Tearmain stands beside the Shes hero. They enjoy eating the raw meat while feasting on the dead Jalfem. Tearmain prefers the thighs. To our disgust, the two diners take their time savouring the feast.

Selenad slaps the wrist of the slave who is reaching to fill Selenad's mug. He says to the slave, "Leave it be. Get out of here now. All of you get out!"

We view the mad scurry of ten slaves rushing to leave the lavish living quarters. Rich scenic tapestries hang on every wall and on the floor are rugs woven from human hair, dyed in violent patterns that Selenad finds pleasing.

Larret Army

When only Tearmain and Selenad remain, Selenad casts a ward against eavesdropping so that no one outside the room can hear what is being said in the chamber. Though, we are inside.

Tearmain places the stripped clean thighbone on the table. He then rinses his hands and face in the warm water of the washbasin, before drying off with a large plush wool towel.

The two settle back into their lounge seats and Tearmain says, "I have a plan. I will reveal my plan to your council on my next visit. You must be prepared to be a leader of the Shes. No hesitation, Selenad."

Selenad laughs, waving off the comment. Replying confidently, he says, "I already lead one-hundred warriors, seventy thieves, twenty giants and giant-kin. What else do you want me to command?" We know he's not prepared for Tearmain's plans.

Tearmain chortles long notes. Calming, he says, "Be in the Council chamber on Spring 5, Bear. I'll let you know then, along with the council. At that time, I will present my commands to you and Shestan."

Observing the two as they continue their social evening and into the morning, slowly devouring the sacrificed slave until all that remains are her bones and hair, we fear significantly for humankind.

Larret Army

With the rise of Stonewire and Imvor on Winter 22 Pine, Tearmain leaves Selenad's home. Selenad spends three hours sleeping before going to the combat challenge ring and competing in six challenges. He kills twelve combatants before becoming bored and retiring to his home again, where he accompanies three of his life-companions for a bit of rough dallying. We feel the pain of the females, but we cannot ease their situation.

Spring 5 Bear

The winter was harsh in Shestan; many clans lost Shes members and slaves to starvation. Many clans ate their own slaves to survive. Yet, here in the Council Chambers, Selenad is fit and healthy – in prime condition. His stable of slaves still overflows, and he has far fewer challengers among the Shes elite now. As those who challenged Selenad began to weaken, we watched him eliminate them.

The council consists of thirteen of the strongest, fiercest, most intelligent, and wisest Shes in Shestan society. These are necessary qualities to survive the demands of being part of the ruling council and internal splinters for superiority, often resulting in death combats. Every one of them bears battle scars.

Larret Army

However, Selenad has the least scars and is the healthiest in appearance. Selenad possesses the wealthiest clan holding, mainly due to his terrifying tactics as an overlord of society. Every leader shows Selenad respect, even though they may not show every other member of council respect. Too many have seen Selenad's combat prowess, and we are all witness to his continual growing powers.

Selenad is no longer a mere local figure or a state hero. Shes, throughout the country, worship him like a god, and the bastard revels in it, flaunting the attention every second that he can. We see his aura growing stronger and brighter every day.

Selenad peers around the table, and he flippantly says, "I think we should bring the god Tearmain here to liven things up. You're a deadbeat bunch … past your time."

Knowing Tearmain was waiting for a cue, he, who is human in appearance, appears sitting beside Selenad.

There are no Alaran humans on the Shestan council. Under no circumstances are humans of any kind allowed in council's chambers. The other twelve council members rise to their feet, drawing their weapons – all except for Selenad.

Tearmain rises to his feet and draws his longsword, smiling. He asks in perfect high society Shes dialect, "Okay, games first. Who dares to challenge me first?"

Larret Army

Two younger Shestan rush Tearmain, expertly feinting and attacking.

Tearmain quickly decapitates the first Shestan attacker, and then the other.

Looking disappointed, he calls out: "Is there anyone more skilled who is willing to challenge me?"

An old bull Shes marches forward, and with guarded finesse, the old Shes draws blood from Tearmain's sword arm.

Tearmain replies by severing off the Shes' sword arm, and then his opposing leg. Following that, Selanad drives his longsword into the Shes' head before the Shes hits the floor.

Again, looking disappointed, Tearmain asks, "Come on, is that your best?"

Two Shes point to Selenad and motion to him that he should try.

Tearmain and Selenad approach each other and shake hands. Then, with arms wrapped around each other's shoulders, Selenad says, "I'm not going to fight my only friend, now, am I?"

A groan erupts from the remaining nine living Shes, and from us. We knew this was coming; we're feeling sad for the Shes.

Larret Army

Tearmain and Selenad take the head seats and Tearmain says, "Sit down, and we'll get this meeting to order. I'm getting hungry. And with the food on the floor, I may eat before we address the agenda. But, I don't want to do that ... business first."

The survivors sit in their seats, and then Tearmain begins. "I am capturing the Dominnion of Kannoral to rule it. The Shespan will sub-rule the southwest as they help capture that region. You will have the northeast when you capture the area there."

We wince as one of the generals' shout, "How the gods are we getting that done? We have two gyno-sphinxes to pass and two mountain ranges to cross to get there."

Tearmain lifts his sword and says, "The Sphinxes are no concern, and Selenad will form an army and formulate a plan to traverse the mountains to the Web Ocean and capture it quickly."

The same general dares to say, "The army is my property."

Selenad stands and walks around the table as the sweating general stands unsteadily. Both have their weapons. We know what is going to happen, and we are aware that the general already regrets speaking.

Steady, Selenad asks, "Who is the army commander?"

Larret Army

The general bows and says, "General Selenad is."

Looking around to the other eight, Selenad again asks, "Who is the army commander?"

All in unison say, "General Selenad is."

Tearmain asks, "Who rules Shestan?"

There is uneasy dead silence for a minute, and then Selenad says, "General Selenad!"

This is followed by nine voices uttering fearfully, "General Selenad."

Tearmain smiles and says, "Good mice, remember this."

We wince at this new gods' presence as he looks around at us.

Chapter One

*New Beginning
After Death*

Chapter One:

New Beginning after Death

Summer 1 Bear

Larret Hamlet

The ground is still muddy from yesterday's torrential rain. The sphere is clear with its souls twinkling brightly. In the air, dangerous breaths are blowing eastward. The cold air freezes the edges of puddles on the hamlet's barren ground. All of this bodes poorly for the future.

Larret Army

Today, the high breaths and cold air have animals taking shelter. Cattle face east with their asses to buildings. Horses lie down on the east side of any shelter they can find. Sheep huddle patiently together in their compounds. Yes, even the wildlife has taken refuge, delaying daily living for the thousands of free life forms. Waves barely break upon the coarse coast, as the waters fight the hard breaths blowing out towards the ocean's blurred horizon.

Yes, today is bad. Several of us have gathered in Goat's Tavern. The respectful tavern will not decline wayward souls, providing us with shelter and warmth. Old Ringus is happy to earn a few additional dusters from his customers.

Ringus is a retired Cleric of Ikerus, though no one in the hamlet holds that against him. Ringus lost his only son to the ruling Lord's army of our Dominnion. Loyal to King Dolan IV, Ringus became a bit reclusive when his son, Jerrid, joined the King's army.

Cobbler Dentin is busy these days, as he has a few new oxen hides to make boots and shoes. When the news spread that Dentin had new hides, our cobbler was mobbed with orders requesting new boots. He actually took six orders for new boots yesterday, alone. The poor man is in Goat's Tavern resting between work projects and getting ready for the next job. He will be going back to work soon. Dentin drinks his dark ale in slow gulps.

Mason Delan is inside Goat's Tavern, as well, having a drink with Cooper Toorp. Our mature Jalfem, Toorp, is happy to have someone to talk with, as she has been idle without orders for nearly a six-day.

As all sit socializing on this miserable day, our group spots Reeve Jeston's daughter enter the tavern's tireless hall. Tripper, looking dishevelled – very much unlike her – walks in briskly.

Tripper spots G and the rest of us. As Tripper rushes over, we can see she is muddy from the gods-breaths and wet ground.

"G! Father wandered off again. I think it is bad this time. We need to find him; it's not safe out there for him to be going for a walk. Even the animals have enough sense to seek shelter. But NO, Father decides to go for a walk – who knows where. I tell you, his mind is gone, and it took his common sense with it. He might be lost; will you all help me find him?" asks Tripper.

Erin smiles warmly, and piping in rapidly, she says, "It's okay, Tripper. Stonewire looks after the weak-minded. After all, the reeve is old. He is over ninety years as far as we can figure. For two Flairs, I will go out in this demon of a day and try to find Jeston. After all, the village needs its reeve."

Larret Army

Eren, the beautiful farmer who practices mage-craft, flashes her stunning ice-grey eyes as she looks to Tripper and then to her table companions.

Bowyer G lowers her head and shakes it, sullen. Slowly looking up to her other two friends at the table, G doesn't have to ask the two priests her question. Silently, they both know G's question and their own answers; they shake their heads in opposition.

Looking back to Tripper, hesitantly, G answers. "It looks like you have two ready to go with you, Tripper. Unfortunately, the other two we need have decided to stay inside Goat's Tavern, milking the place for all its worth with their coin purses. Eren may want two Flairs, but I will do it because you and Jeston helped me last season when the rainwaters lapped up over my shop's floorboards. The water destroyed all three bows I was working on then. Okay, Eren, do you need anything before we start out on this manhunt?"

Eren smiles greedily, simply answering, "Almost ... two Flairs, please ... from either of you. Stonewire must be watching over you, Tripper, for me to even consider this foolhardy excursion. In simple terms: two Flairs and I am ready to go."

G sighs in exasperation. "I just bought you an ale. Won't that do for now?"

Eren looks at G and asks, "Well?" Eren doesn't move to stand. Her ankle length red wool dress barely reveals any change in Eren's breathing.

G frowns and answers, "Okay Eren. The three of us are going to find the Reeve. You get the coins when we get back." G stands and downs the last of her ale.

Eren still doesn't move from her chair as she looks at the bowyer who is dressed in common blue wool leggings, a light blue tunic, and has a well-used longsword strapped to her left side.

Eren laughs. "No, you pay me now, and then the three of us will rescue old Reeve Jeston once again. We will find him and have the reeve home before evening meal."

Tripper looks like she is becoming upset. "Look, the longer you two talk, the farther Father will have wandered away. Now let's go; you can bicker on the way."

G, looking at Tripper, and then at Eren, sighs. Freeing up her coin pouch, she opens it. Looking into her lightweight coin-pouch, G takes out two Flairs. "There you go – your two Flairs from my dwindling resources. Now come on, Eren."

Eren takes the two coins and places them in her own coin pouch.

Larret Army

Barely waiting for her two helpers, Tripper walks outside into the cold gods-breaths. She wraps her light cloak tightly around herself. Feeling the weight of her hand-axe at her side, Tripper knows it may be of no use to her. Tripper took lessons from the men-at-arms of the village. So far, she has not had to use the weapon. She hopes that she will never have to test her skill of the hand-axe.

Close behind Tripper is Eren the Unwilling. Eren is beautiful with a very deceiving youthful appearance; she looks eighteen, even though she is thirty-five-years-old. The Jalfem has braided waist-length raven-black hair and eyes that sparkle like grey-ice. Considering her age, she still has a strong body. She's a Jalfem that few from the village are willing to encounter.

Most people avoid Eren.

But, if you are in a bind, Eren will usually take up the challenge, for a price. Staying with the confrontation until its conclusion, Eren is just the person you want to have with you in a risky situation.

No one really knows Eren's story. She came to Larret Hamlet ten years ago. She began teaching, whenever she can, for pay. Her policy has been: no pay, no aid, no exception.

However, Eren does look after the ancient Shrine to Stonewire without pay. She goes daily to pray and tend to the shrine's needs. The shrine is located in the centre of Larret's central square and has been around longer than can be determined.

Few attend the shrine, which seems to frustrate Eren.

Eren generally makes her living by farming. She has a five-acre demesne and a herd of ten goats. She has two billies, five nannies, and three kids in her herd. Eren supplies a few villagers with fresh goat milk, as well as her own greatly sought-after goat cheese, in three or five-pound wheels. This year, three acres of her holding is in crops – wheat and flax – and the crops are doing nicely.

The youngest of the three women in this group is Bowyer Gena. Villagers have called this Jalfem, 'G', for as long as they have known her, which is going on five years. Few know that her given name is Gena.

The young Jalfem has always been a scrapper. She is studious in her studies of the village life and of her other interests. G started training almost a year and a half ago with the village men-at-arms, using the longsword which she is most comfortable, swearing it is becoming part of her being.

G doesn't think the gods make a difference in the world, often questioning if the gods even exist. She believes that we each have the power to control our lives and that we are responsible for our actions – good or bad.

Walking quickly towards Reeve House, Tripper smiles as her animal companion rushes excitedly towards her. The boar has followed Tripper around since leaving his sow's side as a weaned piglet. The boar's name is confusing to most; Tripper calls him 'Winey'.

Winey, who is now a three-year-old boar, is silent as he runs rapidly toward Tripper.

Tripper reaches down, scratching Winey's forehead as the boar grunts. Winey moves solemnly beside Tripper to follow her.

A relatively strong gust of gods-breath blows harshly, almost knocking the three women backwards.

The walk to Reeve House is only a few dozen metres from Goat's Tavern. Yet, today, the effort of walking seems to be so much harder than usual, due to the breath blowing angrily against them.

Arriving at Reeve House, Tripper quickly opens the door. Walking into the house, the room looks in disarray, more from a lack of an attempt at neatness than anything else. There are two medium-sized blue pottery plates on the dull pine dining table.

One of the plates still has food on it – scrambled eggs and porridge.

Tripper ignores her two rescuers, leaving them outside. Entering into the main room, she picks up a bag from its dark resting place in the northeast corner of the kitchen area.

Returning to G and Eren, Tripper closes the house door as she exits. Facing G, Tripper inquires with a certain boldness. "Which way, G?"

G looks blankly at Tripper and shakes her head. "Your guess is as good as mine, Tripper. Any good tracks that would have guided us are erased in the rain trodden mud. If I recall correctly, Jeston likes to stand on the beach, watching the waves come in during the day. That might be the best place to start, unless Winey is able to track Jeston?" G says somewhat sarcastically.

Tripper frowns shallowly. "Okay, the beach it is."

They start walking eastward with the breaths, towards Laret Beach with its coarse sand and rocks.

Four searchers walk confidently toward Laret Beach.

Arriving on the rough shore, the three women look uneasily around the beach. The shore bares its shells and debris from the ocean, like badges among the small, bleak, brown rocks, set in the varied browns of sand grains.

Larret Army

G looks to the south. Then, walking cautiously southward, she states, "I recall his favourite spot to watch the waves is just down a little way, on the other side of the rock cliff."

It only takes a couple of minutes to search the area where G indicates. The group doesn't find any sign of Reeve Jeston.

Eren pauses and looks west while addressing Tripper. "Did he say anything when you last talked to him, Tripper? How long has he actually been missing?"

Tripper, now on edge from worry, answers shakily, "Father went to bed a while before I did last night. He really didn't seem to want to talk. I got up this morning and prepared our morning meal. When I went to wake Father, his bed hadn't been slept in last night."

Huddled close together for shelter and warmth, Eren, Tripper, and G ponder the situation for a few minutes longer trying to determine what may have happened to Jeston.

Tripper looks sadly at Winey. "Find Father for us, Winey. Please."

No one really expects Winey to find Jeston.

We are all surprised when Winey starts walking north, towards Harpen River. He walks quickly in search of something.

Everyone comes to a rapid decision and follows the boar.

Larret Army

Arriving at Harpen River, Winey snorts in determination. He tests the air with his snout, and then turns west, moving with rapid steps.

Along with the three villagers, we follow behind the boar as we move along the riverbank.

We continue westward until Winey comes to a stop.

Again, testing the air with determination, Winey squeals and walks into the river, swimming out to a tangle of roots, trees, and rocks.

G, appearing a little worried, follows Winey out to the chaotic tangle. Looking into the aggressive tangle of trees and rocks, G finds a soaked tunic.

The tunic, torn and dirty, is stuck on a large branch projecting out from the jumbled roots and trunks.

G retrieves the frazzled tunic and continues to look among the freezing sodden clutter for anything else.

Not finding anything else of importance, Winey and G start moving up the river, working their way back to the bank.

Reaching the shore, G hands the tunic to Tripper. "Was he wearing this last night when he went to bed?"

Tripper takes the tunic. She looks it over, and then simply nods. Holding onto the soaked and torn tunic, Tripper follows Winey, G, and Eren.

Larret Army

Everyone is shivering uncontrollably as they walk into the blasting cold gods-breaths. None of them is accustomed to this type of weather in the summer. They walk onward until twenty minutes later when Winey stops.

Then, walking back to Tripper, Winey sits in front of her.

Realising that Winey is looking for something, Tripper scratches the boar's forehead while reaching into her pouch with her other hand. She retrieves a morsel of cold chicken meat.

Tripper offers the meat to Winey who takes the morsel before stretching out to nuzzle Tripper's left knee. He chews the chicken quickly.

When he is finished eating, Winey stands on all four hooves and runs west along the Harpen River bank.

A stronger gust of gods-breath blasts the area. Leaves and branches are ripped from trees and bushes. There are no sane people out in the fields. The only ones foolish enough to be outside are herders keeping an eye on their animals and these three villagers who are searching for an old reeve.

These three are following a young boar, who seems to know where he is headed.

Eren is the first to spot Reeve Jeston sitting with his back against a rock. Looking out towards the east, Jeston is sitting still. His tunic is missing. In fact, all he seems to be wearing are his leggings. The Reeve appears to be sitting and watching the ground in front of him.

Winey rushes up to Jeston and nudges the Reeve's right hand.

The hand doesn't respond.

Tripper charges to Jeston with a look of fear and a panicked expression on her face. Kneeling down to look at Jeston, Tripper is aware there is no movement from her father.

Kneeling next to Jeston, G looks at Reeve Jeston and then turns to Tripper. "He looks so peaceful, Tripper. But I think he has passed away. We should carry Reeve Jeston home. Eren, let's carry the Reeve to Reeve House."

Eren and G awkwardly pick up the old reeve.

When not burdened, it is usually about a ten-minute walk to Reeve House from these rocks.

Winey follows behind them with Tripper.

Our journey is quiet this time, as is the Toydon custom for the dead, which springs into the minds of both Tripper and G.

Eren is thinking; she is calculating how much extra effort is needed to carry the small pebble clenched in Jeston's right hand. How much extra coin she might be able to charge for the efforts of carrying Jeston home. *Three dusters should be fair … well, maybe.*

Larret Army

Then Eren returns, mentally, back to the others. Her mind is happy with the thought of doing a community service by helping to carry Jeston home, yet making a profit in the effort.

Arriving at the door to Reeve House, the women set Jeston down.

G opens the door as Eren speaks. "I believe Tripper owes us each another three dusters for taking the effort and time to carry Reeve Jeston home. I would like to be paid now, Tripper."

Breathing out heavily, G looks at Eren, "You are a black swan among greater grey swans. You really want to charge Tripper for carrying her father home from his place of death? How do expect people to like you?"

Tripper turns to look at Eren and then G, saying, "I will pay you once you have Father on his bed, dressed and ready for the ceremony, as is the custom of the Toydon. Is that okay?" Shuddering violently, Tripper almost breaks down grieving, even before the preparing of Jeston.

We ask … *how did Jeston die? Was it exposure to the bitter cold of the night? Was he killed? Did he have problems after washing up in the Harpen River? Did his heart just quit? Or …*

With a look at Tripper then G, Eren smiles, and she says, "Okay. Let's get the old man inside and dressed for Toydon Right of Passage." She motions for G to help.

Looking up at the sphere with eyes wide, G has the look of '*why do we bother,*' then she bends down to pick up one end of Jeston.

The old-looking, but genuinely young village priest, Mi, approaches quickly.

Seeing the dead reeve, he looks to Tripper. "Do you desire the usual Toydon Right of Passage?"

Tripper simply nods to him.

Mi smiles calmly. "Let's get started then." He helps pick up the frail body of the late Reeve Jeston of Larret Hamlet.

Together, G, Eren, and Mi wrestle the body through the doorway, struggling to bend him through the portals into Reeve House and placing him on his bed. The group backs up and then Mi frowns as he looks at the group who gathered.

The priest utters, "My, aren't we a group of black swans. Maybe if we help one another, then this time won't be as hard on each of us. Yes … that would be us … The Black Swans. I am sorry, Tripper, that your father has passed away. If there is anything Ikerus or I can do for you in this time of grief, please ask,"

Tripper, looking at the Priest of Ikerus, mutters, "Yah, right."

Larret Army

Summer 2 Bear

The day begins with the appearance of Stonewire and Imvor, and we look towards the spectacular view as the yellow beams of light from Stonewire and the orange-red streaks of light from Imvor break over the eastern horizon. This morning, the sphere is partially covered, but the north breaths are warm and not near as strong as yesterday's breaths.

As we look out over the ocean, there is a calling we hear. To the west, Tripper is announcing the death of Reeve Jeston.

Eren smiles, knowing she has done her part in protecting the hamlet. As per Toydon custom, Eren tied one of her billy goats to the front of Reeve House.

Billy Dolon is doing a fantastic job of defending against possible foul spirits. Plus, the villagers get to see her best billy goat.

He should fetch a good price when the six days of passing are finished.

I suggest in Eren's spirit that we return to Larret.

I have seen the rising of Stonewire and Imvor on so many previous days.

Eren sighs and turns, walking toward the hamlet. I look back to the waters, and I feel the drawing to the unknown realms of the gods.

Eren speaks up. "You know; I don't understand why it takes seven days for a soul to pass on. I mean, we are born, we live, and then we die. It's all part of the cycle of life. The body has stopped working, yet people think it will rise and haunt us if we don't go through a whole bunch of garbage. The reeve is gone … done did."

Eren and I arrive back in the hamlet's market as Tripper finishes announcing his death.

Winey is rummaging around the market's waste, but staying close to Tripper. How often has that boar been considered for some villager's supply of food?

I am betting he weighs close to 160 pounds. There is a lot of meat on those ribs. I sadly consider that thought and the thought that Tripper will not eat today. But, that is the price for worshipping the gods.

Die? I consider it occasionally. To tell the truth, it bugs me to the Seven Hells. I know everyone dies. Why haven't I? I keep going like a stream, not knowing when I will pass over.

We follow Tripper to Reeve House.

She seems to be contained in a world of her own thoughts. She can't eat today and must prepare Jeston's corpse for viewing, which will take place from noon until god-set.

Larret Army

I laugh when the vile Eren starts spouting about the powers of Stonewire. I have learned to tune her out when she starts in about Stonewire protecting those who defend themselves.

If I understand it right, Eren prepared for today by memorizing two mage spells.

Eren seems to have memorized *'Protection from Hunger and Thirst'*, as well as *'Mending'*.

Apparently, she spent almost half an hour studying.

As we walk to Tripper's house, I wonder if Tripper will be left with the house or will she have to move into another home? Will the lord of the hamlet appoint a new reeve soon? What will be the fate of Tripper and Winey? They have no other home; they have no family here. Tripper has few friends after a life of being aloof and treating others poorly. Tripper does have some good qualities; I am sure she does. But I can't think of one right now.

We walk Tripper home as Eren speaks up. "I can help with the preparations, Tripper. What will we be eating tomorrow? Have you thought about the feast? I will prepare some of it if you want. Unfortunately, it will make me hungry, so I will need to eat while I prepare the feast."

Larret Army

Tripper looks over at Eren with a bit of distaste, her mouth tight and straight, eyes squinted. "You can prepare the feast. But you will have to use what Fath …"

Tripper hesitates and then continues, saying, "What I have in the house … nothing more, nothing less. Go ahead, eat the last bit of bread. But leave the cheese for tomorrow, to be served with the feast. Now, excuse me while I dress Father for this afternoon."

Tripper then becomes quiet.

Opening the door to her house, it can be seen that she has done nothing with yesterday's morning meal. The meal still rests on the table mouldering where she had set it for eating.

"Okay, Tripper, I will clean up while you get Jeston ready for viewing. Don't worry, it will all be taken care of." Eren walks in with Tripper and looks around. "Yes. Find food, then clean, then start preparations. The effort should be worth at least two or three Dyns, right?"

Tripper doesn't speak as she goes into her father's room. She looks over at Jeston's old body. Long past his prime, Jeston raised Tripper for as long as she can remember. Finding it odd, Tripper has no memories of her mother. However, Tripper was told that her mother is alive, living west of Larret Hamlet. But who knows how far west. She could be three kilometres away or three hundred kilometres.

Saddened by her loss, Tripper begins removing Jeston leggings in preparation for cleaning and dressing him for the midday viewing.

She spends the rest of the morning cleaning the body and then dressing Jeston in his best clothes. Finished, she steps back from Jeston, and looks over her handiwork.

Father looks comfortable and content.

Tripper looks around Jeston's room. It will be best to clean up the room. Not much work is needed, as Father was very organized and neat, she takes up her new task.

Earlier, back in the common room, Eren's eyes scan over the room. The mess that has taken hold of the room is most unnatural in this house. Luckily, the day was cold yesterday, and the room only started warming up this morning, so the food on the table does not smell too badly, yet.

She decides that the food needs taking care of first. She starts working: cleaning off the table, and then the stove and finally the counter. Once all that is settled, Eren looks around, again assessing the room's state.

The fresh food only needs to be ready for tomorrow morning's daylong feast. *I can work at this, as Tripper is feeding me today and tomorrow.'* The thought rang through Eren's mind quickly.

She smiles and takes a few moments to eat the stale bread, chasing the food with wine that Eren had found under the counter. Watching Eren work, reminds me how strong and agile she is, and how dedicated she is to her work.

Though the villagers know that Eren is a master of mage-craft, few have seen her display her skills. It takes years of dedication and a sharp mind to learn mage-craft.

Eren has both a sharp mind and the patience to get what she wants. The food she eats isn't free, she knows that. At least she is being paid to help Tripper. This is what counts in life for Eren: to get a return for effort or to acquire materials. Her goal in life is to amass wealth, not fame.

Several years ago, during her journeyman walkabout year, Eren discovered the price of fame and bragging. The event almost cost her life. It did cost her two seasons of healing in a respite, and the loss of all her accumulated material possessions. She was left with nothing but her spell tome and a ruined set of clothing – the clothes she had on when she managed to escape the village mob.

People are dangerous and brutal to individuals and things they don't understand. Fear is a strong driving force in society.

Larret Army

In the end, it cost that village when she returned as a certified mage a full year later.

Eren was forgotten, and she happily left the respite after two seasons. Going back to the Mage University for Mage testing was bittersweet. Eren had survived the yearlong walkabout test needed to pass final requirements, and to become a full-fledged mage. But, it came at a high cost, and something she had not expected. She swore never to fall into the same trap again.

With the table, counter, and stove clean, and with food in her belly, she begins the work of cleaning and preparing the room for the viewing of Reeve Jeston. Odd, but she doesn't feel comfortable doing all this work without compensation beforehand. Tripper still owes her three dusters from yesterday. Eren thinks of stopping the cleaning as she only agreed to prepare food for tomorrow's feast.

Looking around, yet again, Eren sees disorganization – plain careless disorganization. In her mind, she is disgusted. *'Nope, can't leave it like this. Stonewire will bless me for this effort and Tripper will pay up!'* So, Eren continues the task while figuring out the price to charge Tripper for her help. By the time midday arrives, the room is clean and organized. Eren is proud of her efforts.

Larret Army

A composed, but dishevelled Tripper comes into the room. Tripper is dressed in her orange wool dress and white leather vest, and looks at Eren. Tripper sighs and says, "Thank you, Eren. It was kind of you to help with this."

Eren smiles and says, "Winey is mine now, or you pay me a Royal Flair for my efforts. It is your choice, Tripper. If you pay up, I will stay and help with the cooking for tomorrow as well."

Tripper looks fit to burst, but she nods. She knows she is going to need folks in the near future. It is going to be rough getting through the next year or so. Taking the last gold coin from her coin pouch, Tripper pays Eren without thanking her or offering any comment.

Not more than ten minutes later, Cleric Jessep Whitestone arrives. Looking a little flustered, he follows Tripper's direction into Jeston's bedroom.

Looking over the deceased reeve, Jess gives a *Blessing of Lorn*. Done with that, Jess departs Reeve House without a word to Tripper.

As Jess is leaving Reeve House, a more familiar cleric arrives – Cleric Mikene Lornet of Ikerus. Smiling, Mi walks into the common room of Reeve House.

He offers Tripper: "I will stay with you through this hard time, Tripper. You do not face this alone. Ikerus and I are here

23

for you and Jeston. When Jeston's Right of Passage is finished, we will then talk about your future in Larret Hamlet." He enters Jeston's room offering a *Blessing from Ikerus*.

As five village guests wander through the house, it dawns on Tripper how unpopular she and her father were in the Hamlet of Larret. She begins thinking about her future, yet again. Does she stay or does she move on to someplace else? *'No, I am reeve until our lord commands otherwise. I am staying. These low-class farmers can't make me leave, ever.'*

So, the folks of Larret Hamlet continue with their way of life.

In the corner of Reeve House kitchen, Eren frowns and mutters, "Yah, right."

Summer 3 Bear

Watching the gods rise we find that yesterday's events spilled over into today. The Toydon Right of Passage for the Reeve continue. Today is the feast day of the Toydon ceremony.

Scattered cover lightly adorns the unmoving sphere. G, somewhat attractive, appears to be middle-aged even though she is only seventeen. Because of her appearance and personality, most people in the village believe her to be thirty or so.

Larret Army

Thinking things through quickly and intuitively, knowing what needs to be done, G helps villagers who ask for her help.

G has been practising with a longsword for over an hour today. The sword feels like an extension of her body. During her practice drills, with no breeze of a gods-breath to give her relief from the heat, she is sweating profusely. The fleeting pass of an occasional zephyr stirs some air, but it is too light to notice.

Hot! That is a mild statement for this day's beginning.

Finishing with her drills, she wonders how things are going at Reeve House. She starts walking home along the trail to Larret Hamlet. We walk north with her, back to Larret Hamlet.

G's longsword is clean and protected in its' well-used scabbard. Her armour is damp with perspiration and deliberately set too loose, causing the armour to make squeaking sounds.

Her ill-fitting armour is an attempt at creating poor fighting conditions for today's drills. Damn, there are a few bruises and blisters from today's practice. The unbalance of her armour forced her to compensate for the awkwardness, something she hadn't experienced since her first few lessons of wearing armour.

Walking idly along the path to Larret Hamlet, G contemplates her new day.

Larret Army

Her house is bare, except for a few rare possessions and the few supplies needed each day. Even at that, it is almost time to clean house again.

G has three longbows currently under construction. The one looks like it might warp on her. She had reset it, soaking it and then putting the bow in the lock vices, but G isn't sure the correction will succeed.

She remembers the first longbow she crafted. It never did feel right no matter what she did to it. That was five years ago.

She has crafted over two dozen longbows, and she has lost count of the number of shortbows she has built over the last six years.

It's going to take a while to properly clean the armour and sword. Her boots probably smell like Winey on a hot day, too.

One of the men-at-arms suggested wearing a backpack with stones in it for practice drills to increase her power and the strength of her coordination. How that will work is questionable. Won't that just throw her off when she practices without the pack later on?

She is getting rather well adapted to her studded leather armour, small shield, and longsword combination.

Larret Army

The Reeve? What is going to happen to the village now? G has a good understanding of the politics of this hamlet, enough beyond the rules needed to live and work in the hamlet.

She knows that the tax she pays is one Flair per year. Her shop taxes are six percent of her income. She knows that the water at the well is safest and costs nothing more than the effort to fetch it. To eat, she must earn enough to buy, trade, or grow the food.

Thinking of this year's seeding of her small garden brings a smile to her. Hopefully, it all grows and survives to be harvested. She is looking forward to the beans and peas the most. The tubers – well what can be said for uninspiring tubers?

A new pair of leggings and a tunic would be nice. Talking with Cobbler Dentin yesterday, the two agreed on two Flairs for a new pair of high hard boots. G. Dentin said the boots would be ready for pickup in twelve days.

Come to think of it, she is hungry. Let's cook morning meal then clean up this equipment.

Yes, another day at the cottage, working with some old wood, and the south fields are looking a little greener today. As she walks along toward her cottage, she suddenly stops.

Looking to her right, G smiles, noticing a particularly suitable cluster of willows growing straight as any she has seen lately. They might be a good source for arrow shafts. She smiles and then continues onward towards Larret Hamlet and home.

Arriving at her home, G finds everything in the house is as she left it. She takes the time to strip out of her studded leather armour and equipment.

She looks over each piece as she sets them out to be tended to once she has cleaned up a bit. Thinking about the work ahead of her, G decides she wants to be seen at the Feast of Passing at the Reeve House. She considers life is a puzzle to be worked out as we go along.

Finished with the cleaning up, G puts on her good socializing clothes: her best light blue leggings and dark blue wool tunic, a pair of soft low boots, and her scabbard containing her friend, her longsword. Shunning her red wool cloak for today, she frowns.

G knows that it is not a good idea to leave her equipment in its current state, so she begins tending to her armour.

Several minutes later, she is finally satisfied that her armour and shield are fit for use once again. Her longsword's edge is keen again, and the sword is properly oiled.

Leaving her home, G walks to Reeve House for the feast. She brings along a basket containing a dozen eggs.

Larret Army

When G arrives, Reeve House is almost empty of folk. Eren, Mi, Winey, and Tripper are the only living occupants of Reeve House.

G looks at the three people. Eren is the odd one out. G would not have expected Eren to come to a Right of Passage feast for anyone. What is she up to? Eren looks very relaxed.

G puts the basket, which was woven from Harpen River reeds, on the counter. There is one other item on the counter – a Holy Symbol of Ikerus. No doubt the Holy Symbol was presented by Mi.

Looking at the table of food, there is a small brick of Eren's old goat's cheese, two loaves of yeast bread, a small plate with goat butter, and a cask of what is probably water.

Doing her duty, G walks into Jeston's room and takes a quick gander to see that all is right. She wants to be sure it is Jeston and that he has not risen as a walking-dead. If he did rise, he'd probably be livelier than he has been for the last dozen years.

'Yup, its' Jeston alright. He still has the big brown mole on his right cheek.' Using water from the basin on the table beside Jeston, she places a drop of water onto Jeston's forehead, as per the Jalnoric Right of Passage custom.

Larret Army

Returning to the common room, G offers her condolences to Tripper. Though G is not sure of the genuineness of what she is about to say, she speaks anyway. "Tripper, I am sorry for the sudden loss of your father, our reeve. I brought a basket of eggs for you. You can keep the basket if you like, or donate it to one of our poorer families who need such items. May life shine upon you; may you find happiness. May you find a husband and raise a family who prospers. Good day, Tripper. I have work that needs tending." *That was sappy, and I don't think I meant one word of it. Especially the part about having work that needs tending.'* She thinks.

G slowly starts to leave without a word spoken to her by Tripper or the others. As she reaches the door to the outside, Mi speaks out. "Master G, may Ikerus bless you for your kindness and goodwill."

Damn, he had to go and do that, didn't he?' G thinks. She stops, and turning around, she looks back. Bowing slightly. "Thank you, Mikene. May Ikerus work with you." She does an about face and quickly walks out of Reeve House.

Outside, G considers her spot in life at this moment. These thoughts fade quickly, and she smiles. *'I have done my duty that needed doing. For now, I think a trip to the reeds for new supplies are needed. I had a basket that now needs replacing.'* G walks home to get her collecting knife and her carryall.

Larret Army

We walk west to the reed bed, at the Olan ox-bow of Harpen River. This has been the harvesting site for at least three generations of weaving craftsmen. Only a small part is harvested each year so as not to over-harvest the best source of reeds near Larret Hamlet, and to not disturb the natural life balance in the area. Her friend brought G here a few years ago to demonstrate harvesting and to show her how the village practices its cultivation of this unique patch of excellent reeds.

Spending over an hour harvesting the proper reeds, G has her load ready in her carryall. She laughs and sits down on top of the high bank of the ox-bow.

Looking down at the river pool below, she notices that across the pool from her are a group of four turtles sunning themselves. She remembers the names she gave the big turtle and the youngest red-back: Gaeren and Tolin.

She wonders if she could harvest the older red-back for food for the village, without upsetting the other turtles' family life.

Looking down, she nods, thinking, '*Yah, right!*'

Larret Army

Summer 4 Bear

We are walking to Reeve House; Mi seems pre-occupied with something. I know what it is, but I am told to please not say anything. I will be silent for now, but things will be brought up later, and someone will get hurt. Mi, the zealot – Cleric Mikene Lornet of Ikerus – believes in fate, and he thinks fate has been altered and not by Ikerus. During his prayers last night, he stumbled upon a piece of information that could alter the fate of the village. But zealot-a-lot wants to ignore that right now, at least until he finishes his current service.

Visually, Mi is forgettable, other than to say he looks old. He has never been ill that anyone can recall. He works with anyone who asks him to, but few do.

The hamlet's villagers don't ask Mi to work with them because, when you ask Mi to help you, you have to listen to sermons on Ikerus until Mi is finished working with you. His steel-blue eyes bore through you, making you feel guilty if you cut the job short, trying to get rid of him so you don't have to listen.

The tall, stocky man can outwork most farm boys, though. So, when there is a tough job that needs long days of work, Mi does get called upon.

Larret Army

His young nineteen years don't deter his drive to share his story and the faith of his god, Ikerus.

As the two day-gods rise and pass through the sphere, travelling to midday, we arrive at Jeston's house to find the door ajar. Looking in, we see Tripper sitting with her elbows on the table and her head in her hands. We can see her shoulders occasionally shudder.

Standing and looking behind himself, and then looking back at the door, Mi frowns with slightly curled down lips as he raises his fist. Knocking loudly, he cheerfully calls in. "Hello in the house. This is a house call from Ikerus and Mi. We have come to see how you are feeling today? Was yesterday's feast satisfying?" He moves as slow as a whisp as he opens the door all the way and walks in.

Jerking with the violence of a leaping toad, Tripper lifts her head. "Why yes, come in. The company of a high-class cleric is appreciated." She brushes the tears from her face with a quick stroke of her hand, taking a look toward the door as he enters.

Winey snorts several short bursts, and rushes straight over to Mi.

The good cleric reaches down and scratches deep on Winey's neck just behind his skull. With a genuine smile, Mi says, "Hello, Winey, nice chops. Going my way?" He bursts out with a jester's laugh and continues in past Winey. Walking directly over to the dining table, Mi sits across from the dejected Tripper.

Slightly fatigued from a lack of sleep, Tripper is deeply mourning the loss of her father.

Turning her body to face Mi, she says, "Good Cleric, I must apologize for my appearance this day ... as you know, I lost my father. Today and tomorrow, I am not able to eat. So, today I tried to sleep, but I was not able to do such. I fear for Father, Mi ... he was not a well-liked man. I realize now that I was not the kindest villager, either ... I'm discovering I have no friends. All I have is Winey and you ... what am I to do? I am reeve now ... until our Lord Ramson appoints one to replace Father. But are any villagers going to obey me?"

Mi is thinking, *Poor Tripper probably doesn't realize how much people dislike her ... or even why they dislike her.* Instead, he says, "Tripper, you can stay at Reeve House for now. However, I am sure that Lord Ramson will help you find a new home ... he may replace your father with someone other than you. Appointing a reeve is serious for a landholder. The reeve oversees the day-to-day business of a landholding when the landholder is absent ... As such the reeve never rests and is held responsible for everything that takes place in their little fief. Let me pray and I'll

34

ask Ikerus to watch over you, Tripper. I'll come here every day to look in on you. You're not alone in the village. Is there anything Ikerus or I can do for you now?"

Eyes watery and reddened, brows furrowed, Tripper looks over at him. "I am reeve, Mi ... there is no other after the Right of Passage. I am going to change some things in the village. I will raise the taxes. Father had them set too low. We didn't have enough to give to Lord Ramson and keep ourselves properly fed."

She looks even deeper at Mi, and she starts walking toward her bedroom. "I need to sleep now ... good-bye, Mi."

The priest remains watching Tripper. Mi's lips curl downward again, tight. Standing, he calls after her. "Ikerus' blessing upon you and your home."

Together, we slowly leave Reeve House.

A voice in the village calls out, "Yah, right!"

Summer 5 Bear

As we walk towards Reeve House, there is little talk among us. The partially covered day gives some relief from the heat. Today's air is warm and pleasant, more like it should be. The eastward breath is much the same as yesterdays.

Larret Army

The day is uneventful, or at least it is unexciting, so far.

At Tripper's house, G is not ready for Jeston's Right of Passage. Eren and Mi are with us and seem lost in their own thoughts.

I wonder what the Right of Passage will do for Jeston, but none of the other lost ones want to answer me. I don't think any of us actually know what happens to the soul after passage.

Do the gods take the soul and put it somewhere safe? Or do the gods send the soul back to a new body? How do I get my final Right of Passage? Or is this what happens to us when we die: we wander around with the living, talking to them, and occasionally changing aspects of fate for the living.

Both Tripper and Eren are alive because I changed their fate in the past.

But are either of them thankful? No! They do not even realize that their fate was changed.

Was their fate actually changed, or was my interference their fate all along? How does fate work? Is there actually such a thing as fate?

I am not sure of the answer, so I will continue with helping my friends as best as I can – to see them carry on living their lives.

Arriving at Reeve House, G knocks on the door for us.

The door glides open.

There on a burial stretcher, Jeston lays with his best clothes on. The same clothes that Tripper dressed him in five days ago. The Holy Symbol of Ikerus is nestled on Jeston's chest, just below his crossed hands.

Glancing over at G, Mi smiles, knowing that in this village, these occasions are rare little gems. Few call for his service, although he is eager to do services for others in Ikerus' name.

Entering, G stands aside to let Mi take the lead now.

After we all enter the house, Eren closes the door.

Looking around, we see Winey laying close to Jeston.

Her eyes still bright red from grief, Tripper sits beside the burial stretcher that holds her father's corpse.

With determination, Mi walks quickly to Tripper, where he places a caring hand on her tense shoulder.

There is a jolt in the room, preceded by a loud crashing thump on the door. It sounds as if something very hard has hit the entry door.

Unarmed, G rushes to the door. She opens it just in time to see the billy goat, Dolon, run toward her, attempting to ram the door again. Instead of attacking the door, the billy goat connects with her leg, knocking her down.

Larret Army

Taking exception to this, Winey rushes at Dolon, while bellowing one of his loud attack squeals.

With a shake of her head, Eren moves to separate the two animals, while Mi quickly moves to aid G.

Laying on the floor holding her leg, G's lips crease downward. Then, even though she must be in pain, her lips turn up to form a grim smile. "That is one for the billy … he won't get away so easily next time."

Kneeling down, Mi peers at G. "How does it feel? Is your leg broken?"

With a snide laugh, G looks up at the kneeling cleric. "Aren't you the one who is supposed to tell me if my leg is broken?"

Shyly looking away, he answers quietly. "I am not a healer. I do not know the anatomy and workings of our bodies. I heal through the power of prayer – through Ikerus. I can try to heal you tomorrow, as I am not prepared for such today." Mi, speaking a little louder so all can hear. "Eren, can you get the healer so he can tend to G's leg. It may be broken."

With a short burst of laughter, Eren looks over. "Two dusters per message, Mi. You know the rules."

With true determination, G tries standing up. Grimacing, she continues her efforts without help from those gathered.

She stands up on her own, and using both legs, she walks to a chair that's near Jeston. "I think I am fine. It is just a bruise to flesh and ego." She offers a meek smile.

Letting out a deep sigh, Mi watches as Eren returns to controlling her billy.

Again, but with more force this time, Tripper pulls Winey away from the goat.

Once the two animals are separated, Tripper looks around outside.

Seeing nothing else out of sorts, she looks down at Dolon and shakes her head in denial.

Closing the house door, those gathered take their positions as needed.

Later, as they wait for the gods to set, there is a knock on the front door.

Before anyone can move to answer, the door opens. There in the doorway is the hamlet's official cleric, Jessep of Lorn. "I heard there is a problem here. I see I am in time to witness Jeston's Right of Passage." He walks in and closes the door just as Dolon rams the building yet again.

With eyes narrowed, Mi looks at Tripper and then at Jess. "Must be spirits trying to get in and claim Jeston … after tomorrow that should end."

The others nod solemnly.

Silent, Jess sits on a vacant seat.

Nothing is said about G's injured leg.

The waiting continues.

There is no chatter amongst those gathered. Everyone, except Jess and Mi, looks uncomfortable being here.

Moving the head of the table, Mi seems eager to get the ceremony underway.

Fingers twining together like a nest of snakes, Jess seems settled and waiting for things to flow along.

Eventually the natural light of both day-gods starts to fade in the west.

Steadfast Mi, still as a stock, stands beside Jeston's body. Then, he looks at Tripper.

He starts the ceremony when complete darkness falls upon the inside of Reeve House.

The ceremony begins with the lighting of one candle, which is placed next to the head of Jeston.

The faint yellow light from the candle serves several purposes. One purpose is as a device of timing. As the candle burns down, each phase of the Right of Passage must be done at the proper moment. One error and the soul will not continue as is intended.

At least that is the general thought regarding the passing ceremony.

Looking over at Jeston, I note his soul rise. He seems ready to leave. Suddenly, his soul shifts in colour.

The greyness rushes through him.

Wait! I remember me going through that change. I am still here. As I watch, things fade slowly at first ... then more rapidly ... I ...

Looking down at my body, I see the candle burning beside my head ... I see light ...

A bodiless voice calls out in a chuckle. '*Yah! Right.*'

Summer 6 Bear

The day-gods have gone to their homes, leaving the world in darkness. The night is lit only by the night-gods in the sphere, along with the brightly twinkling souls. The night is warm, though the east breath had picked up again in the evening.

We look up into the sphere overhead as Dolon runs. Is he chasing spirits? Is he guiding Jeston's soul to the departure of our realm? We don't have any answers to those questions.

Damn the Seven Hells. When we watched the soul depart yesterday, we felt a pang of regret and loss.

Larret Army

With a twinge of laughter, Tripper watches Dolon run wild.

The billy is running straight for the Web Ocean, east of the hamlet. He is running right through the heart of the hamlet, only slowing down to dodge whatever is in his way.

Eren looks alarmed at the goat's running rampage, and she quickly takes after Dolon.

We speculate as to what is happening – Dolon is guiding other lost souls to the ocean – swimming out to release the lost souls with his death.

From such an effort, Dolon will not come back.

Catching a breath, Eren shouts back to Tripper, "If he dies, I demand payment of two Flairs." Eren continues chasing after Dolon.

Stepping outside, G looks to Tripper. "Eren might forget, but I doubt it. Do you have two Flairs left, Tripper? You know that Dolon is headed for a swim in the ocean … can you stop him? Or do you prefer to pay Eren?"

As she watches the goat, Tripper sighs loudly. "I could, but Eren would prefer I don't stop the beast. She informed me of that when the goat was first tied to Reeve House for the Right of Passage. She mentioned something about kind value for that billy."

With a slight single nod, G thinks a moment, and then answers, "If I know our Eren, she will either rescue the goat and claim divine intervention, or let the goat drown. Then, she'll haul it back to her place, butcher it, and sell whatever she can from the carcass."

From beside G, Mi adds in retrospect. "I believe you are right, heathen. The village mage will find a way to profit from this … in her mind at least."

We watch Dolon running headlong until he reaches the beach. Then, suddenly, the goat stops, lets out several bleats, and then turns quickly. We see lights rising into the air from the goat. The lights swirl upward and then shift rapidly; they then dart into the gravel of the beach.

As if mad with rage, Dolon charges Eren, stopping short while the mage stands her ground with a stance that says, '*you dare strike and you become food.*'

Pointing at the duo, Mi quietly chuckles. "Which one will win the test of stubbornness?" As bold as a Goren Hawk, Mi adds, "We should offer an Ikerus Blessing to Reeve House today."

We turn and look from Eren and Dolon, who are locked in a challenge of wills.

Larret Army

Eyes widening, Tripper looks at G. "Should I go and help Eren with her goat? They could be there for a long time, and it is darkening out here. We don't want the goat out-willing Eren ... Eren would never live that down. Right now, I think the goat is winning, though. Eren was out in her fields today, so she is probably tired already."

G slowly shakes her head twice, and then laughs. "We could, but let's let them stare at each other for a while longer. I think Mi was talking to you, Tripper ... something about an Ikerus blessing for the floor of your house? ... I think."

With the abruptness of a springing hare, G turns and follows Mi into Reeve House.

We stand a moment longer and turn to watch Eren and Dolon.

I swear, if one of them doesn't twitch in the next five minutes, then we are going down to the beach and disturbing both of them.

The living can be so immature.

We look over at Dolon and shout out down to him, "Na, Na, Boo, Boo."

Then, we follow the others inside into Reeve House.

Inside the house, we find Mi saying prayers of blessing for the house to Ikerus.

Larret Army

Sitting in a dining chair, Tripper, in her Imvor-orange dress, is looking at Mi, and then she states, "Okay then, go ahead and continue to say your prayers to your god. But it won't bring back Fathe. Please, I would appreciate it if you all left me alone tonight and tomorrow, until the burial procession is ready to take Father to the cemetery and bury him. It will be his last look at Larret from above ground. Really, I do thank you for everything. But I want to be alone with Father. Okay? Please?" She motions for G and Mi to leave.

Looking over at Winey, we wonder about him as well.

Tripper, with an oddity in her gait, walks to her father's corpse and calls Winey over to her.

She sits in a chair next to the stretcher, while Winey eagerly stands and rushes over to Tripper, laying his head on Tripper's lap. He grunts a couple of times, moving his head from side to side.

With deep compassion, G looks at Tripper and Winey. Placing her hand softly on Tripper's shoulder, G murmurs, "It's okay, Tripper. I do understand. You know where my shop is and you know that my house is open for your visits. If you need to talk, come on over. Goodnight, Tripper. I will see you all tomorrow ... I think?" She scratches Winey's neck near his ears, and then walks out of Reeve House.

Larret Army

While in the house, Mi starts his prayer to offer Ikerus' Blessing for Reeve House.

We believe that Tripper should feel honoured, because a priest's blessing, though performed at no monetary cost to Tripper, is not cheap.

From my guess, I would say the material costs alone are around fifty Royal Flairs. Mi needs to go to his Head Temple to get the Holy Water. He can't make his own … at least not yet.

We once asked to accompany him on his next run to Moratan Temple of Ikerus. He never answered us in any way.

…..

We are all rather curious as to the progress outside, near the beach. I can sense that G is finding it funny and wants to go look as well.

True to her word, G walks down to see what the two old mules are doing.

We all arrive to find them still locked in their contest of wills.

Apparently, taunting a goat is useless for us. So, we try to decide on the next step – haunting the goat?

Even though we really don't care, it would be bad form to leave these two here all night.

Larret Army

Wait a minute, to stay here all night locked in a contest of wills? That may not be a bad idea after all.

Good grief, young G has to spoil our fun as she approaches Eren and asks in an idle tone. "I was wondering where I could get a good goat pelt to make a couple quivers for my arrows. Now I see a goat right here, prime for use. What do you think Eren? Just slit his throat, here and now, as punishment for being a bad goat. And, in the process, I get a goat pelt. I think it's a splendid idea ... how tall are you again?"

Eren doesn't change her gaze as she answers. "To the Seven Hells if you think that you are slicing the goat's throat just to use his pelt. Unless, of course, you have three Flairs with you to pay for Dolon, as well as a sharp blade to kill with! Well, you could use a dull blade or a ragged blade, and then he would think twice before charging anyone."

Shouting to the goat in an annoyed tone, Eren calls out, "RIGHT DOLON!"

Eren stands still looking at her billy; she seems to be considering something.

To some degree, whenever Eren considers anything, it is scary for anyone near her.

Eren talks firmly to Dolon. "Okay, if I offer defeat, then YOU will feed me and a couple others in the village."

Larret Army

Maybe this is not a wise choice, as Dolon rears up on his hind legs and tries to bunt Eren.

With a slow reaction, Eren seems to take the butting as an answer to her inquiry, and she falls to the ground in pain.

Also known as Farmer Eren, who is now sitting on the dry ground, she makes a quick decision as Dolon comes up for a second butt.

The now red-faced fuming Mage Eren takes her sling from its pocket. She stands as Dolon lowers his head again.

The goat misses this time as it goes off in a sideways drift.

As quick as he can, Dolon sets up for another butting of Eren.

They both seem more than slightly agitated.

Raising her readied weapon, Eren has her weighted sling securely holding a stone as she strikes Dolon with a solid thud on his shoulder.

Not to be outdone, Dolon, on the other hand, has a bit more skill and practice when it comes to aggression. He impacts Eren in her torso, which knocks her back a step or two and knocks the breath out of Eren.

Stepping back, trying to regain her footing, Eren falters as if stunned for a moment.

This gives Dolon time to evaluate his next attack. The goat backs up a few steps as Eren gathers herself.

Neither the woman nor the goat seems inclined to withdraw. Both want to go on with this, even through the night.

Swiftly, with random aim, Eren takes a mad swing at Dolon with the loaded sling. The sling goes above the goat.

While she attacks, Dolon comes in again, lower this time, striking Eren on her thigh.

Doubling over and grabbing her thigh, Eren falters again but keeps her footing and her anger in check.

Observing the lopsided conflict, G realizes that she may have to step in and aid Eren. Though, she would prefer not to help the mage.

The village bowyer unsheathes her longsword from its well-tended, but much-worn scabbard.

She steps in closer to face Dolon.

Standing five or six feet away from Eren, G calls out, asking, "Shall I step in for either of you?"

Neither combatant answers G. They both remain intent on each other.

With another random wild flick of her forearm, Eren swings her sling with its stone at Dolon, missing badly.

The goat impacts Eren's abdomen, knocking the air out of her.

The stubborn farmer mage falls to the ground and loses consciousness.

Seeing the goat turn to G, G lets out a deep sigh. Looking at Dolon, she says sternly, "You shouldn't have done that."

As the bowyer brings her sword to bare, she utters, "Eren may be annoying and not well-liked, but you don't knock people down that way, goat. Prepare to pay for your efforts." She takes one last sidelong look at Eren, and then quickly steps up to Dolon.

The goat seems to be losing his drive and stubbornness.

With a few circular sword motions, G takes a warm-up swing at the goat's head, intentionally missing.

The goat takes offence to this and drives a hard head-butt into her chest.

The young warrior shakes off the attack, muttering, "Do you concede, beast?"

Thus, these two are locked in another struggle.

Moving toward G, Dolon determines that he feels himself weakening, and then suddenly he decides to run off to his barn stall.

Larret Army

With a quick but painful fluid action, G bends down to check on the mage.

Laying unmoving, not blinking, Eren seems to be breathing, but not aware of the world around her.

With great care, grunting in her effort, G picks Eren up, carrying the limp body of Larret Hamlet's most stubborn and least liked farmer.

Arriving at the local healer's house after several minutes, G shuffles Eren around so that she can knock on the heavy wood door.

G knocks twice while calling, "Repeat customer for yah. Eren has gone down again and seems a little lost to the world at this moment."

An annoyed male voice shouts back from inside the house. "Okay, take her away until tomorrow. Either way, she will wake up or pass away. In both cases, she will be out of my room."

Jostling Eren, G laughs loudly, and then states boldly, "Come on, open up. She's gained ten pounds since the last time I carried her here."

The door opens hesitantly, and Jess stands in his nightclothes. "We don't take freeloaders here, Fletcher." The hamlet's priest of Lorn looks at Eren, and then motions G to bring Eren in.

Larret Army

They walk to the treatment area, and G flops Eren onto the rugged, but sturdy, cot.

Seeing no obvious wounds, Jess chuckles sarcastically as he begins the examination, stating matter-of-factly, "Okay, I don't see any blood this time. You don't mind if I check under her clothes for broken bones? What did she attack this time?"

The fletcher laughs in a short burst and then answers briskly. "She challenged the Soul Goat of Jeston's ceremony of Right of Passage. You are aware of what I think – that the ceremony is a complete waste of time and resources. Anyway, she was challenged by the billy to a contest of wills. Then, after several hours, Eren proceeded to break the rules of their contest. She tried to negotiate with an animal who can't think beyond food and mating. The animal decided that negotiating was grounds for an actual physical combat duel … guess who won?"

With that, G laughs again and winces slightly. "I was stupid enough to speed things up, and the goat got me as well while I was driving him off. But, I believe that even though I was injured, I won because the goat retreated."

Hesitating, Jess looks up as he is checking for any broken arms or legs. "Did you see where the combatant was struck? I am not finding anything broken, so far."

Rubbing her cheek, G ponders this, somewhat uncertain, looking over at Eren. "I believe that she was struck in her chest, as was I. Dolon aims high ... and hum ... right leg ... also, the butt that knocked her out ... it connected with her abdomen."

Unimpressed, Jessep frowns. "Okay, I am unable to check for internal damages ... unless I open her up. That could be interesting, even though I have no formal skills in the surgical art of healing. So, I will need to do what Lorn grants me and hope it works. Let's see ... I think I prayed for a healing prayer two days ago. Stand back G, or even better – go away. No, on second thought, stay here, as I might need you to protect me from a mad farmer, yet again. Remember, she pays three Dyns for every day she is here, including the full price for a partial day. This means before the new day begins, by our forefather's reckoning."

G laughs heartily as she starts to walk out. "Jess, you work that out with Eren. She holds the strings to her coin purse."

Jess frowns, as he sadly offers G, "Good night, G. See you in the morning?"

With turning to look back, G returns the statement blandly. "Yah! Right!"

Larret Army

Summer 7 Bear

The east breaths blow across the land with less force than yesterday. The gods have the sphere clear, showing a mixed canvas of several streaks of yellow, orange, and red. Today, the unsettling part for us is the ice that has formed around the edges of the ponds. There has been a definite drop in temperature. But it is not cold enough to create a crust on the ground of Larret Hamlet or in the fields or forest of Laret fief.

This weather brings an issue in itself. It seems that the lone digger of Jeston's grave wants to leave the chore of filling in Jeston's open grave for someone else to do because her fingers are cold.

Tripper hasn't deemed it important to make proper arrangements, leaving such tasks to others.

In this case, Mi has been left with the task regarding the grave. He found a villager who was willing to dig the grave in exchange for cancelling her back taxes, which amounted to three Dyns.

Today, the gravedigger has decided that the weather is too cold to fill in the grave, unless her next year's taxes are forgiven as well. However, Mi feels that returning the soil to the cold dark hole, in the dimness of night, is not worth five Dyns.

Larret Army

The funeral procession will start towards the grave in a little while. Mi observes those gathered, and though he is sad at the turnout, Mi gets ready to lead the way.

Tripper is still in the same dress as she has been since the morning they went looking for her lost father. She is sitting near the burial stretcher.

Winey is laying on the floor beside her.

Tripper desires the procession should start near mid-day.

Mi watches those attending.

Four other people are here, in addition to Mi, Tripper, and Winey, G is here, as is Eren and her bruised ego. Also, Cooper Toorp and Cottar Denain are present.

Denain is here as part of his bond to Laret fief. Besides, he has nothing better to do today. His wife is absent from the service; she is working her loom to make a new bolt of cloth.

Mi has a thought before he starts services. Therefore, he approaches Denain. "Excuse me Cottar Denain. May I speak with you?"

The middle-aged farmer looks up from viewing the ground. "Yes, Priest Mikene?"

So far so good; Mi smiles. "Denain, we seem to have a small task that needs attention. We are willing to pay a fair price for less than a day of work. Would you be interested?"

Larret Army

Denain looks at Mi and starts to speak. Then he hesitates and looks at Jeston and Tripper. Turning back to Mi, he answers, "Is it proper to talk about work at a burial ceremony?"

Nodding, Mi answers, "In this case, yes, Denain. We are looking for a strong man to fill in the late reeve's grave. It pays four dusters if you are interested."

For a moment, Denain ponders the offer. That amount would pay for a new sickle. He considers the offer for a moment longer. *'I could also get Lensa a new brush or comb.'* He makes his decision. "Priest Mikene, I will do it for five dusters."

Closing the deal, Mi frowns while offering his arm to clasp. "Done – five dusters to you for filling in Reeve Jeston's grave today." The verbal contract is set between the two men.

Happy that the grave issue is settled, Mi is ready for their journey. He wanders over to Tripper. "We are ready, Tripper. The service will start now."

Walking to the foot of Jeston's stretcher, Mi starts the ceremony. First, Mi acknowledges the gods – all nine of them. However, Mi places his emphasis on Ikerus.

Next, he transitions to calling on the world to attend to Jeston's return to the gods.

As he finishes that phase, he motions for G to take up a position at the head of the stretcher. Mi grasps the foot poles of the heavy wood and canvas stretcher. The two of them lift the carrier and start out, toward the path to the South Cemetery of Laret fief.

The ceremonial group walk on the path along Laret's coastal shore. The procession respectfully walks the half-a-kilometre in silence, listening to the natural sounds around them.

Life continues around Laret fief, even through the mourning of Reeve Jeston and his last travel in physical form.

Jeston arrives at the cemetery in fine form and without incident.

The group walks to the cold dark deep grave. At the graveside, they find a middle-aged woman. Actually, the woman is older than middle-aged. Upon closer viewing, she looks to be sixty-years-old or more.

The Toyfem looks very similar to Tripper. This stranger to the hamlet quietly watches the solemn group approaching.

We recognize her, but none of the others seem to. This could get interesting.

G and Mi set the stretcher down on the cold, dry ground near the open grave.

After he walks up to Jeston, Winey lays down with his head near Jeston's head. The boar groans once, and then he falls silent.

Larret Army

The mourners look over at this unknown woman who is intruding. She remains quiet, and no one seems willing to address her.

Solemnly intoning the rituals of the Toydon, Mi proceeds with the final actions for Jeston's body.

With the last spoken sounds of the service, G and Eren heft Jeston's stretcher, moving it over the grave. Then, they lower the whole works into the shadowy grey ground.

Diligently, Denain picks up the old shovel that rests on the mound of excavated soil.

Once Jeston is resting securely, both women back away and Denain begins the process of shovelling the mound of loose dirt into the hole, and onto the deceased man's frail corpse.

Peering at the stranger, seeming to be more curious than the others, G asks the woman, "Welcome to Larret Hamlet of Laret Fief. Who might you be?"

Replying slowly, the woman answers G's question. "I am Jeston's sister-law. My name is Tenasin. I have come to see that the news is correct – Jeston has finally deceased. He outlived my sister by about twenty-five years. Our family can now rest, assured that justice has taken its payment from Jeston."

A little shocked by this statement, Tripper speaks up. "I am Tripper, daughter of Reeve Jeston. How do we know you are who you say you are?"

Tenasin smiles while replying, "You don't, but I do. Jeston was my brother-in-law for six years before Endna passed away. I believe the last item for the ceremony is the will of Jeston being shared with us, here at the grave. I was told there was a child from my sister and Jeston. That would be you, Master?" She enquires as she points to Tripper.

Going into a funk, Tripper is shocked by this news, and she merely nods. "Yes, I am Reeve Jeston's daughter. I was told that my mother lives west of here – is still alive, and that she had no other family. I don't believe your claim, Tenasin."

Tenasin smiles and then smirking, says, "That is fine; you do not need to believe that I am your aunt. I am here to close a chapter in the history of my family. You do not need to be part of that history." She watches as Jeston is covered over by soil. Knowing the superstitions of small villages and hamlets, Tenasin remains quiet.

A smile forms on her face as she says gleefully, "Good-bye, the murderer of Endna. Justice will now be set right. May you never rest in an un-life for what you did to my sister! May her curse end with your passing on this day! Enda Lon, daughter of Jeston Lon, may you and Jeston Lon never find peace in your life. I leave you with this note: your father killed many people in his life and left a curse on each that he killed. Those walking-dead may seek you out now. But I hope the gods send the walking-dead through to their passing before they find you. Your father left your mother dead and cursed. Your salvation will be in finding your mother and putting her to rest in a Right of Passage. Then, and only then, will you find your life settled."

Turning to the road that leads back to Larret Hamlet, Tenasin doesn't wait for responses. With purpose, she walks towards Larret.

Tripper seems not to notice the others at the grave. She is lost in her own thoughts. Suddenly, Tripper looks up from the grave and seeing Tenasin walking toward Larret Hamlet, Tripper rushes after the woman.

We rush after her, remembering who we were.

Mi watches Tripper hurry off. Then he turns to the rest of the participants from the procession. "Well, folks, that almost sounded like a will being spoken. However, I have here in my hand the last will of Reeve Jeston Lon of the Hamlet of Larret as he dictated to me to record. A copy is in Lord Ramson's possession as well. I could open this and read it word for word, but I know what is in the will. I need two of you to listen and confirm as witnesses to the reading of the will. G, how about you for one? Eren, you look like you need to sit a spell. Considering last night's escapade, you should be resting. Will you be the second witness?"

We watch as Eren lowers herself slowly onto the grassy ground. It will be cold sitting on the dark grassy ground, but Eren sits anyway. She looks at G, and then at Mi.

Just then there is a snort and Winey rises to run after Tripper.

Eren speaks up, trying not to laugh. "Sure, I will witness the reading of Reeve Jeston of Larret Hamlet's will. The usual fee of three Dyns for such service, though."

At that, G sighs and shakes her head. "Perhaps you should mention that to Tripper before we continue. But you do know that once we leave the grave, an unread will is no longer valid. It is legal only if one person reads the will and two others witness the reading. We will seek out Tripper to get three Dyns for you later. Really, Eren, you are a pain in the arse! When will you do something for someone just because you feel like it, not because you are getting paid? I bet you have a chest full of Dyns and dusters in your home. Are you simply greedy, or are you angry at the world?"

Eren laughs, and she answers. "Both."

Larret Army

Eren is ready to listen to Mi reading, while she says, "Cottar Denain, you heard all that, right? I will be paid three Dyns for the service of listening to and witnessing the will."

Denain, remembering who supplies his family with goat cheese and butter, replies, "Yes, Master Eren, you are going to be paid three Dyns for sitting on the cemetery grounds and listening to Reeve Jeston's will."

Eren smiles broadly. "Good, then we are ready to start."

Clearing her throat, G offers, "I haven't said yes, yet. What about Denain being the first witness? I think he is perfect for the job. I just don't want to witness a statement that might bind us all to something that I don't agree with. You know what I mean, folks? What about it, Denain? Or what about you, Toorp? You're respected in the hamlet."

Eren laughs softly. "A mere cottar as a witness to a Reeve's will? You know that no one will listen to him later. The village cooper? Where is the sense in that? She is a busy lady of the village."

Cooper Toorp laughs, answering the question. "At least I am not freeloading off of other people's pains, Eren. I actually work for my earnings. Which, by the way, you are short on your payment for that last keg I built you. You're short … just imagine that … a whole three Dyns short. G, I will stand in for you on listening to the will. Thank you for your help a couple of days ago in collecting new wood for building barrels."

Eren looks over to Toorp. "I disqualify you because you slandered me in public. It's not three Dyns I still owe you, it's only twenty-seven dusters. So, be quiet … Cottar, you don't need to answer either. You're not qualified to witness a reading of a will."

With sharp looks at the gathered folks, Eren says, "I think that leaves you and me, G. Afterwards, we can collect three Dyns for you as well. Or, you can donate it to me if you feel guilty about accepting the coins."

With several sarcastic laughs, G turns to Eren. "Nice try, Eren. Both of these folks are qualified to witness the reading. It might have been better for you if you hadn't mentioned the debt you owe Cooper Toorp. I nominate Cottar Denain as the first witness. Do you second the nomination, Mi or Toorp? Cottar Denain do you accept the duty?"

Simultaneously, Cooper Toorp and Priest Mikene second the nomination of Denain.

Denain looks at each person who is present at the graveside, and then looking at the dirt he is shovelling, he smiles. Putting down the shovel, Denain walks over to join the rest of the small group. "Indeed, I do, Fletcher G. I will take the duty of first witness to the reading of Reeve Jeston Lon's last will. Jeston can wait for me to finish covering him up."

We laugh with G, as she states approval. "It is then set. Priest Mikene of Ikerus will read the last will of Reeve Jeston Lon, deceased from the Hamlet of Larret. Cottar Denain is the first witness, and Farmer Eren is the second witness. Thus it is settled, the bearing of witness to the reading. Mi, please proceed."

Stepping beside Eren, with quick cheerful laughs, Cottar Denain then says, "By all means, please do continue reading, Priest Mikene."

Mi clears his throat again. "Okay, as per Reeve Jeston's will, all his physical possessions will be traded for coin at the earliest opportunity. The funds are to be given to his only daughter, Enda Lon ... what possessions have not been converted to coin will be distributed to villagers. Enda will only receive the coins from Jeston's estate. No other physical possession will be handed over to Enda ... Enda, also known as Tripper, will be on her own from this day forward. Thus, is the will of Reeve Jeston Lon of Larret Hamlet."

We think sadly. '*Yah! Right!*' We watch the group walk back to Larret Hamlet.

Denain remains at the graveside to cover over Jeston.

Most of them are thinking about the future of the hamlet. So much is left unanswered, and no one volunteers that they have not heard from the Lord yet. So, it is assumed that no one in the hamlet has heard from Lord Ramson.

However, it takes three days to walk to the Lord's Dartoln Village. An immediate return would hinge on Lord Ramson actually being home in his manor.

At best, it would be six days after Jeston's death before we'd get word from Dartoln. It is uncertain if Ramson will respond at all, or even if he is available to attend to the passing of the reeve at this time.

You know, I think Tripper got her due in life. But it is still sad to see this happen to anyone. She may contest the will, but she can't win. I really am not sure what her reaction will be: anger, yes; frustration, probably; fear or dread, maybe. But we don't foresee a positive response from Tripper.

. . . . .

Ah! Well now, we are at Reeve House. The door is closed as we approach. We are curious as to the day's end.

G gives a sharp knock on the door and listens.

At first, there is no sound from inside. Then, shuffling can be heard from beyond the portal.

G knocks again, harder.

Larret Army

There is a thump on the door as a grunt is heard from inside. Of course, the grunt can only be one thing – Winey. Which means Winey and Tripper are home, but she is not answering visitors.

Frowning, Eren opens the portal.

Tripper sits at the wooden table where her father and Tripper had shared meals. As far back as Tripper can recall, that same table has always been in her life. In-depth discussions were had at this table. Now she seems to find strength from sitting at the table.

Edgy, Eren looks at G and says, "Bad timing, or right timing?"

With slow light steps, Eren sighs and leads the way into the house. G looks around, and then at those following her. She turns to Tripper and says, "The will was read and witnessed, Tripper. It doesn't look good for you, girl. You owe me three Flairs and seven Dyns. I would like to collect them now."

Moving swift, G slaps Eren's shoulder hard. G says, "What she is saying, Tripper, is that the estate you believed to be yours, isn't yours ... it has been divided another way. Tripper, unless Lord Ramson decides you will be the new reeve, you're going to have to find a new home. You won't be totally broke, though. Most of what you and your father owe to others can be

66

paid. This will leave you with a few coins to travel with, but nothing else. You will have to move your books and items. Everything your father owned will go up for sale tomorrow. I am sure Eren and I can help you. But I am giving you a few days before I come to help you. If you want help before then, please come and find me."

Summer 8 Bear

It is around midday, and everyone seems to be busy on this cold, overcast day. The east breaths have picked up again. The fishermen have decided the gods-breath is too brisk to go out on the ocean.

We saw G working in her shop a short while ago. We think she has decided to abandon the bow that is twisting on her.

This morning, she went out to the willow patch that she noted a few days ago. She harvested about forty arrows worth of willows. Taking the willow shafts to her shop, she began getting them ready for crafting into new arrows.

Away from her cottage, Eren the Unwilling hasn't been seen today. But that means little, as she is probably planning the demise of another incantation.

Larret Army

As we watch Mi praying in the church of Ikerus, there are sounds of riders approaching Larret Hamlet from the west.

A couple of the villagers try to spot who is riding in.

Entering the Hamlet as the riders' pace slows, they head directly to Reeve House.

It is Lord Ramson with three men-at-arms. They stop in front of Reeve House, where Lord Ramson and his escorting riders dismount.

Lord Ramson is not an impressive appearing man. He's an average Jalmal who is quite forgettable. He doesn't appear as if he might inspire folks readily. His mature appearance indicates a man nearing midlife years.

With Lord Ramson are two Jalmals and a slightly younger appearing Toymal.

All four walk up to the door of Reeve House.

At the closed portal, Lord Ramson peers at the door, where he can be heard calling in an upper-class Jalnoric accent, "Hello in the house; is anyone home?" Lord Ramson waits.

After no apparent response, he reaches out, and he opens the door into the old house.

This house is accustom to authority residing inside. We once asked the house how old it is. The house didn't respond.

Larret Army

We guess that houses don't have spirits or souls. Either that or it was sleeping when we asked.

Now, with the door to Reeve House unlatched and open, the boar, Winey, startles Lord Ramson.

Clumsily, Ramson steps aside as Winey stops and blocks Ramson's passage to inside.

Winey is snorting and bellowing as only an angry boar can.

Her complexion ashen, Tripper with a slouching posture, walks up to Lord Ramson. She looks up to Lord Ramson and then taps Winey twice on his head, between his ears.

Winey snorts twice, standing his ground, but he goes quiet.

As Tripper invites Lord Ramson inside, two town guards, alerted by Winey's commotion, arrive at Reeve House. The guards, Nela and Enda, approach with caution.

The two town guards are outnumbered. It has been some time since there was trouble that needed the skills of a warrior.

We determine that something interesting is going to happen, so we tell Mi. He needs to see what is taking place in Reeve House.

Looking up from his task, Mi spots the congregation of military folk gathered at the front door of Reeve House. This is enough to give him the initiative to see what he can get into.

Larret Army

On our way to the house, we see the gathered guards speak, as only guards will. They stand ready as Lord Ramson enters Tripper's home.

Lord Ramson closes the door after Tripper sends the boar outside.

We all knew this has been coming. Nevertheless, it is a bit of a rude awakening for the hamlet to see Lord Ramson, Lord of the Web Shireward and Liege of Larret Hamlet, and Laret Fief, arrive after the unfortunate death of Reeve Jeston.

Arriving at Reeve House, Mi addresses the men-at-arms. "Good day to you, and Ikerus' blessings upon you good folk ... and you too, Winey."

The visiting guards look at Mi and then at Winey. Then, the guards burst out laughing.

Morlan, one of Lord Ramson's escorting guards, looks to Mi while offering his forearm in greeting.

The other two begin to relax as well. "Well, it has been some time since we met, priest. It is nice to see a friendly face here. It is dire business – this death – the loss of a reeve. Lord Ramson wants to talk alone with Tripper for a bit before he decides what he is going to do here."

We laugh while uttering, '*Yah! Right!*'

. . . . .

Larret Army

The villagers watch as Lord Ramson and Tripper stand in front of the small crowd.

Denlan Tavern rarely sees such a large gathering. People stand jostling each other as the seats are all occupied.

With impatience, she holds up her hand as Tripper demands quiet. The crowd hushes, waiting impatiently for the news to be provided. Looking at the folks in the room, she starts speaking, hesitantly. "You are all aware that our Lord Ramson has come to Larret. Moreover, you know why ... so, I will leave it to him now. My father's spirit thanks you all for your cooperation over the years. Good evening." She sits down near the three guards who came with Lord Ramson.

As he remains standing, Lord Ramson waits until Tripper sits. Then, he begins speaking in refined Jalnoric, revealing his nobility. Such fine Jalnoric is rarely heard in this area.

Not even Reeve Jeston used the dialect. "Okay, as you know, I am Lord Willis Ramson. Larret Hamlet and Laret Fief are part of my Shireward. As such, it is my duty to protect and manage Larret and Laret and their citizens. The reeve, who had been appointed so many years ago by my father, has recently passed away. You, I am sure, are all aware of these things ... you also know that his only surviving kinfolk is Enda Lon – also known to you as Tripper. It now falls upon me to appoint the

71

new reeve. In the past, the custom is that kinfolk are appointed to the reeve's office. Also, that the reeve is appointed for the lifetime of that person. Reeve Jeston had been reeve until his death. During your lifetime, most of you have known no reeve other than Jeston. I feel we need new blood in the office of reeve. Tripper has agreed to step aside for another to take the position as reeve. Your new reeve will arrive in twenty-eight days. You must see that the hamlet is ready to receive the new reeve. I saw much that needs upkeep. But records for the last five years are sketchy at best. When the new reeve arrives, he will go through the hamlet's records, including each villager's account. Villagers are accountable for proper upkeep and records will be held to account. The new records will reflect an accurate state of Larret. Thus, they will be able to set taxes and fees. We will then know the actual status of Larret."

"Tonight, after gods-set, I will answer nine questions. Choose who you want to be the person to ask the questions and what the questions will be. If I am not approached at gods-set, the questions will be forfeited. Do you all understand? Do at least two or three of you understand?'

There is an uncomfortable silence.

Tripper stands a moment later and addresses Lord Ramson. "Lord Ramson, I think it would be better if we appoint a person to ask the questions."

She looks out over the crowded room. Pointing to G. "Will she do, Lord Ramson? Her name is G. She has a fair-handed approach to those in this Hamlet."

Folding her shoulders in and shrinking back a bit, G looks around, ready to bolt. But there is nowhere for her to escape to.

Lord Ramson looks over at G. He motions for her to stand.

She looks at Tripper as she hesitates. Then G stands, straight and tall. With command, G says evenly, "I am G, Lord Ramson. If others agree, I will step into the task."

Raking a sharp look at G, Lord Ramson ponders this for a while, and then waving his hand. "You will do. Now I am leaving to go to Reeve House. Be there before gods-set, G."

Lord Ramson and his three guards work their way through the crowd towards the door. It is slow going for the four men. Eventually, the crowd starts to part, allowing the men to leave the tavern.

Meanwhile, G makes her way to the front while Lord Ramson and his men are leaving.

Once up front, frowning, she asks half-heartedly, "Anyone else who wants to do this?"

There is a rumbling of comments as the crowd begins to thin out. Looking out at the audience, G can see most of the villein's and tradesfolk are here. They seem troubled. There are a couple of half-villeins and a few of those ever-so-timid cottars. About twenty folks are remaining in Denlan Tavern.

With a deep command, G clears her throat as she looks out at those gathered. She motions for quiet. "Eren, can you sit here and record the questions that we decide to ask Lord Ramson, please?"

Remaining seated, she shakes her head negatively. Eren the Unwilling answers, "A scribe's wage is one Flair per sheet, G. We would also need quill, ink, and material to scribe upon. Parchment might do best in this case. The quill is two Dyns, the ink is eight Flairs, and the parchment is two Flairs per sheet. How many sheets do you want?"

Frowning dejected, G answers curtly. "Don't worry then; I will remember the questions. But what are we supposed to ask?"

Looking out again at the people gathered, G wonders a few things as we watch. "Does anyone have questions to ask Lord Ramson?" She asks as more people are leaving Denlan Tavern.

No one responds and after several minutes, only eight people remain in Denlan's.

With a downturned expression, G appears disappointed in her task.

She is becoming concerned because she hasn't heard anyone ask a question.

The bartender of the tavern, Deana, approaches G. "Master G, it looks like you're left with a tab of thirteen Dyns, and no one is actually talking with you … I see Cooper Toorp sitting with Cobbler Dentin. Villein Rataln, the old Jalnoric clan head, is by himself, mulling over a tankard of water. I see my husband watching you. Petre is thinking about what brew might be best to prepare next. Cottar Denain and his son are watching you; I believe that they are wondering about their future in Larret. Both of their futures are in question now. Denain's contract as a Cottar is almost ended, as of Autumn 1 Bear. So, right now, you have a small gathering. They are not interested in upsetting Lord Ramson, so they do not ask questions. As the sailors and fishermen say, 'don't rock the barge, or you might fall off.' You're the captain of this barge right now G … it looks like you're also the oarsmen. Anything you want to ask, then go ahead and ask. Remember, you have nine questions. One question might be: who is the next Reeve?" Deana waits for the Dyns to flow into her hand.

We wait as G opens her pouch and shakes her head in puzzlement. "Why would you serve people who haven't paid, Deana? Why am I paying for others?" She looks into her pouch and frowns more. We know her funds are getting low again. She needs to sell another bow or two. Picking out a single gold Flair and three silver Dyns, G hands the coins to Deana.

Standing briskly, G walks directly over to Denain.

With a friendly smile, G begins. "Well, my friends, it looks like the middle-class is generally not interested in our future. How about you two? Tairry, are you prepared to go away and look around the Dominnion, or are you staying home to work the family estate? Denain, I know that your contract is over on Autumn 1 Bear. So, both of you have a stake with the new reeve and with Lord Ramson. Both of you could petition Lord Ramson. One petition for each of you would use two questions. I don't think you would have to pay the usual petition fees if you do it today."

Tairry has an amused expression on his face as he looks to his father. The lad turns to G and says, "I think my petition might fall upon deaf ears. But I actually have two petitions to ask, G. The first petition is a for contract as a half-villein, and I ask for ten acres. The second is a little more personal, but I think you know what my request will be. In the past, you have listened to me for several hours about it. I want to marry Deslora, Villein Timmen's daughter. I know a cottar marrying a villein is rare and frowned upon, but I feel we would be strong assets to Larret. Also, it would offer Lord Ramson more tithes and more income from Larret and Laret … right, G?"

G and Tairry know that these issues will probably fall on deaf ears with Ramson.

But G has a feeling that today things may be different.

We don't always have a *'feel'* for things that are different. But yes, we agree with G.

G responds to the young man, knowing she's had a crush on him for over a year. This may be her opening. "Sure Tairry, let's take this to Ramson … both petitions. Denain, what about you – maybe renew your bond? Even increase your holding?"

Denain watches G curiously, as G watches Denain's son. Denain isn't slow; he sees G's desire. But Denain won't interfere; Tairry has to learn on his own. "Well, G, I think an increase in holding on a renewed bond of twenty years sounds like an idea. What do you think?"

We understand Denain's thoughts, and we respect him enough that we won't share his thoughts with G or Tairry.

Larret Army

Long ago, Denain lost his first love to the parasite that ravaged Larret Hamlet. So many people died that year.

Yet, Lord Ramson still hasn't employed a full-time healer for Larret. The hamlet needs an actual healer, not one of these one-shot priests. Denain's love, Anelda, died after suffering for four days with terrible pains and bloodfires. Her whole family perished that year. She was simply the first one to go.

Still locked with her eyes on Denain, G knows that Denain works hard and has earned the right to half-villein status. She will fight for him on this, but she also feels Lord Ramson will ignore his petition.

However, we never know what Lord Ramson is thinking. By the casual way in which Denain spoke, G thinks Denain believes the petition to be a longshot if it's even considered.

Halfhearted, G smiles politely. "Okay, I will take these three petitions to Lord Ramson and see what comes of them. Is there anything else?"

A soft voice speaks from behind G. "I would like my house back. I would also like to petition to be the new reeve, Gena."

Turning rapidly, G rises with a confused expression on her face. She views the older man standing near her. He, too, is Jalnoric, maybe forty years old. She remembers him through a fog in her mind. Looking him over, she says, "I won't take either of those requests to Lord Ramson, Uncle Trevour. But I will ask for a new home and nintey-year cottar bond. Will that make you happy?"

We know there is something not right here. G definitely is uneasy – maybe even angry about something.

The man speaks up, "Sure, that will work Gena. Will that be a debt-free bond, or are you going to see to it that I owe a bond that is more than I can afford?"

With aggression burning in her face, G looks the man over again. He wears clothing that appears to be close to rags: a rough wool tunic faded to a greyed red and a pair of old wool trousers faded to a greyed blue. His cloth shoes are well worn.

We can feel G's intense anger, mixed with fear.

For the first time since we have known her, G doesn't stop to think about her actions. She strikes out with her fist while saying, "My mother told me about what you did. I don't believe that you've suffered enough yet, UNCLE TREVOUR. Starvation while suffering should do you well."

Her hand flashes out, and she strikes Trevour's shoulder, almost knocking down the half-starved man. He makes his attempt at regaining balance as he blinks, still standing in front of G.

Uncle Trevour, grim-lipped with a raking gaze, simply stands and watches G.

With a step back, G appears under control again.

The young woman peers at the outcast who is called her uncle. She closes her eyes to settle down, and she mutters angrily, "Please go, Uncle Trevour. You're not welcome here." She opens her eyes, staring at her uncle.

Denain, quiet most times, stands and walks over to G. "G? Do you need help? Who is this man with the outcast mark? One who dares to talk to you?"

Silent, G remains glaring at Trevour.

With a nervous tick of his lips, Trevour lowers his gaze. He stands there, waiting for his fate.

Then, slowly, with patience, he speaks again. "I am sorry, Gena ... truly, I am sorry. It wasn't supposed to happen ... please forgive me?"

G spits out, "You raped my mother – your own sister. No kidding, it wasn't supposed to happen. Why Lord Ramson only outcast you, and never hung you, I don't know."

Trevour sobs. "It was your mother's request to outcast me so that I would suffer."

Feeling G's anger rising again, we can only answer, '*Yah! Right!*'

Larret Army

Well! We look at the doom and gloom club who are gathered here. The four haven't spoken a single word for a few minutes now. We watch them as they curiously watch each other. Who will speak first? How long are we going to draw this out?

There is a soft cough coming from G.

We turn to her and smile. When this young girl does that, we know that G is going to speak thoughtfully, even if the thought is out of place in the conversation, or, as in this case, lack of conversation.

She smiles timidly while G looks at Lord Ramson. We shrink back, knowing that the last time Lord Ramson was here and he had this look, Larret lost two cottars.

As for G, we haven't seen such determination from her before. An almost commanding presence flows from her posture. Her back is straight and stiff, and her arms rest firmly on the table, but are relaxed.

"Lord Ramson, for this meeting, may I address you by your given name, Willis? If so, you may use my given name as well. I am not G in the eyes of the gods. My name is Gena. For these questions, I humbly ask that we use our given names, those given to us by our ancestors." G waits with patience while watching Lord Ramson. She observes Ramson as only a youth would: with curiosity, as well as a small amount of respect.

Ramson nods as he intently views G. "So, the village asks an old child to negotiate on their behalf … interesting. I think we can use our given names: Willis and Gena. Yes, I agree."

He waits patiently for G to speak again.

Both of the selected seconds look shocked at this but keep silent.

Delan almost has an expression of fear on him – his mouth slightly gaping and eyes widened, face reddened.

Morlan, shocked, jolts back in his seat, wondering if a good outcome can be had with such familiarity on G's part towards Lord Ramson.

A little relaxed, G is humbled with Willis' answer to her. She smiles. "Willis, my lord. The hamlet has been given an opportunity here. I am afraid that most are too scared to say or ask anything of you. I, on the other hand, have my freedom. So, if necessary, I can move on. I know that would leave me with a bit of hardship for a while. But I also have no family here and no fear of the road that leads to the next place. The villagers did not choose a humble old man who is afraid to speak his mind in addressing you, my Lord. I ask that we start talking now, you and me."

Larret Army

Delan quickly places a hand on G's shoulder, in fear for her safety. Ramson is known to be harsh when pushed. She must be more careful. Delan shakes his head slightly as he turns to look at the fletcher of Larret Hamlet.

There is a chuckle from Lord Ramson as he looks directly into G's eyes. We are unsure of what he look for in her eyes, but he smiles. "Good. I see the hamlet actually chose well. You will stand up for your villagers. As you know, you should have nine questions ready to ask. I have no idea what the questions are, but I do want to sleep tonight before I set out for home tomorrow morning. So, by all means, Gena, speak your mind. I won't promise to listen to any silly childish questions. But I will attempt to humour you this evening." He nods to G, and then takes a drink of his tea.

As she gives a bold smile, G appears to relax slightly more while she answers him. "Willis, as you say, we have no time for childish questions. Therefore, neither one of us will waste the other's time. I am not sure if you know my second – Mason Delan of Larret Hamlet. He is an excellent village mason who is here to keep me in check and not waste anyone's time. Though, I have to say that I haven't addressed Mason Delan with the things I am about to speak to you about."

She turns to Delan. "Fear not, good Delan, if the rod is used, I will be the one receiving the lashing. If you are uncomfortable with this vigil, then please leave me with Lord Ramson, and leave us to our devices. You will not be looked ill upon, not by me."

Ramson bursts out laughing heartily. After calming down, he addresses the others. "You would face me alone? Or would you like my man-at-arms to stay? Yes, Mason, if you feel ill at ease, please do go. We don't want anyone getting into trouble because of this girl." Ramson laughs more.

With furtive looks at each of the two, Delan is not sure if they are serious or only having fun at his expense.

Now smiling, with a twinkle of mischievousness in her eyes, G calmly turns to Delan. "Remember, I can look after myself. I believe it is custom for each party to have a second at these meetings. I do appreciate you being here. But you do have more to maintain than I do, Delan. It is your choice to stay or leave."

Frowning nervously, Delan looks at G, and then offers. "I am sorry, G, I know you should have a second here, but I have my shop and family to consider. This is about asking Lord Ramson questions that might ... be difficult to sit through. Sorry G, maybe you should have had Mi or Jess with you on this."

That said, Delan stands, turns to Lord Ramson, and while bowing, he adds, "Good evening, Lord Ramson. May you have a pleasant sleep tonight." Quickly turning, Delan exits Reeve House after giving G an apologetic look.

We have gotten to know G; she is up to something.

With a throaty sigh, G turns to Willis. "There now, there is no threat to you, Willis. I feel more comfortable as I can say what needs to be said. We can say what we want without someone going into shock. How is my aunt?"

Giving a nod while smiling cheerfully, Willis then says, "Well, it's good you remember who you know, Gena. Your aunt Mitila is doing fine. How are you getting along here? Is there anything you need? You know, child, it has been some time since you were home, and I think your aunt would enjoy a visit with you. I forgot how spunky you can be."

Knowing that Willis is giving her a compliment, G smiles, something he saves for very few. She looks to Morlan. "And you? How do you fair these days, Morlan?"

Before Morlan can reply, G faces Willis again. G continues. "I am doing well here. I think what I need is Larret to have a reeve and the villagers to settle down again. Aunt Mitila may get a surprise one day; I am getting the itchy feet that our family seems to get in our youth."

Larret Army

Man-at-arms Morlan sighs deeply from his abdomen. "Why? Why do you two do these things? I am fine, Gena. Your aunt sends her well-wishes, even if Lord Ramson forgets to tell you. But as usual, he did not forget." Morlan laughs humorously.

We are confused. Did G know she would be chosen to speak with Lord Ramson?

G says eagerly to the two men. "For one, I still remember the lessons you gave me, Morlan. I remember my family … I remember my duties. My duties include helping Laret Fief and Larret Hamlet to prosper. Who … wait! I know you, Willis, if I ask a question now, you will count it. You will probably be true to your word and only allow nine questions, and then you will send me away. Well, I have some questions, and some of the questions are in the form of petitions that get asked of a Reeve or the Lord. First, I am really curious as to who is going to be the new Reeve?"

Willis smiles evilly, and his eyes narrow. "You remember, Child, the rules of conduct we worked out when you were twelve. I reserve to answer that question later. From you, I will listen to petitions today. My, how you have grown up since the last time we met. When was it? Was it five years ago already?"

Larret Army

The three gathered in Reeve House talk late into the night, trading questions, answers, ideas, and the occasional shot in jest. Finally, issues are settled and G walks home.

Entering her home, G refrains from lighting a lamp. Quietly, she walks to her bedroom, passing her guest. With a look of sadness on G's face, she pulls the blanket up to Tripper's shoulders without waking the woman.

G retires to her bedroom for some much-needed rest.

Thinking, as she's going to sleep, that everything is settled and that Tripper is not Reeve of Larret Hamlet. The negotiating for the petitions were tough. Even though Lord Ramson is Gena's uncle, he didn't go easy on her, just as he said he wouldn't.

Willis gave into several issues but then shocked G with his final point – a statement G will need to think about overnight. Her uncle was moving quickly for her. He wasn't wasting time, and that scares our young G.

As G lay in her bed, she thinks, '*We are too young for this. He has to be joking with me.*' G is unable to sleep all night.

We, of course, say, '*Yah! Right!*'

Larret Army

Watching the gathered villagers in the central square of Larret Hamlet, we smile. It seems Lord Ramson has decided to make a statement and some decrees before departing Larret Hamlet. He is stern looking as he stands near the Shrine to Stonewire. Lord Ramson holds up his hand as eastern breaths blow on clothing and bodies.

The sphere is partly cloudy; we expect it to rain today. The breaths are strong enough that no barge will travel today.

Lord Ramson calls out to the crowd. "Would G, Eren Molan, and Enda Lon please come here to me now. I will make my decrees once all three are standing with me."

The crowd seems curious as to what is going to happen. Some whisper, wondering if G is going to be punished for some slight to the Lord. Tripper? Why her? The one they are most curious about though is Eren. The Lord has had no contact with Eren on his visit.

Tripper arrives on the stage first, standing next to Lord Ramson's left side, while G is a close second as she stands to our Lord's right hand. As usual, Eren lives up to her nickname, being last.

Larret Army

Eren the Unwilling was named such, as she volunteers for nothing and does little to help others unless there is a profit in it for her. Eren looks as confused as the rest of those who are gathered here in the hamlet's square.

Lord Ramson motions for Eren to stand with G. He then clears his throat as the three stand in their places. "Citizens of Larret Hamlet." He bellows out to almost two-hundred gathered villagers. "As you are all aware, Reeve Jeston passed away Summer 1 Bear. Thus, leaving Tripper to maintain his position as temporary Reeve of Larret. I have spoken with Tripper and Gena; they are aware of my concerns about the future of Larret Hamlet. I have relieved Tripper from holding the Office of Reeve. In doing so, I have also appointed your new reeve. Now hear me. I appoint Reeve Gena of Larret Hamlet and Laret Fief. She has asked that the one who is known as Eren Molan be appointed beadle of Laret Fief and Larret Hamlet, as well as a lead herder of both. Reeve Gena will take up her position starting Summer 8 Bear 1st Cycle II Succession of King Dolan IV. Gena will also stand as a woodward until Gena can arrange a new woodward. You will pay proper attention to your new reeve. I have full faith in my choice of appointments. Reeve Gena will be working with the beadle and herder, Eren, for the season, making a proper accounting of Laret Fief and Larret

Hamlet's assets and citizens. I expect full cooperation with these two. I tell you now that if I have to return this season to oversee any of this, I will be very upset with the parties responsible. Now Reeve Gena would like to address you." Ramson nods to G as he turns to her.

G looks out at the people of Larret Hamlet. Maintaining a stoic expression, she calls out. "Lord Ramson has asked me to speak with each household to discuss the household holding and to record such discussions. Many of you will receive newly assigned bonds. I will be talking to each household about their future in Larret Hamlet and Laret Fief. A few offices of Lord Ramson's appointment will be dealt out to the involved people. I have accepted this post of reeve for Larret Hamlet and Laret fief. Many of you know me from dealings we have had. I know most of you, and I am familiar with your families. I will not lie to you; some of you will be disappointed, even angry with the decisions I am going to hand down. Do not fear, no one will be left out in the cold without a home this season. But a few will need to decide their future elsewhere."

Turning to Eren, G says, "Thank you, Eren, for accepting the offices as discussed this morning. I hope we can work well together. I know I will learn much while we work together in the coming seasons."

Larret Army

With two confident steps forward, G walks around Lord Ramson, and she approaches Tripper. G hands Tripper a small sack. "Tripper, this is as per the will of your father. All possessions of your household and his have been sold. This is your estate as he wished it. It is a few Flairs and some Dyns. You will now find your own way in the world as a free person. If you desire, we can talk about a future here, or you can move on. That is up to you."

Hesitantly, Tripper takes the sack as she looks at Lord Ramson and then G. "If we could talk, I would appreciate it, Reeve Gena. I lost my father and my home. It appears I have even lost a place in Larret."

She walks away, towards Goats Tavern. Her head hanging low, Tripper walks slowly with Winey at her side.

Turning to the Lord and Knight-commander, Earl Ramson, G answers. "I now fully accept the office of Reeve of Larret Hamlet and Laret Fief, working in your name, as our liege Lord Ramson." She is stuck between a smile of excitement and a frown of concern.

For one brief instance, G thinks, '*If a sixteen-year-old can rule our country, then surely, I, being a little older, can manage a mere village.*'

We think, '*Yah! Right!*'

Chapter Two:

The Dead Aren't Done

*S*ummer 10 Bear

We were thinking, but it hurt, so we quit.

The thoughts went such that, G is a young woman who seems to understand things even before she has finished the thought. G is above average in appearance, but not beautiful. She has ice-grey eyes and waist-long raven-black free-flowing hair. She is shorter than average and has a light build, hiding a strength that allows her to work heavy loads for long hours, effortlessly.

This all conceals the fact that G is only seventeen-years-old, even though most who meet G believe her to be about thirty-years-old.

In comparison to G, the beautiful Eren the Unwilling thinks for hours before pulling it all together and building on what she discovers. Eren is beautiful with her ice-grey eyes and striking facial features, matched with raven-black waist-length braided hair. Eren is often outfitted in an ankle-length red wool dress, in contrast with G's common-like blue tunic and leggings.

Eren, the same age as G's mother, may be thirty-five-years-old, but with her attitude and looks many who she meets believe Eren to be eighteen or nineteen-years-old. Eren is muscular and hardy. Being tall and stalky, she can work alongside any farmer, performing the long hours of hard work. She appears to work effortlessly, and can accomplish the work of two men. She tends to her goats nimbly and smartly, gaining the milk from the nannies to make her much sought-after cheese that the villagers eagerly pay for.

Here, in this place and time, G rules.

"I don't care. We are going to go through each family, starting with the cottars. We will list every person in their household, their current ages, including all kind owed with all debts they have, as well as any notes that should be in their bond. Then we will deal with the half-villeins, followed by the villeins and then freemen and others. We are doing that starting today, Eren. I have negotiated a few petitions with Lord Ramson. He explained that as Reeve, I am free to alter any contracts I feel need reworking. So, when you're done your prayers to your non-existent god, we will get started. I think twelve sheets of parchment will do, right?" G iterates again to the less than happy Eren.

Perched on a chair near the large wooden central table, Eren looks over at G. It is strange to see these two attempting to work together, especially with their roles reversed. We are not sure why Eren was singled out from the village to work with G. But, be damned, she is determined to do the job correctly.

Eren looks at G, while asking, "So, if I have it right, you take any coins owed to the hamlet and fief, as well as any owed to Lord Ramson, and divide it into two lots. One lot is for Lord Ramson, and one lot is for Laret Fief and Larret Hamlet. Lord Ramson's lot is seventeen percent of the full total. The second lot is for the working of the fief and the hamlet, for the things that need taking care of. Also from this lot comes our pay: three Dyns per day to me and five Dyns per day to you. Plus, you and I receive a bonus of one percent of the fief's profits, correct?" Eren looks ready to explode, then starts laughing hysterically.

Finally calming, she adds, "Plus, we keep our places, rent-free. This is too much. I see we need to work hard for ourselves. I want a horse by the year's end." She continues laughing.

G looks at her partner who will be working with G to manage the hamlet. "Come on now, let's get ready. Keep the records honest, Eren. We don't want trouble from Lord Ramson, do we?"

Eren and G look around Reeve House. All of Tripper's possessions are now gone. With the aide of the hooded lantern, the light source sitting in the middle of the table, Eren looks around the room.

The stove is burning, heating the house, as the two women search the house. There are four rooms. In the centre of the structure is the large low-ceilinged common area. There are two rooms to the west of the central room and one to the east.

The east room is dark with the door closed. The footprint area of the room is ten feet by twelve feet. The walls are lined with several well-used deep shelves. The room contains supplies, such as food, water, the ale barrel, and other storage items. Miscellaneous items, such as clay plates, bowls, pewter utensils, as well as the much-used copper cooking gear, sit on the shelves. Last night, G added her cooking gear, including bowls and a birch cutting board.

Larret Army

G and Eren made a full accounting of the house last night, and quite a bit had to be thrown out, as it never sold because it was unusable.

In considering the two rooms on the west side of the house, the women had finally agreed that G would occupy the bedroom that had been Jeston's, while Eren claimed the sleeping quarters that Tripper had used. Both rooms are ten feet by fifteen feet in area. Both rooms have small shallow chests lined with shelving, and each has one shuttered window.

The room in the east has no window. The common area has two windows on the north wall and an exit situated in the south wall.

G is resigned to purchasing a new bed soon. For now, she will move her old feather mattress single bed over from her house. Her own bed is in need of small repairs, but it will work for a couple of more seasons.

Eren looks at G, and then she speaks up. "It's time to go; see you after my meal."

We chuckle, *'Yah! Right!'*

Larret Army

Summer 12 Bear

After a light knock on the door of Reeve House, G opens the portal and is surprised to see a destitute child. The child looks to be Jalnoric and female. But the ragged clothes and dirt make it difficult to be sure in the dusk of the day. She doesn't recall seeing this child before. G can see that the child is distressed and possibly hungry.

"Hello, can I help you?" asks G.

We watch the child, sadly knowing we must stay out of this one. Influencing G has been forbidden in this instance. We watch and tell G nothing.

The youth stands a moment watching G, and then she says, "Mamma is missing. She went missing three days ago. Pappa went looking for her two days ago. I can't find them. Please, will you find Mamma and Pappa?"

Still new as reeve and young herself, G is unsure how to respond. Her heart tells her to take the child in, clean her up, feed her, and ask a few questions. So, she says, "Come in. What is your name?"

The little person hesitates, and then slowly steps into the house.

The gods are nearing their resting place for another day.

Larret Army

G and Eren had been dealing with villagers since nine o'clock in the morning until just past eight in the evening. G had no idea that their job required so much attention to people's behaviours and situations.

From over half the villagers, she has recorded the things that Lord Ramson asked her to record. G is finding that the records from the former reeve are terribly incomplete and wholly inaccurate. Deaths were not recorded; births were not recorded accurately, and the status for folks was out of line with their contributions and holdings.

It is all a mess.

G thinks to herself. *'Two more days to finish this. Then we have to inform Lord Ramson of the results.'*

Sitting the child at G's table, she returns her thoughts to the present. Less than twenty minutes ago, Cottar Ilnn left, having declared Ilnn's father had passed on, yet there was no official record of it.

Tripper and her father had been very lax in record keeping.

"Can I get you something to eat? My name is G ... what is yours?" asks G, while watching the child.

The child responds as she sits at G's kitchen table, which Eren and G had used as a desk. "I am Genella. My mamma's name is Elina. She is old. Pappa says she is thirty years old. Pappa is a good pappa. Why doesn't he come home? I am good. I know I am. Mamma and Pappa are missing. Please bring them home. Please G."

.....

G sits up in bed, looking out into the dark of her new Reeve House bedroom. Larret's usual night sounds play around her. Trying to recall where the little girl is, G gathers her senses and realizes the little girl was only a night-dream.

G reaches for her mug of Harpen water that sits on the nightstand beside her bed. The room is too dark to see the nightstand or the mug, so G relies on memory and reflexes. But when she reaches for the mug, she is unable to find it.

The nightstand is where it should be, but there is no mug. "Damn! Did I forget the water?"

Swinging her legs out and setting her feet on the floor, G feels the wetness on the floor. She shakes her head and sighs. "Well, there is the water."

Standing slowly, G orientates herself using the frame of the bed. Facing in the direction towards the door, she treads lightly, so as not to cut her feet on shards of the pottery mug. Not even two strides away from her bed, G's foot strikes into a person on the floor.

Larret Army

Kneeling, trying to recall if she settled anyone on her floor last night. All she remembers is her night-dream of Genella.

Reaching down, she hears, "I am sorry Mamma; I didn't mean it."

Maybe it wasn't a night-dream? Perhaps the little girl is having night-dreams?

G quietly says, "It's okay, Genella. You're safe." She feels the girl's shoulder, and the girl flinches. 'Odd.' thinks G.

G quietly asks, "Are you awake, Genella?"

There is a mumble, but no other answer.

She decides the girl is still asleep. Standing, G carefully steps over the girl on her floor. Finding the bedroom door, she opens it.

Exiting the bedroom, G feels that the air is fresher in the common area of the home.

The souls outside in the sphere shine through a window's open shutter.

With the small amount of light in the room, G walks carefully over to the window. She looks out into the night, recalling the sad story of Genella. Genella's family lives in the woods, a fair distance south of Laret, near the south swamps. They have a house for the three of them. Genella has no siblings. Her pappa hunts most days, just to feed the three of them. Her mamma sits for hours, not moving or talking. Four days ago, Genella's mamma was yelling at Genella's pappa, saying that she was tired and wanted to go to a village and live.

G realizes that the child may have misestimated the time, as the girl said it took her two days to get here. Genella started walking two days after her pappa left. Genella's pappa went two days after her mamma.

As G figures it, Genella's mamma has actually been gone for at least five or six days. Genella's folks may have already returned home, but G doubts they have.

With a brief shudder, G recalls the things that her uncle did to her mother that had her uncle branded an outcast. He would never be allowed home again. Many people were angry, and G was very confused, as well as a little upset.

So, she can imagine how Genella is feeling now.

Walking to her cupboard, G picks up a mug, fills it with water, and then sits at her table.

We feel her sadness and anger. G has a tough choice to make. She's been reeve since Summer 8, and already she has to talk with each villager, sorting out the mess that has built over the last six or so years. That task isn't finished yet.

Now, she has a young girl, about ten years of age, who has come to her for help. The girl's life is unstable and definitely uncertain at this point.

G wonders who will look after Genella.

Our voices are almost in unity as we say, *'You, G'.* Tonight, our voices seem to go unheard. Maybe G is blocking us out.

She takes a couple sips of water, as is G's custom when trying to figure something out. G is a young woman, not even considered an adult yet in some cultures, and yet G has been through plenty.

Now, G has taken on a job that a much more experienced older person might even have trouble with. We think that Lord Ramson chose G because of her lack of experience, possibly bringing new ideas and flexibility, but determination to the position.

Laret needs more than Ramson realizes. Laret needs G, but G must remain a stable influence.

Already G has changed several contracts and has had to deal with the financial difficulties of several households. These last few years, hardship has been all too common.

Many households are barely holding on to their lives, with little to eat. Many are unable to support themselves in their current situation. So far, G has dissolved three households, not renewing their contracts, and giving the families involved a little aid in kind, but informing them that there is no future in the village for them as a household. She had to inform these households that they would do better as part of another clan's household or in another village.

G now whistles that little tune she does when she is coming to a difficult decision.

We think she might be right about this. '*Yah, right!*'

Summer 13 Bear

We are watching the gods rise up into the sphere. Listening to G this morning was akin to watching the chaos of a school of frightened Tarbot fish – they're all going in different directions without actually colliding.

We weren't allowed to influence her decision, so we're proud of G's solution.

Walking out of her bedroom, G is followed by Genella.

Genella saunters over to the table and sits on a chair, while G opens the house door for Eren, who is slightly tardy.

G looks outside and notices Cottar Billup walking towards Reeve House. He, too, is slightly late, as both of them were supposed to be here fifteen minutes ago.

Larret Army

These long days are wearing thin on G, but she realizes that there are only a couple of more days of this and then the task will be finished.

Addressing Eren, G hands her a Dyns. "Can you go to my house and bring Tripper here? I have a job for her if she is willing."

Eren takes the Dyns, knowing it is probably from G's own fortune. She steps outside and then looks up at the sphere. She sighs, seeing the cover in the sphere and feeling the chill in the air. However, it is warmer than yesterday. The east breath has settled down a little. Eren walks down the slope between the buildings, towards G's house.

Ten minutes later, Eren arrives at the house she intended, and she knocks forcefully on the old wooden door, rattling it.

A grunt answers her. There is a pause, and then an answering human voice, "Come in," is heard, as well as the click-clack of a boar running across the wooden floor.

Not being one to stand out in the cold needlessly, Eren enters the house.

Upon gaining entrance into the house, Eren is greeted by the boar.

Winey snorts and nudges Eren. The boar seems a little friendlier today.

Tripper says to Eren, "Please let him out. He needs to go for a bit of a run. Come on in, Eren."

Eren lets Winey exit before closing the door. With the door closed, Eren laughs. "I am not here to visit, Tripper. G has sent me. G says she has a job for you if you want it. You're supposed to go over to Reeve House."

Tripper frowns sarcastically. "That traitor is offering me work? Why should I take her up on it?"

She gives a devious smile as Eren views Tripper. After some thought, she answers Tripper. "Because you're hungry and need food. Winey didn't go outside just to go for a run; he went out to forage for food. Your table has a bowl of thin pottage on it for your morning meal. Do I need to go on? Come on ... I have work to do; I want to get it finished ... let's go, Tripper."

Eren turns around to open the door to leave.

Tripper takes a deep breath. Angrily, she replies to Eren. "Tell the traitor that I will be there sometime today."

Eren looks back at Tripper. "Don't wait too long; others are looking for work right now as well."

Arriving back at Reeve House, Eren enters and finds G in discussion with half-villein Moore.

The old Jalnoric serf is asking that some of his household's labour obligations be forgiven this year. Instead, Moore offers

427 dusters, claiming they need the time to catch up with their holding's work. This is their entire purse of spare coins; they have no more.

Eren walks in. "Okay, let's start from the beginning so I can record this."

G turns to look at Eren as Eren prepares to record the proceedings. "Well? Is she coming over?"

Eren nods her head as she sets the inkwell in a convenient spot on the table. "She'll be here, but don't expect it to be right away. Tripper still has her pride."

Moore looks at each of them, but he says nothing.

The proceedings continue again for the third day.

Once Moore leaves, and before their next head-of-household arrives, G and Eren discuss Cottar Billup, getting that business settled.

Reeve House door opens to show a neatly dressed daughter of Jeston. Tripper's hair is brushed, and her clothes are relatively clean and tended to. Tripper closes her eyes, and taking a deep breath, she sighs and then opens her eyes.

Stepping into Reeve House, Tripper looks right at G. "Eren said you have work for me. What is it?"

Larret Army

With a sharp piercing looking, G turns to Eren. "You told this impolite, rude, callous girl that I have work for her? I didn't know."

Swift as a sparrow, G turns to look at Tripper. "If you rephrase that into a more polite question, then I MIGHT answer it."

Again, Tripper swallows and stares at G. "I am asking if you have work for me, Master Gena."

G frowns sadly. "She's not even calling me by my proper title. Do you believe the callousness of this girl, Beadle Eren?"

Smiling slightly, Eren nods, but she remains silent. We think for her well-being, it is best that Eren not voice her thoughts.

Seven Hells, we're not repeating them.

Tripper lowers her gaze but says nothing.

G addresses the peasant free woman. "I do have work for you, Tripper. The work is important, and I won't ask anyone other than you to carry it out … my chamber pot is full."

G trips on the last part of that, breaking out into a broad grin. "Seriously now, a young girl's parents are missing. I thought someone with your skills might be able to help find them. This young girl's name is Genella. Her parents have been missing for about six days as I figure it. Apparently, they live near the south swamps, two days away. Can you help Genella, or should I ask someone else?"

With narrow eyes, Tripper looks at Genella. "Obviously, her parents cannot pay for a mage. How do I get paid for doing this? It's not considered work unless there is pay."

G smiles broad cheek-to-cheek. "I am so glad you're volunteering to help Genella, Tripper. I am sure there is a cow or some other animal somewhere looking for an owner. But we can deal with that later. Are you, or are you not going to help Genella?"

Before Tripper can reply, Eren pipes up, saying, "I think Lord Ramson's guidelines show that a mage can be hired for two Flairs a day, or for up to a total of fifty Flairs for an assigned job longer than twenty-five days. Looking at our budget, I believe we can pay for twenty days at most. Am I correct Reeve Gena?"

G frowns with sadness. "Two Flairs a day? That is more in one day than she is going to earn all year. But I do understand that we have such a proposal in our budget. Okay, Tripper?"

Tripper laughs confidently. "I can do this in ten days or less. No matter the length of time to fulfil, it will be fifty Flairs, whether five days or twenty-five days."

Eren looks over at G and nods her head once.

Larret Army

G sighs shallow from her chest. "You drive an expensive deal, Mage Tripper. But I agree, upon confirmation of completion of this work, you will be paid fifty Flairs. Please scribe that in the village log, Beadle Eren. Oh yes, make an additional note that Mage Tripper has only twenty days to complete this work or she will forfeit the contract."

Tripper pales slightly, but she is confident it won't take even ten days. So, she nods in agreement.

G says, "Sorry, I didn't hear your answer."

Tripper swallows. "I agree to those terms. I accept the work."

G digs into her coin pouch and pulls out two Flairs, handing the coins to Tripper. "For expenses. Now please go; we have our own work to deal with. Take Genella to see the village, and find a decent dress for her to wear. Thank you, Tripper."

Genella leaves with Tripper, and the dreary day of reeve business continues for Eren and G.

Tripper and Genella search around and eventually find a rugged but clean and functional dress for Genella. The dress is sea-blue in colour with a red embroidered bird on the left shoulder.

Genella weeps as she puts on the dress, telling Tripper she has never had such a pretty dress.

Larret Army

'*Yah, right!*' we ponder.

Summer 14 Bear

As she looks out of the window, G peers at the souls in the sphere, almost wanting to worship one of the gods this morning.

Yesterday at midday, Tripper left Laret, headed south with the young girl and one man-at-arms.

The man-at-arms, Tesser, is a Jalmal on the older side.

G recommended that Tripper takes Tesser – a forty-five-year-old man who has taken the time to learn tracking and forest survival skills, and he has military experience as well.

We know G's dilemma, and we understand her guilt. But, we also know there is nothing more she can do for Genella.

Having second thoughts, G is frustrated even though she knows it is too late to change her decision. Eren should be here in about an hour, and G is still dressed in her nightclothes.

Filling the water kettle and stoking the stove fire, G sets the kettle on the stove to heat up. She continues to the bedroom, carrying an oil lamp to light her way. There, she grooms and then dresses in the same skirt and tunic as yesterday. Last night,

110

to prevent her clothes from further wrinkling, she had carefully laid out her clothes.

'That longbow for Nesseb needs finishing tomorrow. Hopefully, I will get back to work on it today. It is already overdue by two days.' G is generally conscientious about her work and schedule. However, the agreement was made before she was appointed reeve of Laret and before Jeston passed away.

A knock on the Reeve House door alerts G that someone has arrived. She finishes the last knot of tying her shoe and then walks out of her bedroom. Closing the bedroom door, G moves to open the front door. She is mildly shocked to see Mi.

We sent Mikene so he could talk with G, so he can hopefully settle her mind and spirit.

He is one of the few villagers who G actually trusts and actually cares for. Mi is strongly drawn to G, spiritually and emotionally, though neither has told anyone, including each other, about how they feel.

We are the only ones who know how they feel; the two don't even realize their bond with each other.

The Cleric of Ikerus looks up to see G, and he slowly smiles while reading into G's expression. "I am sorry. I can leave, G, if you want. It's just that I was doing my morning prayers to Ikerus, and I felt that I needed to come and see you. I am not even sure why. I can leave; sorry to disturb you."

Mi turns to leave, but he hesitates halfway through his turn, looking embarrassed.

G places a hand on Mi's arm, saying, "Come on in, Mi. I am about to have my morning tea. The water should almost be ready."

She removes her hand from his arm. It's her turn to suddenly look a little uncomfortable, but it passes. "Come in Mi; don't catch a cold out there. You didn't even wear your cloak. Come on in now."

As G backs out of the doorway, a small field mouse runs out of the house through the open door. She moves, intending to let Mi into the warm house.

The cleric hesitates and shrugs as he pivots around to enter Reeve House. He finds it hard not to smile. "Tea will be nice. I have a few minutes to visit."

The two settle down to tea after laughing about their brief awkward moment. The sight of the mouse running out had lightened the mood. The two village leaders are together again to talk about the community and their current work.

G speaks about the little girl and about sending Tripper and Tesser to escort the girl and help find her parents.

Larret Army

Listening to the story, Mi smiles. "I think that is a wonderful way of dealing with the situation, G. It shows wisdom and compassion. I think the villagers' current view of you has been a bit harsh; this should lighten them up. Most reeves would have sent the child to the church or to a village home as an orphan. I suspect you are right about the little girl, Genella – that she is now an orphan, left to her own skills and smarts."

"Mi, I heard that you are tending to the Right of Passage for half-villein Norn. Do you know how he died? How far along is the Right of Passage? If you can, I would like the funeral taken care of before nightfall," asks G, Reeve of Larret.

Mi fumbles with his next thoughts, but says, "I believe he passed away from old age. He was 102 years old, after all. It happens eventually to all mortals. Jess is tending to the Right of Passage of Norn. I think it will be all taken care of by gods-set."

This sounds right to G, so she makes a mental note to talk with Jess about it today.

There is the now familiar knock of Eren the Unwilling on the door.

G calls out, as is a habit now, with the arrival of her assistant. "Come in, Eren."

Quick, G stands then makes three mugs of tea, setting them on the table. G also sets the small honey pot and a small spoon on the table.

Eren opens the door and walks in. She sees Mi and then looks at G. "Trouble already this morning? Good morning, Cleric Mi."

Mi smiles. "Actually Eren, I ran out of prayers to say this morning, so I came to visit G. Good morning, Beadle Eren."

Both G and Eren sit at their usual business seats to drink their morning tea.

G says, "One of the fishermen left three fish last night. I cleaned them already and will cook them for us today. So, Eren, if you and Mi will eat midday meal with me, I would be honoured."

Mikene smiles. "Of course, I will share a meal with you."

Eren looks at Mi, then to G, and smiles. But she only says, "Fish sounds good. I will bring milk from my goats to go with the meal."

Mi offers with a grin. "I will bring the bread – freshly baked yesterday afternoon."

We watch and listen to the forming friendships. '*Yah! Right!*'

Larret Army

Summer 14 Bear

We watch Tripper walking with Genella; both are quiet and sullen. As Genella follows Tripper, the girl is not sure what is happening. Tripper is still put out because of recent events in the village. But this job will provide her with food for a season or two. She just won't be able to expand her craft until she acquires more coin. Now she finds she is saddled with a little girl who probably has no hope of seeing her parents again. They are now trying to find those parents. In the least, G could have provided Tripper with a better tracker.

She sent Tesser back to Larret after he had confessed that he couldn't find Genella's tracks anywhere along the edge of the woods, nowhere along where Genella said she had come through.

We think, *Umm hum, yeah a lot of good a Laret tracker would do you.'*

Several hours into their journey, Tripper looks up as she hears crackling in the woods off to the east of their path. Those damn birds fluttering again. Tripper ignores the sounds.

Genella lets out a loud scream as an appendage wraps around her torso.

Tripper stops quickly and turns to see a creature holding Genella secure in its arms. Then, Tripper realizes what the creature is.

Tripper is uncertain as to what she should do, but tries to relax the situation by speaking to the creature. "My Lady, please, the child means no harm. Perhaps if you release her, then I can give you a bit of food?"

The creature speaks out in frail jalnoric speech, "This is my child; you can't have her. She is mine, I say."

Tripper stops, realizing that her thoughts are right. This pitiful creature is a woman. It is a little difficult to determine her race, but it is a woman and most likely an adult.

Not sure as to how do deal with this, Tripper lets her natural instincts take over as she settles her arms to her sides. "I am sorry. I didn't catch your name. And the child's name is what?"

The creature offers. "The child is Genella. She is mine … I don't … remember my name. I am her mother. Her father tried to kill me … he pushed me into the swamp to die. I … I don't want to die. I want Genee to have a real home. Take me with you to a home. Take me to a village. Take me to a safe place. Take me to a safe place, Lady."

Larret Army

The little girl squirms. Turning, Genella looks at the creature. Looking into its face, Genella brushes mud and debris from the face, revealing a woman of several decades of age who might have been pretty at one time. "Mamma?" calls out Genella.

The voice, now firmer, answers, "Yes, Genee, it is me, Mamma. Where is your pappa?"

The little girl shivers. "Pappa left me at home. He didn't come back ... I was so hungry. He didn't bring me any food, Mamma. He left me there as you did. Why did you leave, Mamma? Why?"

Genella begins crying, and so does the creature who is known as Mamma.

Tripper is uncertain what to do.

Then she begins doing something that she might not have done several days ago, Tripper unslings her pack and waterskin and takes out some food. She looks at the creature again.

With a heavy heart, she offers the creature food and drink.

The creature lets go of Genella, who now clutches and clings to her mother while leaving the woman's arms free, so she is able to eat and drink.

Seven hours of walking into the woods with Genella, and already Tripper is reconnecting the child with her mother.

117

Larret Army

At least Tripper hopes it is true – that this is the girl's mother.

The woman slowly eats the hard bread, relishing each bite. She's obviously hungry, as if she hasn't eaten for some time.

Soon, they set out walking, until Tripper guesses that it is time to find a spot to camp. She spends an hour looking in an area but finds no place to rest for the night.

Continuing on, Tripper finally finds a place somewhat suitable to camp, deciding that a fallen tree can be used as a lean-to. Tripper clears a small area for a fire and makes a nest of moss and reeds for the other two to sleep on.

She is trying to understand ... there she goes again, '*analyzing the situation*' she calls it ... we call it, '*thinking about nothing*'.

The day-gods set in the west before Tripper can finish setting up camp. But, she should have enough fuel to get them safely through the night.

We watch the three settle in for the evening, wondering how safe they will be through the night.

This is, after all, called the Dark Woods of South Laret. Few people venture here, even during the daylight hours. Few come back after a night out here.

'*Yah! Right!*'

Larret Army

Summer 15 Bear

The three night-gods are in the realm of the sphere when a noise alerts Tripper that something is amiss. Their fire had died a while ago from lack of fuel, leaving the trio without light other than the night gods and the souls of the dead.

Tripper peers into the darkness beyond their little camp. The creature from the swamp is sound asleep, and Genella is curled up close to her for shared warmth.

Looking out into the darkness, Tripper fears the night, and that fear is playing on her mind. Her thoughts even cause us to have fear.

But we know what moves in the dark. A young weasel, curious as to what is in the camp and its occupants, is investigating the camp.

.....

The light of Stonewire and Imvor eventually bring ease to Tripper's mind. Tripper is shivering from the cold, as well as from exhaustion. She did not sleep after the sounds caused by the strange movements woke her.

The distraught mage watches Stonewire rise, as her charges stir.

Genella informs Tripper that she is hungry, so Tripper offers Genella a bit of her own food and water.

The creature, who seems to have drawn in Genella's favour and trust, also stirs from her resting.

Tripper looks the woman over. She looks like some walking-dead swamp monster.

Something strikes Tripper as odd. The woman looks so much like Tripper does when Tripper looks at herself in a mirror. But that could be for any number of reasons. Tripper's family do not originate from this area, but someone related to her might live out here.

With no more thought about the resemblance, Tripper offers the dishevelled woman bits of food and some water.

For now, do we continue to their home to find Genella's father, whom this woman claims tried to kill her? We listen into Tripper's mind, as she is deciding what their next action for the three of them should be.

She looks up into the sphere – the planes of gods. Then, with a decision made, she watches as the east gods' breath whips the cover overhead.

Tripper says, "Okay, let's go back to Larret. I found your mother, Genella. So, I have done what I promised and was hired to do. The job is done."

To Tripper's dismay, Genella starts to cry. She calls out, between gasps of crying. "Pappa … I want Pappa … we find Pappa … now … Mamma, we find Pappa …"

The woman, who's sitting on the damp ground watching the little girl display her distress, shows no evidence of emotion. Silently, the woman stares at Genella. Slowly, as she sits there watching the girl, the light comes to her eyes. "We can go to Larret and get food, and then we go find Pappa. Okay, Genee? We find Pappa, and then ask him why."

With a sharp twist, Genella turns to the woman. "Mamma, you find Pappa? You find Pappa, and we all be together again. We be together like before, in home, like before. Like before you left."

The woman, looking at Genella, nods her head in slow motion and sullenly answers. "Yes."

Genella slowly stops crying and looks at the two adults. "Okay, we go find home to be good. We go now." She stands up, and looking around, she begins walking before either adult can stop her. "Come, Mamma and other woman. We be going home now."

We think. '*Yah! Right!*'

Larret Army

Summer 16 Bear

Yesterday, we watched Genella lead the two adults through the woods for the whole day. She took them on a route that would have confused even the best scout or ranger. As the gods were setting below the horizon, leaving the sphere, the trio stepped out of the woods into a clearing.

This clearing contains two buildings, one of which appears to be a house, the other an outbuilding that could be a small barn or storage shed.

Genella laughed and shouted, "See, I find home. We stay and find Pappa tomorrow."

. . . . .

Now, with the morning dawning upon the world, the trio know that morning brings new hope for one little girl, despair for her mother, and frustrated confusion for their rescuer.

Life can be entertaining and sometimes funny. But today, life isn't being those. Instead, it has placed a burden upon three people who don't realize it yet.

Tripper crawls out from under the blanket made from a deer hide. She stands up and looks at the child who is sitting on her own bed, watching Tripper.

Genella speaks. "I know where Pappa is. He called to me to bring you. We go to Pappa now, Tripper Lady. We talk to Pappa; he tells us why he leaved."

Tripper, as a mage, is accustom to the unexplainable. She looks at Genella, and even though she knows better than to ask, she asks, "When did you talk to your pappa, Genella? Why did he leave again, before waking me to tell me he was here?"

Genella shrugs and replies. "Pappa says bring you. He tells you there himself. Pappa not be able to come home now. We go to him. Then we go to your home, Tripper woman."

Tripper stretches a little. Sleeping on a dirt floor, under a deer hide blanket, with no pillow or straw was a little uncomfortable.

Now, things do not always go as planned. Which is something Tripper is well aware of these days. The *'plan'* was to take Genella and the woman who says she is Genella's mother, home to Larret. Once there, let G deal with the situation.

We smile. *'Guess again!'*

The woman saunters over to Tripper. The woman has cleaned herself up. The clothes she wears are not a lot better than yesterday's, but at least they are clean. She stops near Tripper, and looking at the mage, she says, "We need to find my life-companion. He has something I need ... I need to say good-bye before leaving him to the woods and swamp. I know where he is."

Tripper closes her eyes while frowning in frustration. But heck, she has six days left to return to Larret so she can collect her reward. The Flairs are important, now that her father is dead and she wasn't appointed reeve. '*Yes, Father is dead.*' She has to look after herself as no one else will.

Tripper looks at the little girl and then at the girl's mother. They don't have anyone either. They have to look after themselves, and now they both look to Tripper to help them. Is this fair?

Tripper has a dilemma, and she has no one to help her. Yet, these people want her help. Can she do it?

Can Tripper do something for others without help from anyone else? G and Eren had always helped Tripper when there was trouble – specifically, all those times when her father wandered off on his own. But there is no one else here, other the little girl and this strange woman.

Tripper smiles. '*I am smart enough to be a mage. I can do this. I don't need anyone's help to aid these people.*'

"Okay, I will help you some more. But, if we haven't found your man in two days, I will return to Larret with or without you. So, let's do this."

Larret Army

Tripper looks for confirmation from both of them. Then it dawns on Tripper. *'I don't need their approval. I am making a decision that affects myself. It is me making the decision now.'*

The woman suddenly smiles. "I remember; I'm Elina. My name is Elina."

Tripper sighs. *'One step forward.'* She says, "Okay, we leave now. Elina, if you know where your life-companion is, then please lead the way … how long will it take to get to this place?"

Elina nods. Standing, she heads for the door in long strides. She stops at the door, turns around and says, "Genella, come along. We have to say good-bye to your Pappa. He can't look after us anymore."

Genella, with tears forming in her eyes, looks at Tripper. "Okay, Mamma, I coming. Pappa needs our help, right? We go say bye, then find a good place to live?" Genella stands, and then gesturing to Tripper she follows the older woman.

.....

We watch as Tripper looks at the body strung up in the old poplar tree. The two females said it was Genella's father.

His death doesn't appear to be a suicide. The skin on his legs is peeled away – from his hips all the way down to his feet.

This was not a voluntary or accidental death.

125

Larret Army

A bucket rests on the ground near him, full of what is most likely his blood. The blood is now jelled and crusty. The bucket of jelled blood appears to be at least six days old.

Genella looks up at her father. Her eyes follow the rope up into the branches which are a good seven or eight feet higher over his head.

Tripper turns away from the bucket to look over at the woman, Elina.

Elina appears to be in a state of abstract horror and in deep shock. She has stopped in her tracks. Her eyes are swollen with tears, and the tears begin to flow.

Genella walks boldly to the corpse that is hanging in the mature poplar. As she stands peering up at the corpse, she speaks. "Pappa want down ... Tripper woman, please bring Pappa back to Amara?" Turning around, and then looking back to the corpse, Genella laughs and says, "Yes Pappa. Tripper woman help you leave after you come down. She powerful woman."

Tripper, feeling queasy but knowing the child does not understand what has happened to her father, walks forward and looks the area around him over. She notices the long hemp rope is tied to another tree close by, while one end of the rope is tied to the man's two wrists, which are tied together stretched above his head.

Tripper shivers nervously. The man died in great pain. But why? By who?

Untying the simple slipknot at the tethering tree trunk, Tripper struggles to slowly lower the man. Even though the man had bled out and is missing a large part of his skin, he still weighs over two-hundred-fifty pounds. Bracing herself, it is all Tripper can do not to get pulled up by the rope as the dead man comes crashing down.

As he settles onto the ground, Tripper starts to relax a little. She is glad it has been awhile since she last ate.

Elina stands frozen staring at the corpse. She hasn't moved since first seeing her life-companion's mutilated body.

Winey suddenly breaks into the clearing and snorts roughly.

Tripper smiles while still trying to hold in her meagre stomach contents. The mage scratches Winey's neck as he joins her at the corpse.

As the initial shock leaves, Elina suddenly begins to moan and weep. She returns to the harsh reality of what has taken place. Elina walks forward while looking around. "He's dead? Really dead! Why? It was only a gold locket filled with a grey powder and a pin. The pin was simple and dull. It wasn't even a good iron pin ... why would he do this? The man ... he came looking for it after Darius brought it home, saying it was laying on a stump north of the farm. The gold locket had to be worth hundreds of Dyns, maybe even a dozen Flairs. But to kill for it ... why Tripper? Why just for gold? It's not worth killing for. And to do this ... the man must be a demon of the gods."

Now that the body rests flat on the ground, Tripper feels queezy as she takes a closer look at the corpse. The deceased is totally naked, and his genitals have been removed as well. It looks like – Tripper looks away at the thought of it – the genitals were ripped off, or a very rough dull or ragged item was used to remove them.

As Tripper considers what she has to do, she looks again at the body. She finds it easier not to think of the body as belonging to a man. If she doesn't think of him as a person, it helps Tripper to deal with this.

Finally, she releases the end of the rope. Tripper looks around and notices a rough wooden bowl. Inscribed inside the bottom is a dark rusty substance. Looking inside the bowl, she sees symbols of three straight parallel lines; each line is about two inches long. Below the lines, is a small bit of grey powder; about a quarter of an ounce.

Now what? Tripper is not a priestess; she cannot do last rights or the Right of Passage.

We volunteer, hoping that Tripper is listening. The Right of Passage takes time and belief. These three need to believe in the man and have faith that we are sending him on to the god's planes.

Sighing, '*Yah! Right!*'

Summer 17 Bear

Tripper walks sullenly into Larret Hamlet, followed by an excited young Jalnoric girl and her tired but cheerful mother. They are happy to be in a settlement. The two walk into the hamlet with an air of success, tempered by the reality of their situation.

The woman's life-companion, who is the little girl's father, is dead – never to return. He died with much pain and suffering – so gruesomely – at the hands of an unknown butcher.

Tripper leads the two directly to Reeve House.

Reeve House sits on its little plot of land on the western side of Larret Hamlet. Arriving at the house, Tripper almost enters as if the home was still hers.

She draws back, looking at the door suspiciously, and yes, forlorn, as it's not her home anymore. She doesn't have a home anymore, much like the two who are following her.

Standing straight, Tripper knocks on the softwood door. A dull thud is heard and then it is answered by a shout. "Enter." The voice from inside is recognized as G's.

Tripper looks at her companions and then down at Winey. She nods. Reaching out, Tripper releases the door's latch and opens G's door.

Looking inside, Tripper calls. "G, it's Tripper. I have come back within the agreed upon timeframe. In fact, I am early. But you're not going to like it. May I enter with my charges? They both could use a meal."

G walks out from her bedroom over to the entry. She looks outside to the two refugees and then to Tripper. "You and your companions may enter, and I will get all four of you a meal. Please, introduce your company to me."

The hamlet's reeve starts towards the kitchen. "Also, please close the door once you are all inside. Wipe your footwear off."

She puts a pot of water on the fire and begins cutting up some tubers that were harvested this season. She cuts the tubers into smaller pieces, so they cook faster. Next, G adds three carrots chopped into small pieces as well. She stokes the stove's firebox.

With that done, she turns to her four guests. Pointing to Winey, G calls to him. "Bed, corner."

The pig snorts and then ambles over to the corner that used to be his until recently. Winey lays down on the cold, dry floor to wait for his supper.

The time is about halfway through the fourth watch of the day.

G has taken to this job of being Reeve. Although she was initially reluctant, the young Jalnoric woman has attacked her new responsibility with full gusto, making her best effort at sorting out the contracts of each household. One more day should have it all finished, and then she can send her report to Lord Ramson, liege of Larret Hamlet and Laret Fief.

Suddenly, Genella runs over to G and cries out. "Lady. We found Pappa. Tripper woman helped find Pappa and Mamma. Pappa gone now to see the gods."

While they wait for the one-pot meal to cook, G looks over at the three dirty and tired travellers. She chuckles to herself, noting even Winey is dirty this time.

Pouring cold water into one of her wooden basins, G places the basin on the table. She fetches a wash towel and some soap powder. "Everyone takes a turn at cleaning up. Except for you Winey, the river waits for you. Genella, you're first, then the woman and finally Tripper Lady. Got it, everyone? I have one wash towel, so you need to share it. I will get my two drying towels for you to share as well. Sorry, it's not hot water; I know how good that might feel right now. But for now, we will use the cold water … okay, let's go; we have work to do."

Genella looks at the others and then shakes her head. "No! … Mamma first, then Genee, then Tripper Lady."

G smiles in her most benign fashion. "Okay, it can be done that way. By the way, Genee's mamma, I am Reeve G of Larret Hamlet. Welcome, I hope you are well. You can stay here tonight; we will sort out things tomorrow."

The dishevelled woman responds in a polite respect. "Thank you, Reeve G. I am Elina, Genee's mamma. Her father … well, we found him … dead in a tree. Skinned like an animal. They got him … those creatures that call themselves men. They got Genee's pappa, and they tortured and killed him dead, keeping him in pain for a long time. They did things …"

She stops talking and starts washing her hands, arms, and then her face and neck. She's sullen, as if deep in thoughts that are not about the here or now. Visible tears roll down her cheeks as she dries her face. "He wasn't always the mean, nasty man he became. He didn't deserve to die that way … he tried, he really tried, G. He did … really! He just wanted a place for us … away from the rules and those who watch others … some freedom … safe from thieves and bullies who call themselves our lords of the realm. But they found him … he didn't have a priest send him on his passing … he wasn't a mean man … really … he wasn't." Elina goes silent as she finishes up, putting the towel on the dining table.

Genee listens to her mamma talk. She replies, "Pappa not mean, Mamma. He just hungry and afraid of bad men. But bad man found Pappa and made Pappa dead."

G looks over at Elina and says to the mother and child. "It's okay now, you're safe here. We will figure something out for the pair of you. For now, rest and settle for the night."

Looking at Tripper, G says softly, "I would like to talk with you. Please, lets' go for a short walk outside."

Tripper grimaces sharply, but nods slowly in acceptance. "Winey, stay here. We will be back soon."

The two women step outside and G closes the door as Genee steps up to the basin to wash up.

Walking towards the Stonewire Shrine, G is fully expecting Tripper to follow along.

133

Halfway to the shrine, G talks without slowing down. "Okay, let me understand all of this – the woman, Elina, is Genella's mother? Right?"

Tripper just answers, "Correct."

They briskly continue on, G quickly stating, "Genella's father, who is Elina's life-companion, was murdered by someone, but you don't have a clue who did it, or how many were involved? I hear that it was one, but in another statement, I heard it might have been more than one. You confirmed that he is dead?"

She swallows hard as Tripper thinks back to the memory of the body that the three of them found hanging in the small glade in the woods and swamp. "Yes, there is someone dead in a clearing south of Laret. The human male was skinned from the waist down. It appears that he was alive while he was being skinned. We took him out of the tree that he was hanging from. We tended to the corpse as best we could, though he did not receive any Right of Passage or any last rights. The woman and child claim he was theirs."

She gives a harsh sigh as G stops. "Can they stay with you in my house, until we figure something out for them? ... oh! Yes, I have this for you, Tripper." Deftly G reaches into her belt

134

pouch, pulling forth a largish coin sack. "Your coins for doing this – as promised, Tripper."

Tripper eagerly takes the sack. Weighing the pouch roughly in her hand, she nods with approval. "Thank you. Is this why we went for a walk to a shrine of a god? I know you don't talk with any of the gods, G. Thank you for the coins. The two can stay with me if that is your wish. But don't expect any further aid to them."

With an abrupt turn, G turns to look at Tripper. "For starters, my beliefs are no one else's business, but you are right about the walk. There are three extra Flairs in there for you as well."

We chuckle. *'Yah! Right!'*

Chapter Three:
Tripper's Journey

*S*ummer 18 Bear

It is the morning and the two day-gods, Stonewire and Imvor, are rising into the sphere overhead, following a path set out long before humans arrived upon Quantos' North Amara.

The pair of day-gods usher in a strong east breath, chasing across a partially obscured sphere. This day is starting out warm, but many barge captains will be carefully judging the strength of today's breath to determine if sailing is going to be safe for their vessels.

136

Larret Army

With sidelong glances at Tripper and Jess, G has already invited them into G's kitchen for a morning tea. She takes a slight inhalation to gather the scents. G determines that the two made sunflower green tea. The two have already stoked the firebox of G's stove, warming the room and adding the taste of smoke to the air.

As G enters the warm main room from her gloomy bedroom, she sighs. "What now you two? You wake me at gods-rise for a mug of tea? I think not. Tripper, you were paid last night for finishing and solving the puzzle, so I am unclear as to why you are here. And Cleric Jess, priest of Lorn, why are you here?"

Tripper speaks first. "Reeve G, or should we call you by your given name now? Reeve Gena … I asked Jess of Lorn to come here with me – to talk with you and petition a boon from you." Tripper looks apprehensively at Jess.

We know what is coming, but we don't know what G's response is going to be.

Turning back to G, Tripper says, "Jess and I ask that you accompany us to the site of the deceased Jalmal, Darius, to offer him proper last rights or a Right of Passage, so he doesn't rise up and terrorize Larret or the surrounding lands. I suggest that

Genella and Elina stay with Mi until we return. It should take only three days."

Jess, in agreement with Tripper, nods to G.

Sighing, G takes up the mug of hot tea and sips the steaming liquid. She smiles, thinking that whoever made the tea is good at it; they made it the right strength. It was probably Jess, as most of the time, Tripper has a hard time just boiling a pot of water.

Returning her attention back to her unwanted guests, G responds coldly. "You barge into my house, on the first day that I can have any semblance of resting, to ask me to go on an errand to find and put a dead man to rest? You're sure now? You are asking me to go, why?"

Jess speaks up quickly before Tripper can stumble on her own words. "Well, Reeve G, by Tripper's account, the man died a horrid death. He was not given a Right of Passage or even last rights. So, we all know that he will rise up as a walking-dead of some sort and torment anyone he finds. I hope that the best he can achieve is returning as a ghoul or zombie. But, ghosting is possible with such a traumatic death. Tripper is, by her accounts, a Mage of a bit of power, but she is unable to defend herself. I am a Cleric favoured by our god, Lorn. So, I cannot lift a weapon in combat, even for defence. So, you see, if anything violent were to happen, we might both perish in the woods or swamps, along with Darius. Now, I have watched you in your daily practices with your sword and bow. I think you can defend us without a problem. We seek you simply as a defender for the faithful. Please, G?"

G looks over at Jess. The pious priest of Lorn can spin yarns without much effort. Then G turns back to Tripper. "Let me eat and think about this. Now get out of here so I can gain focus, you conniving patrons of Larret. Come back at midday. I have three contracts left to deal with, before sending my report to Lord Ramson. Out … now!"

Jess smiles and utters softly. "I knew you would agree. Thank you. I will be ready for midday, all equipped and prayed up."

Bearing an angry frown, G replies, "I didn't say yes, Jess. Now get out. I'm hungry, and I get testy when I am hungry. If you don't let me get ready for the day, you might see the skilled swordsman from the blade's end. Out … both of you! … now!"

"Thank you, G," calls Tripper, as she quickly opens the door to leave Reeve House.

"I didn't say yes, NOW DID I!" calls G.

We smile, '*Yah! Right!*'

… ..

Larret Army

Tripper understands the value of coin and kind, but not social grace or friendship. We understand her dilemma, as it is now a bad time for Tripper. It's a bad time not to know the grace of people, or worse, to be alienating those she needs.

The trip out to the marsh to discover the dead man, to find the father of a young child and life-companion of an outcast woman, was long. Tripper discovered on her journey that doing good for others, in return for kind or coin, is not always what we expect.

The man was found hanging from the branch of a tall mature poplar tree. He was dead and had been partially skinned. The killer had drained and collected the blood of the dead man, using it for some sort of ritual. If the ritual was magical or priestly, Tripper didn't know, but the reaction of the man's life-companion indicated that the man's life-companion knew. Through discussion, it was discovered that the family was out in the middle of the marsh, living a less than sustenance living because they had been trying to escape from a particular group of very vicious people. It seems the family had been found by these people, and the man paid the price.

Tripper had walked the two female survivors back to Larret Hamlet, with Winey, who had suddenly found and joined the group in the clearing with the corpse. Most of the trip back was uneventful, more so than the journey out had been. The young child led the way back to Larret. For some odd reason, the child seemed to know the path.

The journey was uneventful for the small troop until the ambush by some walking-dead folk. The walking-dead were a group of skeletons left by an event in the distant past. Their remains had lain unblessed by any creature or god for many years.

In the unhappy surprise situation, Tripper's group happened by the site of the massacre, and the skeletons rose to make an attempt on the lives of the travellers. The rotting ropes, clothes, armour, and weapons of the skeletons made little physical impact upon the travelling group. However, the emotional impact was much more immediate.

Tripper unexpectedly imposed herself with a bold command between the living people she was escorting and the rising mob of walking-dead. Thinking quickly, using her high intellect in the arts of mage-craft, Tripper let loose a spell of enough power to debilitate the three leading skeletons, leaving two still attacking.

Winey saw to it that one of the two skeletons soon returned to the ground, thus leaving one skeleton to deal with.

Larret Army

Unfortunately, the remaining skeleton had melee skills when he had been a living breathing person, and he seemed to have carried his skills into the unlife. This skeletal leader retrieved a shortsword from its rotting leather scabbard at its side and aggressively approached the travellers.

Winey and Tripper eventually prevailed by defeating the skeleton.

.....

Tripper has become well aware of life's unfairness. With the passing of Tripper's father, with her first paying job, and with her being relieved of any associations in Larret, Tripper wonders what is going to happen to her. We rather expected this for her, considering all the sheltering in life she received. Tripper became a mage through the efforts of her father and herself, but against the better judgement of others.

.....

G, Mi, and Jess are walking with Elina through the Dark Woods to the southern swamp. They are finding this distressing. We feel the spirits moving, too. But we aren't aware if G can feel us.

The group is following a relatively straight path when they come upon the skeletons encountered earlier by Tripper and Elina.

Larret Army

Mi and Jess help the dead pass on quickly, finishing off the trio's day.

The group of four camp at this spot, waiting for morning.

Summer 19 Bear

G wakes her companions well before Stonewire's yellow beams of light break the eastern horizon's southern hemisphere. She wants to be travelling with the first shafts of Stonewire's light, well before Imvor's orange-red shafts of light break the eastern horizon's northern hemisphere.

The foursome walk briskly through the dense woods of the Dark Woods, finally arriving at Elina's home. Elina follows a path, leading the others to the grove of her dead life-companion.

Arriving near the clearing, the stench of rotting flesh is overwhelming even before the group enters the grove.

Spotting the corpse, they see the seething mass of maggots on the body, and Jess immediately vomits his day's meal.

G says, and we agree with her. "Looks like you two have your work cut out for you. We can't take him back. What do you suggest?"

With the stench and the sight of the crawling mass of maggots, Mi gags back his own vomit. He advises. "Leave him

143

be. He'll be a skeleton soon enough. Whatever Tripper or the killers did have kept him from rising."

Elina drops to her knees and vomits, crying out between hurls. "You can't leave him there … no matter how horrible he became."

Swallowing back more vomit, Jess suggests, "Perhaps we can pray for his safety to Lorn."

Mi says, "And to Ikerus, and that'll be enough."

The two priests grudgingly pray near the dead man. Then, the four rush away from the scene, leaving the man and his lost spirit behind, to figure out their situation.

We wish them luck.

Before returning tomorrow to Larret Hamlet, G and the group spend the last few hours of the day in Elina's house.

Summer 18 Bear

Walking westward, Tripper watches the sky while wondering, *Why does the cover travel east? So much has happened the last few days since father died. His death was a huge shock. Events afterwards were even more shocking. There was the arrival of the young girl and the journey south to the swamps. We found the girl's father, skinned from the waist down and hanging from a tree. The man's blood had been collected in a wooden bucket for some unknown purpose. With no priest to give last rights or a Right of Passage, I did what I could. The walk back was no less harrowing to our group, consisting of me, Winey, the girl and her mother. The entire trip back I felt uncomfortable and nervous."*

Returning to Larret Hamlet, Tripper was rewarded beyond the promised reward, and then she was asked to do another quest – deliver a package to the hamlet's liege Lord.

It's a three-day walk if the weather is good and if there are no interruptions.

It is now on the second day of the journey, and the breaths are blowing stronger than usual for the season. The cover is darker, almost red. Through the cover, the light of the gods is blurred.

Winey squeals for attention and Tripper looks down at him. "What?"

They have been walking along the shore of the Harper River. Winey has now stopped and is looking towards the water.

Tripper follows Winey's gaze out over the surface of the river. Out in the river is a small barge that is slowly floating by, with a man lying awkwardly on the deck. The man is not moving. An arrow shaft is protruding from his right arm. There are two more arrow shafts lodged into the barge's surface.

Larret Army

Counting for a moment, Tripper observes as the barge intimately floats by. "Damn," Tripper says with harsh resignation. She looks at Winey crossly. "Guard."

Tripper places her pack, along with her shoes and her other items, except leggings and tunic, neatly on the ground.

Wading out into the shallow river until the water is chest-high, Tripper then stops. She is upriver from the barge now, maybe twenty metres away.

Resigned to rescuing the man, Tripper struggles, attempting crude swimming. Occasionally, she is able to touch river's bottom. Eventually though, she arrives at the edge of the barge.

Tripper struggles as she tries to pull herself up onto the barge. Once onboard, Tripper rests for a few brief moments.

Looking over at the body, she shivers. Tripper is too late; the man is obviously dead, and he appears to have been dead for a few days. He is already decomposing, resulting in a horrid scent and the purplish coloured skin of a slightly bloated body.

Holding back her vomit, Tripper compares this to the dead man she found hanging in the tree of the swamp. This one smells worse, but he doesn't look so revolting.

With a loud groan, Tripper stands and starts looking around the barge. There is an arrow lodged in the body's right

146

arm, piercing the main artery. He died by bleeding out. It may have taken a minute or more, but he didn't have a chance of surviving.

Tripper looks around and sees an oar lying on the deck. She picks the instrument up and starts oaring the barge to shore.

Ten to fifteen minutes later, Tripper beaches the errant barge. Contemplating her next action, now that she is ashore and the barge is safe, Tripper is fairly surprised as the corpse slowly stands.

The walking-dead starts to head directly towards Tripper. With its arms flailing erratically, striking out at Tripper, it begins attacking her.

With no weapons in hand, other than the oar, Tripper reacts without contemplation. Dropping the oar, she starts by firing off two missiles of energy at the corpse.

The impact of her magic is still inspiring to us. The light from the impact brightens, and then it is gone.

The dead man stumbles momentarily.

As he stumbles, a silent attacker bowls into his body, forcing him off the barge and down into the river water.

Neither Winey nor Tripper had time to think about their reactions.

Larret Army

Tripper reacted as any mage with such resources might: by using magic as powerful as possible to resolve the situation quickly and decisively.

For Winey, it was all about protecting Tripper – his herd mate and the one who helps him obtain food.

Tripper realizes that the corpse is still an issue, though most likely not a problem for her anymore. If it survives, it will need to find a way out of the river, and then seek its next prey. It may look for Tripper; but from what she understands, they don't think beyond what they can currently see. It's their anger at the world that keeps them active.

Tripper ponders the situation quickly. She looks the barge over and then shaking her head, Tripper sighs. Back ashore, she walks to her belongings and picks them up.

Tripper and Winey continue their trek, leaving all the items that were on the barge, aboard the vessel. Well, everything except the corpse.

The day wears on. Tripper, on a couple of occasions, thinks about the incident. She considers the arrows; she believes they were crudely made by someone with little skill. All three arrows appeared to be made by the same person. So it might mean that their supply is limited.

Larret Army

Tripper has no false sense of security. She knows that whoever attacked the barge is still ahead of her on her journey.

It is only a couple of hours to gods-set when Tripper stops at a decent location along the river to build a camp for the night. She begins to gather debris to fuel a small fire, but she soon changes her mind and stops. Tripper doesn't want to set up an invitation for anyone in the night, especially not here, considering the walking-dead man they encountered not too long ago.

Taking out some jerky and a biscuit, Tripper swallows a rare drink of water from her waterskin. She laughs at the thought of a river full of water, yet she rations the water from her waterskin.

The night's darkness rolls in as Tripper settles with her back to one of the larger trees. To her left, she has her pack placed beside her. To her right, Winey is curled up to her in swine style.

Tripper sleeps well, but very light, through the night. She is only disturbed once from her slumber, when an owl flies by and ruffles Winey, rousing the boar.

Larret Army

Summer 19 Bear

They awake as the day-gods rise and shine their light.

Tripper and Winey stretch. Both their stomachs grumble as they seek food – a simple thing to take care of in the past.

Winey wanders off into the woods.

Because of the barge incident, Tripper considers that she lost some travelling time yesterday. She decides to ration her food a little tighter. Taking out two carrots that were from her garden, she eats the carrots slowly.

As she finishes eating, a much more energetic Winey returns.

They gather up their energy and belongings to continue their trek west.

The gods' breaths are blowing strongly to the east. Today would have most barge captains keeping their vessels docked or anchored for the safety of their vessels. Most wouldn't tempt fate or the gods today.

The day's travel, though cool, is relatively uneventful for Tripper and Winey.

At near gods-set their destination comes into sight.

Tripper decides to push through the dusk, hoping to arrive in the village. She estimates there is about another hour of walking.

Having entered the cultivated areas of the village, the pair have found a road of sorts. They follow it towards the village.

Stopping short, about one-hundred metres out from the village, a ghastly sight is present: two crucifixes with bodies mounted on them, stand along the road.

Two young Toymal, both appearing to be about twenty years old, are mounted on the crosses. Both are only dressed in leggings, with no other adornments.

Getting closer as she attempts to pass by, Tripper can see that the blood that has run down the wood is still relatively fresh.

Yes, both men are dead.

On the ground is a collection of items, including a crude bow with a quiver containing eight arrows, which are very similar to the ones that were used in the attack on the barge.

Tripper doesn't know if she can relax or not, but she does walk into the village, looking for a tavern, an inn, or some form of lodging for the night.

Walking to what appears to be the village centre, Tripper looks around and smiles as she sees a building that is obviously a tavern. *Where else better to find information in a village than the local tavern. And luckily, there is still light shining from the windows of the building,'* thinks Tripper.

Walking over to the tavern, Tripper notices the sign, depicting a mug, above the door. Tripper opens the door, and the warmth from inside wafts out, striking her with a promise of comfort and an opportunity to relax. Tripper's stomach grumbles and signals to her the need for an outhouse.

Thinking it over, she decides that currently, a place to sleep and put her things is more important. She enters the tavern room, walking to the counter where an old Jalmal is standing.

She speaks up confidently. "Excuse me, please sir. I am looking for lodging for one night. Where might I find such?"

Turning to look at Tripper, the man smiles a toothless grin. He squeaks. "Yes, of course, I have a room. It'll be two dusters. The pig stays in the stable, not in here. That will cost one duster. I can supply a meal for you at the cost of three dusters, and ale is two dusters. What do you like?"

Tripper briefly thinks about this. She feels his attitude was rude in his reference to Winey, but she decides a room and food are more important than changing the man's outlook towards her boar. She replies, "I'll take the room, stable, food, and two ales – all for a Dyns."

Larret Army

The man points to a door in the far wall. "Your room is there. You can go to the stable out back and put your pig in a stall. Food and ale will be on a table when you come back in."

Tripper hesitates a moment and then nods. She pulls out a Dyns and hands it to the man. "Thank you."

With a gesture for Winey to follow her, they walk out and around to the back of the tavern, locating the small stable.

Winey goes to a clean stall, roots around in the straw, and then lays down for the night.

Tripper rubs Winey's back for a few minutes. Then, she stands, and she sadly utters, "I will see you in the morning, my friend."

Tripper slowly returns to the inside of the tavern. It is a building with the universal signage of a tavern, but it has no name.

Carrying her items, Tripper proceeds to her room, where she sets her gear on the only bed in the room.

Returning to the tavern room, Tripper sits at the only table with food and drink on it. She tells us that she thinks it will be a long night. Tripper is one of the very few folks of the realm who acknowledges our existence, never mind one who is willing to speak to us, or of us. Her beliefs are touching to us.

Larret Army

Before retiring to bed, she makes use of the outhouse and says goodnight to Winey one last time.

Summer 20 Bear

Tripper wakes to a loud squealing from a voice she recognizes. It's Winey's squeal – the squeal he makes when he is alarmed by something, and when he is feeling threatened.

Quickly, Tripper gets out of bed and dresses. She rushes out of the tavern and around to the stable.

She finds two Jalmal boys wrestling with Whiny as they try to lead the swine away.

Tripper automatically acts by striking out with her hand at the closest boy. Catching the side of the boy's head, she connects so hard that Tripper knocks him over.

The second boy is slightly in shock. He reacts by letting go of the rope attached to Winey, yelling for help as he runs away.

The boy who has been knocked down curses while shaking his head. Putting his hand to his cheek, he looks at the furious mage. Tripper has a look of being ready to burn the boy on the spot.

Upon seeing Tripper's gaze, the boy freezes for a long moment. Then, with caution, he evenly says, "Sorry Master. Is this your pig?"

Tripper glares hard at the boy while answering coarsely. "Yes. Don't repeat your mistake a second time. Be gone."

Winey darts over to Tripper and the swine snorts anxiously and rubs up against her leg.

Tripper bends over to inspect Winey as the boy runs away. Untying the rope from Winey's neck, Tripper chuckles, confused, as she feels bad for striking out at another person.

She walks with Winey to the room she is renting. The mage happily settles Winey on the floor, near the bed.

Tripper sits on her bed, looking up at the night sphere through the room's only window. She notes that the night's three gods are in their late positions; indicating the time is just before the rise of the day-gods. There are two day-gods – the greater god Stonewire, and the intermediate god Imvor – and they over-shine the three lesser night-gods. Tripper estimates it is another two hours until the yellow light of Stonewire rises and is joined eight minutes later by the orange-red light of Imvor.

As she is sitting on the bed, Tripper considers the work that brought Winey and her here.

Larret Army

The local Lord of this village is known for his short patience, as well as his refusal to meet anyone before midday. Lord Ramson is a generous, though difficult man to deal with. Being as he is the Lord of Larret Hamlet, and the Earl of the Web Shireward, it would seem a bad call to anger him.

Tripper smiles as she dresses and cleans herself up.

Ready for the day an-hour-and-a-half before gods-rise, Tripper leads the way, and they both exit the room.

Winey and Tripper walk in the darkness towards the manor house, setting out to conduct business with Lord Ramson.

As she checks the package to be delivered, Tripper makes sure the package still contains the proper items.

The yellow light of Stonewire is not present in the sphere yet when Tripper knocks on Lord Ramson's manor house entrance.

Several seconds later, the door roughly rattles opens. A young blurry-eyed Jalmal scowls as he looks at Tripper. In a rough voice, he just asks, "What?"

Tripper frowns rudely while answering the disgruntled youth. "I am a messenger here to speak to Lord Ramson. I am from Larret Hamlet. I must deliver this message before Stonewire rises into the sphere. Do not delay me."

The young Jalmal shakes his head coarsely and says, "Not possible."

Shaking her fist, feigning anger, Tripper exclaims loudly. "Possible and going to happen. I have news for Lord Ramson from Larret. Lord Ramson will be even angrier if he receives this after Stonewire rises above the horizon. Do not delay, lad. Show me to a room to meet Lord Ramson and see to it that the Lord is present soon."

The youth is flabbergasted and flustered by this outburst of authority and command from a stranger. Stalling for a few moments while he thinks, the youth nods anxiously. He then commands, "Come in then. Who do I say is interrupting Lord Ramson's slumber? You can wait in that first room on the left. I will see if the Lord will see you. That is all I will do."

Tripper almost reconsiders her actions, but then she realizes that the boy is laying the responsibility of Lord Ramson's anger squarely upon her shoulders.

"The message is from the Reeve of Larret Hamlet. I am her personal village mage. Do not delay, boy," commands Tripper.

Looking down at Winey, Tripper kindly says, "Come, Winey, we will see Lord Ramson now. He will see us in a short while."

Larret Army

The youth, shaking his head side to side slowly while looking down at Winey, turns away. He leads the two newcomers into the first room on the left.

Entering the expansive richly furnished room, Tripper and Winey are in the manor's Great Hall. In the centre of the chamber is a long poplar table, flanked by six poplar chairs. There is no mistaking which is Lord Ramson's chair.

Tripper walks over to that chair and sits upon it. She sets the pack beside her seat. Waiting in the cold room with only one candle illuminating the area, she ponders Lord Ramson's possible response.

Approximately ten minutes pass, and then a grumbling Lord Ramson enters the dimly lit room. He looks around and spotting Tripper, the healthy mature Ramson frowns angrily. "So, Tripper, what couldn't wait for midday, which is when I typically hold court?"

Tripper stands up firm. She slowly answers in a dry tone. "Your command and also the matter of the death on the river, just east of the village. Your last instructions to Reeve G was to have the records updated for Laret Fief and Laret Hamlet and to have them delivered before tomorrow. I have about twenty minutes before you consider the records late."

Larret Army

Tripper picks up her pack from beside Lord Ramson's chair, as Lord Ramson injects tersely. "A dead man on my river?"

Tripper hands a set of parchment sheets over to Lord Ramson.

Tripper says in a cold voice. "Yes, I encountered a walking-dead just one day east of here."

Lord Ramson frowns as he considers the news. "How did you deal with the walking-dead man?"

Tripper, with a serious expression, offers, "Winey pushed him into the river while defending me. The corpse is still active … here are Reeve G's records for Larret Hamlet and Laret Fief, as you requested."

Tripper pulls a second bundle of parchment out of her pack, placing the documents on the hall table. "On time … as dictated by you." Settling back down on to Lord Ramson's chair, Tripper waits patiently for Ramson's reply.

Looking Tripper over, Lord Ramson is quiet for a minute or two. Then, he tells Tripper in a cold tone. "Thank you, Tripper. You can tell Reeve G you completed your task successfully on time. But before you return to Larret Hamlet, I have another task for you. Find and dispose of the walking-dead, and then report back to me. After that, you can return to Larret."

Tripper laughs loudly as she looks down at the table for a moment. Not looking up, Tripper replies. "Lord Ramson, I have no desire to return to Larret, nor do I have plans to do so. But, for a handsome price of say … a morning meal and ten Flairs worth of kind, I will seek out the corpse and dispose of it properly. No pay, then the corpse continues its unlife as it is now. I still have no desire to return to Larret, after you took my home away from Winey and me."

Lord Ramson smiles mischievously. "Of course, you're angry at me for removing you as reeve of Larret Hamlet. You never asked why though. That fact deeply disappoints me. I removed you as reeve because I see much more potential in you. As a reeve, you'd never develop into the person you can be. I believe you can be a mage of some power and skill, which would have been wasted as a reeve. I like you Tripper; you have the stomach to do what you think needs doing, even breaking the rules as set out by your Lord. We both know that the report wouldn't be late until gods-set today. We both know you came here, at this time of day, to see if I would throw you out or if I would get angry with you. But we also know that you were promptly reporting the walking-dead. So, really, I can't be angry if I truly am a competent lord. Tripper of no address, you are a Freeman now with no ties anywhere. Enjoy it, as very few can claim that status. After morning meal, I will give you your Freeman papers. You can join me for morning meal. I agree to your terms for dealing with the corpse." Lord Ramson rises from the chair without any further speaking.

Tripper, a little confused for the moment, moves to stand as well. Ramson looks at her as he starts walking away to leave the room and he gestures for Tripper to stay seated.

The Lord walks out through a far door and is gone from the Great Hall.

We laugh, as we've known about Lord Ramson's plans for a while. But we couldn't tell the living.

Tripper's response is pretty much as we expected. Though the walking-dead wasn't in the plan, Ramson did make the issue easier for both humans.

Tripper waits patiently, wondering what Lord Ramson's plan is.

.....

The candle stub burns out, letting off its last sputter with a small grey puff of smoke as Stonewire shines its yellow light into the Great Hall.

Larret Army

Lord Ramson casually enters the Great Hall, yawning as he walks to his chair. Sitting, without acknowledging Tripper or Winey, he calls out loudly. "Gerris, we're hungry. Bring some food and drink. Tripper is thirsty, and we owe her a meal. Bring us bacon, porridge, and mead as well."

Looking at Tripper, Lord Ramson asks, "Are we feeding the pig? Its name if I recall correctly is Winer? Or something like that … Oh yes, I recall, Winey."

A young Jalmal brings in a pitcher and two silver goblets. Setting one goblet on the table in front of Ramson and the second in front of Tripper, the lad then fills both with warmed mead. As the lad fills the goblet for Tripper, Lord Ramson idly says, "Bring a basin of water for the pig and three pounds of oats. Quickly now."

The boy looks at Winey, and then at Lord Ramson. "Yes, My Lord." He leaves the room, leaving the pitcher of mead on the table near Ramson.

Lord Ramson sighs after the lad leaves the room. "Sad really, they don't understand. They can't. We need our Winey's; they are the only ones that we can rely on not to change. You and I understand that Winey will die protecting you. And he knows that you will do the same for him, Tripper … I had a Winey of my own, a long time ago. He was a worg named

Assino, who I rescued from poachers on my father's land. The poachers had killed Assino's mother and three litter members. He was the last one living, and the hunters had a rope around his neck, dangling Assino up in the air. I earned my reputation that day as I flew into a mad, furious rage. I killed three of the poachers before they could put Assino down and the rest tried to run. I let them go, and I took Assino home. He didn't wake for days. Three days I tended to him, hoping he would be safe. My father instructed me to kill him, to stop him from suffering. I said that he will live, and I took him to my room, hoping for him to recover. On the third day he opened his eyes, and from then on we were inseparable until he died three years ago. A war party of Shespan cornered Assino, my father's cousin, and me. The cousin was useless in our defence. Assino perished in the battle. We had killed all but one of the Shes. I dragged the bastard back here alive and put him on display. I never fed the Shes, nor did I give him drink. He died from starvation in the stocks. The villagers fear me even more now than they did before that. But you, Tripper, wish to defy me, even challenge me. That takes guts, and I respect that, even understand it."

Tripper did not expect such forwardness, nor disclosure of such a personal nature, from a Lord who is respected and feared by so many. She looks at Winey, who is laying quietly beside Tripper.

Looking up at Ramson, Tripper quietly responds. "Our tale is not so harrowing or interesting. Actually, Winey came from a healthy sow with a litter of twelve piglets. He just sort of chose me. He started following me around and wouldn't stop. After trying to send him away, I finally let him come with me. After a week, I started calling him Winey and fed him bits. I guess we just became friends, and I accepted him. But you are correct: we will die for each other; it is just accepted and understood. But how did you know? And why did it take until now for me to realize what Winey and I have? I couldn't lose him now; it would hurt more than the loss of my father. Do we just accept it and keep going when one dies? What did you do when you lost Assino?"

Lord Ramson appears to not be listening, even looking like he wasn't going to answer. Then, suddenly, he takes a deep breath while turning to Tripper. "Maybe, just maybe, you might understand when I say: they took Assino's mortal life, but he is still with me and always will be, even after I pass on."

Ramson looks down at the table with a look that's hard to understand. Suddenly, the two look up at each other and they smile.

Tripper says, "I do understand. I have seen what the spirits can do. It makes me happy to know that Winey and I will never be apart. Thank you, My Lord."

Ramson chuckles. "Master Tripper, you need not call me lord anymore. Assino, Winey, and you and me have an understanding. I know of only one other person who would understand – your old friend and now the Reeve of Larret … Gena. She had a black swan companion that was taken away from her by her own family. They wanted her to settle down and take her duties seriously. They killed and cooked the swan. They fed any who would come to their feast to celebrate G's rising to journeyman bowyer. Her family made a mistake doing that. She left after her family held the feast. All who ate meat from the swan became ill. Her family who ate from the swan died. She has no one but her aunt and me. G is my niece, and I mourn the loss of her un-named swan as much as she does. Go back to her after you are done with the walking-dead, and become her black swan in Larret. If you do, you will have a friend who will die for you. And, for love of the nine gods, don't tell her that I told you about her black swan. I will disown both of you if you do, and I will deny the swan."

Tripper comes back to being Tripper and laughs. "No one would believe me, never mind understand it."

Plates of food are set on the table in front of both animal masters. Looking at her plate, Tripper frowns, and then she looks at Ramson. "Really, My Lord? You really did have bacon cooked up."

Ramson laughs and replies, "Of course, what would my servants and peasants think if I did otherwise? I would lose much hard-earned fear and respect. So, shut up, eat the food and know it's not from Winey's family."

We chuckle in unison with us saying, '*Yah! Right!*'

The day started out very different for Tripper and Winey. They challenged their lord, but instead of being reprimanded by Lord Ramson, he rewarded the pair and gave them work.

Tripper and Winey were instructed to find and deal with a wandering walking-dead. Then, he offered them both a morning meal, and the three of them discussed the events of their pasts. They discovered shared beliefs and abilities, and a common understanding of life and its powers.

A couple of hours after the meal, Lord Ramson stands and excuses himself, leaving the room to Tripper and Winey.

After a few minutes, the serving boy enters the room, announcing, "Master Tripper, will there be anything more for you?"

Tripper smiles and answers him. "We will be leaving as soon as we have a lunch packed for us to take."

The youth frowns as he leaves the room. Several minutes later, he returns with a lidded wicker basket. Placing the basket on the table, he turns and walks out, leaving the two strangers.

Curious, Tripper lifts the lid of the basket and looks inside at the contents. Inside the basket, she sees a fresh loaf of bread, a brick of cheese, and a wineskin. Resealing the basket, Tripper picks up the container. With Winey by her side, they walk out, ready to leave the manor and the village.

Tripper and Winey return to Tripper's room in the tavern, where Tripper retrieves her belongs.

They begin the walk east, towards the barge's last known location, believing that is where she will begin her search.

The walk is uneventful in the beginning, though Tripper finds the barge is farther along than she recalls. It is nearly eight kilometres east along the river.

Discovering the pirated barge at near gods-set, Tripper begins the search for the walking-dead.

Tripper, not being a tracker, finds the search much more challenging than she expected. However, Tripper made a promise. She might be a little like an uncut gemstone. Each stone has a story and a shape that it belongs to – rough but powerful. It strikes Tripper as funny, how she understands that Winey has a nose with a high sense of smell. She knows Winey can find truffles easily, even though they grow underground on tree roots. But she doesn't know how to command him to use his ability to smell things for tracking.

Walking onto the barge, Tripper begins looking around. She finds the blood that is days old. An old folded tarp lies on deck. Moving aside the tarp, Tripper finds an old weather-beaten chest. It isn't locked, so Tripper opens it. Inside the chest are several coins, two old wooden mugs, two wooden bowls, as well as an old iron cooking pot.

Confident that the dead won't miss the coins, Tripper sorts out the twelve coins – a few Dyns and dusters – and places them in her pouch.

Deciding that she is still no closer to finding the walking-dead, Tripper contemplates returning to shore. But, she stops suddenly.

Standing in front of her, right there on the shore, is her target. Her reaction is revulsion mixed with fear. Quickly, she retrieves the object given to her for this event. Tripper, remembering the words taught to her by the cleric at Lord Ramson morning meal table, and she begins the chanting. She breaks open the seal on the vial while walking off the barge and toward the creature. With vigour, Tripper begins to spray the contents over the walking-dead corpse.

Tripper can almost swear that the corpse is smiling at her. As the last drops leave the vial, Tripper finishes the chant. Not sure what to expect, Tripper sighs as the corpse falls to the ground.

Wondering what actually goes on in walking-dead minds, Tripper contemplates what to do next. The easy part is done. Tripper decides to use the Jalnoric Right of Passage.

She is almost knocked over as Tripper is impacted on her leg. Looking down, she sees Winey anxiously looking up into her face. He snorts twice, and an odd thought comes to Tripper's mind. *'Winey just said 'yes' to me, but everyone knows animals don't talk.'*

He snorts twice again, pushing Tripper over. Tripper is on the verge of getting angry, and then she breaks out laughing as Winey snorts the same sounds as before. She is now sure that Winey is saying, *'yes.'* It strikes Tripper that the dead don't always stay dead, so why can't animals talk?

Winey snorts, *'Yes'* again. Then, Winey looks around, and he begins digging with his snout and hooves.

Tripper shakes her head as she gets herself up off the ground. It dawns on Tripper that the pig is digging a grave.

Tripper questions her sanity. Is she so desperate for love and company that she is attributing human abilities to an animal? Has the loss of her father finally taken its toll?

Tripper ponders whether they should retain the barge, or if they should continue with their journey on foot. She laughs at the fact that she even considers the barge as a salvage possession. Finding a camping spot, Tripper puts all her travel gear on the ground.

Dragging the body over to a place near where Winey is digging, Tripper lays it out ready for the three-day Jalnoric ritual of Right of Passage.

Looking over at Winey, Tripper spots him looking at her. She asks out loud. "Do you understand what I am saying?"

The pig snorts quickly. *"Yes."*

Tripper smiles as Winey continues to dig the grave.

Beginning the ritual, Tripper settles down for the next three days of work. She has settled into doing the full task properly.

Summer 24 Bear

Tripper ate the last of her food this morning. She has been drinking river water since yesterday afternoon.

Larret Army

As Stonewire and Imvor start their daily journey, Tripper looks the fresh grave over. Hopefully, they did the whole thing correctly. Without any food, she will be hungry for a while. But Tripper made a promise. She knows that what she is doing is right and that she will be okay.

The two travellers walk in silence, westward, along the riverbank. Tripper looks down at Winey several times on their journey. Tripper is amazed how she and Winey can communicate to a higher degree than she had previously realized.

Lord Ramson is a man of miracles, and he is a much smarter person than Tripper had believed. Tripper thought Lord Ramson was a man who is mean, overbearing, and an unthinking noble. Instead, she found a man who is deep with possibilities, who thinks ahead, considering many eventualities. He is not as simpleminded, or as cruel, as Tripper had expected. And, strangest of all, he understood her and Winey as partners. He had given them a freedom she never knew to be possible. That's how life is: the unexpected is common.

Larret Army

Summer 25 Bear

It is a hot wet summer as we watch the blossoming Mage Tripper grow into a more aware person. She is changing from the sheltered naïve abusive person she grew up as.

Tripper always knew that Winey was different, even considering him special, but Tripper did not know why until lately. The pig had helped her find her father when she asked him to. Winey had protected her, even saving her life several times while risking his life.

Walking along, on this midday of summer, we watch the path ahead. We would like to warn the duo that something is ahead. But matters such as this have been ordained by our pact with the world and the gods – we cannot interfere. In the past, pushing that barrier almost got us served with disbandment. That's not good from what we hear, and it results in drastically severe punishment for any of us.

The sphere's cover shadows mask the trail ahead as Tripper and Winey round the bend in the path along the meandering river.

Tripper has dogged it for an hour now, as she is not sure she wants to return to Larret Hamlet. What waits for her there is nothing. However, she agreed with Lord Ramson to go back and carry out the task set to her.

She only needs to return to Lord Ramson and collect on his end of the bargain. G will be happy, while Eren might disagree. Tripper is even thinking of acquiring Mi's help with his god's aid in this task. It just doesn't sit right somehow. In Tripper's mind, something is missing from this job.

In recent events, Tripper has witnessed the savagery of people. The dead man in the tree was skinned from the waist down. Even his toes' skin was peeled completely off, following the removal of his toenails. If that is how the people of the world behave, maybe father had the right idea. As that thought passes through Tripper's mind, Winey nudges Tripper, urging her forward along the trail.

The shadow doesn't wait for Tripper to meet up with it. Stepping out from its hiding place, the zombie walks with purpose, straight towards Tripper. Realising that the creature is the second dead man from the free-floating barge, Tripper almost panics.

Reaching for her axe, Tripper stops the action. Instead, she stands proudly straight and tall.

Winey steps in front of Tripper to be between his master and her threat.

Larret Army

As the walking-dead continues to move closer, Tripper moves her hands to chest level, and then bringing her thumbs together to touch, she fans her fingers wide in front of her.

Winey snorts aggressively, pawing the ground in front of him.

The walking-dead comes to a halt in front of Winey. As the zombie begins to reach downward to claw at Winey, a squeal by Winey keeps its attention, and Tripper calmly calls forth, "Unto."

Suddenly, leaving Tripper's fingertips is a 120-degree arch of flame that erupts in a fan-shape, outward from Tripper's hands. The flames reach out five feet, igniting the clothing and body of the walking-dead.

There is a loud gush of air from the lungs as the zombie's lungs heat up. Its flesh and clothing burn. Hopefully, as it falls to the ground, it is permanently deceased this time.

Winey and Tripper stand and watch the corpse burn to ashes. Tripper reaches into the pouch that Lord Ramson granted for her use. She pulls out another crystal vial, and she pours nine drops of the liquid onto the ashes. There is brown smoke and sizzling as the spirit is released from the body, completing transference into death for this creature who was once a man.

Now this leaves the question of who killed the men. The arrow killed him, but someone had to fire the arrow from a bow. It will be difficult to discover who the culprit was, as the witnesses are dead and this soul has undergone separation from the body and spirit.

We shudder, as we know who it was.

Going back the way she had come, Tripper picks her way along the river's bank, trying to locate the barge again and the place where she had previously buried the walking-dead. Finding the barge still beached along this side of the waterway, Tripper concludes that it is still unattended. Thinking that maybe someone else might have claimed salvage of the items, she looks up at the two day-gods.

Tripper decides she will make camp for her and Winey. She looks farther along the beach. The barge is a sturdy vessel used for the transport of people and items from one place to another along waterways.

Walking cautiously up to the vessel, Tripper looks for signs of other possible walking-dead. With no walking-dead in sight, Tripper and Winey step onto the barge, yet again.

There are three distinct separate pools of blood, all about the same age of hardening. Recalling which blood pool Tripper observed earlier, she looks at the others to possibly gain more details, and to determine if the blood indicates that the wounds killed their owners.

The second pool shows signs of lots of bleeding from possibly two separate injuries. Marks and scrapes of blood indicate the body slid off the barge. The body was not dragged, pushed, pulled, or otherwise moved by anyone else.

The real puzzle is that there is a third set of blood pools. Yes, pools, as a group of three smaller pools of blood indicate a person with three distinctly separate wounds fell onto the barge deck here. The curious part is that the individual had apparently stood up sometime later and walked to the edge of the barge, leaving boot prints made in blood. The tracks might belong to a female or youth with smaller feet. It also appears that the individual rose to his or her feet using their own power, and walked off without aid or force.

In the dim fading light of Stonewire and Imvor, Tripper notices another item of interest: muddy canine footprints in several places on the deck. The canine prints follow beside the person who departed from the barge.

Tripper examines the canine prints closer. She is somewhat astonished to be able to determine that there were two canines aboard the barge.

The gods cast long shadows over the world.

Larret Army

Tripper lights her small hooded lantern. Looking at Winey, she asks somewhat haphazardly, as if not expecting any response from her male pig. "Stay on board or make a camp on shore? I think staying on board would be best."

The early start yesterday had made for a long day. Lord Ramson had been quite entertaining in the morning as the three shared morning meal. The noble eats well. He had provided eggs, bread, honey, porridge, as well as bacon. All the rich food was unexpected and very much appreciated.

Tripper suspected that in most places, the meals would have cost over five Dyns each.

What was even more amazing to Tripper, was being treated as an equal by Lord Ramson. Tripper was regarded as a valued guest, even though she had been rude. The conversation had been wide-ranging and very informative for Tripper. It was apparent to Tripper that Lord Ramson was determining how educated and knowledgeable Tripper is. Tripper enjoyed the meal immensely, finding it ended too soon. For the first time, we saw Tripper happy and enjoying her moment. Winey even maintained a quiet presence while lying beside Tripper's chair.

Ramson asked a few questions about Winey, but he never suggested sending him out of the manor.

Larret Army

Yes, it became an even longer day as Tripper waited for the Cleric, who Lord Ramson had requested supply Tripper with two vials of holy water. Lord Ramson had sent a young boy to inform the innkeeper to refund Tripper's meal and room fees and to inform the innkeeper that Tripper had another day and night of food and lodgings when she wanted them.

Tripper thought that her father had a high rank in Larret – a rank in which she never really expected to rise to. The villagers only tolerated Tripper, and no one treated her with respect – except G and Mi. But here, in Dartoln village with Ramson, she was treated as nobility and as an equal to Ramson.

Winey walks over to stand beside her, disrupting Tripper's memories and returning her thoughts to the present. With sighs only a pig can make, he lays down on the edge of the tarp that is covering the cargo of the barge. He looks up at Tripper, snorts twice, and then settles his head down, closing his eyes. Apparently, the discussion is over, and a decision has been made regarding tonight's resting place.

Tripper chuckles. Going ashore and grabbing her pack, she steps back on her newly acquired barge. Settling herself down in the centre of the barge, Tripper sets the lantern on a crate. She closes the hood on the light, allowing only enough light to escape so she can see as she opens her pack, but not enough, hopefully, to gain the attention of anyone passing by.

Summer 26 Bear

Morning sweeps in quietly upon the two sleeping companions aboard the salvaged barge.

Winey stirs first, rising to his feet from where he had been tightly curled up next to Tripper, doing so unobserved, as the hooded lantern had burnt its fuel out, over two hours ago.

Stepping up onto the river's bank, Winey quietly walks a short distance into the woods and does the things all creatures do at some time or another. Finished with relieving his digestive wastes, Winey returns to find Tripper sitting with her back against a largish wooden crate.

Tripper peers at Winey. "You may have been right. It was more comfortable on the barge, and the canvas tarp was a decent blanket." Tripper says casually, not expecting to be understood.

Again, Winey conveys his understanding by nudging Tripper's feet off of the tarp.

Being somewhat intelligent, as humans go, Tripper is beginning to question Winey's intelligence and his understanding of what she says to him. She is starting to understand that her animal companion – her best friend – does understand what she means and that he is intelligent enough to form responses. Tripper shakes her head slowly, believing as humans usually do, that nothing else can think or be as intelligent as humans.

She thinks casually. *'Tomorrow will come eventually, but today has freshly arrived, bringing its events.'*

Not being very familiar with a watercraft, Tripper awkwardly stands, pointing to Winey. "Wait here. I will be right back. I have something to do, and then we can continue to Larret, travelling the Harpen River by using our new barge with its load of cargo."

Tripper smiles. Hurrying, she walks off the barge, up into the dusky woods, much as Winey had.

Several minutes later, Tripper returns dragging her foot through green grasses and plants. Stepping onto the barge, there are bits of fresh scat still adhering to her shoe.

Tripper gives Winey a frustrated look. Pointing at her foot, she angrily asks, "Was that yours? Nice place to put it."

Tripper swishes her foot back and forth in Harpen River's warm, lazy flowing water, trying to finish cleaning the offal from her old footwear.

Larret Army

Winey squeals slightly. We know the squeal is in humour, and Tripper suspects as much.

Tripper steps into the centre of the barge, taking quick stock of what is on board. Tripper then picks up an oaring pole. With great effort, she pushes the barge out into the current, starting their journey to Larret Hamlet.

Summer 29 Bear

Tripper spent two days navigating down the waterway. Beaching the barge on a sandbar once, it took her three hours to get the barge unstuck. Winey helped by digging and pushing.

It is the middle of the day, Summer 29 Bear, when Tripper beaches her barge onto the bank at Larret Hamlet – home again.

Tripper does not recall a time when she was so hungry. She walks to the edge of the hamlet of Larret. She watches as people go about their daily business. Tripper is looking forward to arriving at the house that once was her home. She knows things have changed more than she ever believed possible. This short trip taught her so much about the world and life. She no longer blames G for Tripper's demise. In fact, Tripper now understands what had been set in motion long ago. Looking at the hamlet's centre, she smiles broadly, as she now has more coin than she could ever have imagined.

Walking to the Goat's Tavern, Tripper enters. Taking a seat at an unoccupied table, she waits. The old man, known as Old Ringus, now looks different to her. He seems wiser, stronger, and with more experience than she knew existed – more than she can know now. This trip taught Tripper a different aspect of life and showed Tripper that people are not always what we see. She has a greater understanding of Old Ringus, after learning about his past from Ramson. Now, she ponders all this as she waits patiently.

"Excuse me, I would like service, please – an ale and plate of hot food," says Tripper, as the Jalfem life-companion of Old Ringus passes by her table.

The other three patrons in the tavern turn and look at Tripper, and then they frown.

The tavernkeeper's life-companion brings a mug of ale, setting it on the table.

Lorri says flatly. "Two dusters for the ale, and one Dyns for the hot food."

Tripper smiles with a broad grin. "Yes, of course. Two dusters now, one Dyns when I receive my hot meal. For that price, it better be freshly butchered meat, and not fish."

This tavern's server is startled.

Tripper retrieves her pouch, takes out two dusters, and hands the coins to Lorri.

Later, after Lorri places a plate of chicken and vegetables on Tripper's table, Tripper hands Lorri one Dyns for the hot plate of food. Eating her meal, Tripper doesn't feel a need to have attention.

The tavern door opens several minutes later and in walks the hamlet's reeve.

G smiles when she sees Winey and Tripper. Walking over to Tripper, she sits at the table with the two returned travellers. "Welcome back, Tripper. Was it a good trip?"

Tripper eats a piece of the perfectly cooked chicken. Looking casually at G, she chews her food politely. Nodding, she swallows and then takes a bite of the fried tuber. Tripper chews the tuber well, swallows, and then places her fork on the table. "Thank you, and to answer your question – yes and no. We encountered two walking-dead that we had to tend to. We delivered the records to Lord Ramson on time. The Lord and I talked at great length. I learnt a lot from Lord Ramson. Thank you for sending us on the errand … I am going to tell you now that I will be staying in Larret for some length of time. I need a new home; can I rent your house?"

Larret Army

Eyes wide with a stunned look, G hesitates for a few moments. "You are staying on here in Larret? The house can be yours for, four dusters every thirty days ... that sounds fair."

With a short nod, Tripper calculates the coins needed. Taking up her coin purse, she pulls out six Dyns, placing them in front of G. "That should cover rent for one year, right? I would like possession as of right now. I will come to Reeve House to sign the agreement after I finish moving into my new home."

Wondering what transpired on Tripper's trip, G smiles. She is glad to see Tripper settle in with new confidence. Taking the six coins, G stands while saying, "Come to the Reeve House when you are ready. I'll clear my possessions out of my place once we sign the contract."

Still smiling, G leaves Goat's Tavern.

Things are not going to remain the same, this is certain.

Two hours later, Tripper sharply knocks on the door to Reeve House.

The reeve actually opens the door, instead of calling out for Tripper to enter. G is wearing suitable clean clothing, and Reeve House is neat and clean. On the table is a pottery pitcher as well as two mugs. The room is comfortably warm. She greets Tripper. "Come on in, Tripper. If you like, you can scribe the contract to be the occupant of my house ... we can talk while you scribe."

Giving a sagely nod, Tripper enters her former home, answering, "Thank you very much, Reeve Gena. I think we have much to share with each other today. If you trust me to scribe the lease for your house, then yes, I will do so."

After a sidelong look at Tripper, G makes an observation. She then glances over at Winey and says to Tripper. "You are different now, Tripper. What happened on the trip? It's like you know who you are now, and you have decided that you are okay. I am sorry to hear you had to deal with walking-dead. They must have been difficult to deal with alone?"

Watching Tripper, and knowing what is inside her mind, we smile at her new outward confidence.

Sitting at the table, Tripper smiles genuinely. "Neither of us is alone, Gena. We are simply black swans in a world that fears black swans."

Sitting, G looks at Tripper suspiciously. "What do you know about black swans, Tripper?"

Tripper bows her head slightly while replying, "It's not a good idea to eat a black swan, as one might get sick or die. Families are torn apart and members die."

Eyes darting about, lips quivering, G looks at Tripper, and then her expression lightens, but falls into an expression with tight-knit brows and narrowed eyes. G's face flushes and her eyes widen.

Tripper remains seated as Winey lays on the floor next to her chair. Lord Ramson prepared her for G's reaction.

"It's okay Gena; no one else will bother you again. Lord Ramson told me why he removed me from the reeve's house. Also, that he knows and understands about Winey. I know about Assino and about a black swan. We three are aware of each other's secrets. I want to apologize for my previous behaviour and words. I have a better understanding now, and I am here to work with you as the village mage, and hopefully be your friend. You have Winey and me at your service, for as long as you will allow us. I mourn your past losses."

Through slit eyelids, G looks at Tripper suspiciously. Then, speaking softly, she says, "He told you about the black swan?"

Tripper answers in a gentle voice. "How I learnt is not an issue right now. I offered not to tell anyone. I was asked to keep it a secret. So, the black swan shall be our secret. Very few know who you are. And, back at your previous home, few know where you went. No one in Larret, but Winey and I, know your secrets. I am now a Black Swan for you."

Standing quickly, G walks into her storeroom, disappearing into the darkness beyond. She returns in short order to the central room, carrying a keg and two silver goblets. Setting both goblets on the table, G pops the bung of the keg. She fills the two goblets full of red liquid. The liquid is glittering translucent in the light of the room, and unfamiliar in appearance to Tripper.

With a firm gesture, she hands one goblet to Tripper. "This seals your oath to never mention my swan ever again. If you do, Winey will die horribly. That is the oath you are swearing to by drinking this blood wine. The last time someone swore an oath with this wine, they broke the oath and died a prolonged and painful death." G is glaring hard at Tripper. She waits while holding her goblet high.

As she smiles, Tripper picks up the goblet without hesitating. "Salute to the Black Swans and my oath to never mention your past loss."

Listening carefully, G then corrects Tripper. "No, the oath is to never mention my swan, ever, not just the loss of the swan. Never mention the swan ever again, Tripper." With her goblet still raised, G watches Tripper's eyes.

Tripper begins to drink without added comment, but G places her free hand over the goblet. "Swear."

Tripper smiles. "You follow your uncle's smarts, Gena. I swear as you asked. I will never mention your swan, living or dying. But our Black Swans will become well known, my friend."

Both drink from their goblets. G re-bungs the keg with a new cork.

They sit for several moments watching each other, and casually wait. Then, simultaneously, both smile and nod. The two masters have arrived at an agreement.

Lying beside Tripper, Winey snorts his agreement.

Tripper believes she understands the snort to be Winey saying, *'finally.'*

Both masters laugh and turn to Winey who is watching Tripper.

We laugh and say, *'Yah! Right!'*

Chapter Four:

One Strange Moment?

*S*ummer *31 Bear*

Strangely, life doesn't affect everyone the same.

Today, Jess is out for his daily swim in Harpen River. It has rained all morning and well into the afternoon. The high humidity from the rain and now this heat is causing stress for everyone. Jess sees his afternoon swim as an opportunity to cool down and rinse off his sweat.

Swimming back toward shore, Jess notices someone slowly running, as if exhausted, along the shore.

189

Larret Army

Standing up, Jess takes a closer look and hears the deep, shallow breathing of Cottar Milsep Milsap. Behind him are four silent creatures who are not breathing and are staying close to Milsep as if herding him along.

Looking closely at the race, from his position of standing thigh deep in the river, Jess' breathing sharpens and heart races as he feels fear and anxiety. So, he remains silently standing.

Milsep stumbles and two of the creatures take the opportunity to strike him, knocking down the cottar.

Jess, frozen on his spot, waits as the four creatures overwhelm Milsep, attacking him fiercely.

One of the walking-dead creatures turns to Jess and starts walking toward the Cleric.

Pulling forward his holy symbol that is hanging from his neck, Jess begins chanting and praying to Lorn to stop the creature and send it away. We feel that Jess' fear is intense as he chants desperately to Lorn, his god of choice.

Jess is a healer. He is not a warrior for a reason; he fears conflict to the extreme. Creatures who are going to attack him are confronting Jess, and all he has on him are his leggings and his holy symbol.

From inside his leggings, Jess feels a warmth flowing down his legs. Jess continues to chant as he stares at the walking-dead on Harpen River's shore. This action draws the attention of the other three walking-dead, drawing them away from Milsep.

Milsep lays unmoving, but he is breathing.

We look into the cottar's mind, seeing the broken spirit.

The four walking-dead moves toward Jess. Their attention is now on a cleric who is chanting for all the courage he can muster, as water flows by and carries away the stain of his fear.

They stop and watch for a moment. Then, all four turn and walk away, back along the riverbank, in the direction from which they had come. Making no sound in their movements, they soon disappear out of sight.

Jess lets the water finish washing his stain away before going ashore to tend to Milsep.

Kneeling down next to the cottar, Jess touches Milsep's chest. The wounds don't look severe, and none of the wounds are bleeding badly.

Milsep is unconscious from exhaustion, and by Jess' guess, he will be for some time.

At a loss as to what to do, Jess tries to lift Milsep, but he can't lift the man off the ground. It is about half-a-kilometre from here to Larret Hamlet. The heat and moisture make exertion so much more intense. Also, what will happen to Milsep if Jess simply leaves him here while he goes for help? Will the walking-dead come back? Or did they leave permanently?

Jess tries to recall what he knows about the walking-dead, believing these ones were zombies of a sort. However, Jess doesn't remember hearing anything about zombies who hunt or travel in packs.

Standing up, after attempting to place Milsep in a comfortable position, Jess puts on his own tunic and shoes.

With setting a brisk pace he begins to walk east, towards Larret Hamlet, this seems to be the only action available in Jess' mind. So, he leaves Milsep, hoping he remains safe.

.....

Arriving in Larret hamlet, about three-quarters of an hour later, Jess rushes to Reeve House, hoping Reeve G is home.

Knocking on the door, Jess waits. Hearing footsteps behind him, Jess turns to see G approaching from her own house.

"Reeve G, Cottar Milsep has been attacked and lies injured half-a-kilometre away near Harpen River, west of Larret. Come quickly with a cart and help ... please!"

With a grip of Jess' shoulder, G tries to console the man. "How many attackers and how severely injured is Milsep?"

Larret Army

Blinking several times, Jess begins to settle down. Hesitantly, he answers her. "I think there were four attackers … all were walking-dead – the zombie type … Milsep was unconscious but still breathing when I left him near the river. I turned the walking-dead, but I don't know for how long … they were chasing Milsep … knocked him down … and viciously attacked the cottar … tearing at him with their hands … he may not live if we don't hurry."

"Go inside, sit, have a mug of water and a bun. I will be right back, Jess." Turning, G heads to the hamlet's watch-house.

In the watch-house, G finds Daren and Lesna in idle chat talking with Tarrel.

G commands, "The three of you, gear up. We have some trouble, and I need your help to look into it. We are going west, up the Harpen River. There was an attack by four walking-dead. I am going to find Eren. We will need her goat cart, as there are injured involved. Go to Reeve House as quickly as you can."

Without waiting for questions or replies, G closes the door and heads for Eren's garden plot, as that was the last location G recalls seeing the hamlet's mage and beadle.

Walking quickly towards Eren's garden patch, G notices the mage working with a goat from her herd. "Eren, we need your help as beadle. And, we need your goat and cart to move

193

injured people. It pays one Dyns for the day – no arguing. Meet me back at the Reeve House."

G turns to head back to Reeve House.

…..

The muck and wetness would deter most, but the crew gathering at Reeve House expect such days to happen. The three guards are prepared in their leather armour, small shields, and shortswords.

Eren is in her orange robes, and she has her prize billy goat, Dolon, harnessed to the goat cart.

Carrying a small shield, G is attired in her well-tended studded leather armour, and she has her longsword strapped on. Oddly, being a bowyer-fletcher, she has yet to learn an archery skill.

Dressed in his robes of Lorn, Jess has his silver Holy Symbol of Lorn prominently displayed.

The response group starts out in the humid heat towards the victim of the assault – a man who's been left lying unattended for over two hours.

The billy goat manages to keep up with the humans. An hour later they arrive at the location to find the bloating corpse of Milsep, just where Jess left him.

Milsep rises and starts walking towards Jess, who is leading the group. Silently, Milsep reaches for Jess.

Jess freezes on the spot as he panics.

First to react is G as she swings precisely with her longsword, critically slicing into Milsep's leg, almost severing it off.

Lesna quickly moves in, stabbing with his shortsword, widely missing Milsep.

Swinging back around, full circle, G aggressively and sharply cleaves at Milsep's leg again, dropping Milsep enough to stop him from attacking any further.

At the same instance as G attacks, Milsep misses his attempt to attack G.

With a sigh of relief, Daren watches as Milsep tumbles haphazard to the ground in a crumbling heap of already rotting flesh. The cottar has been dead for less than two hours, but just now his spirit is separating from his body.

Unfortunately, the spirit is lost, doomed to the life between. Milsep's spirit will never know the freedom of the beyond until it's given last rights or a proper Right of Passage. We watch him join us in the in-between.

After cleaning and sheathing her longsword, G gives a cursory look around the area for attackers. "Okay, put him in the cart and let's get out of here and return to Larret Hamlet. This place gives me the willies, worse than the night the spirits tried for Tripper's father."

Daren and Tarrel sheath their shortswords.

Tarrel lifts Milsep's hips as Daren lifts the corpse's shoulders. Together, the two lift Milsep onto the goat cart.

Everyone is ready to start back towards Larret when an eerie cry is heard upriver. It's a sound like the crying of a hungry baby. But the village has no babies who are so young.

With gods-set approaching, and considering the unknown number of walking-dead out wandering, G has a dire decision to make.

All turn to G as she looks in the direction of the sound. The concern and fear on the faces around her makes a choice easier. "Let's get back to the village; we already have one dead to deal with."

Sighs come from all those gathered.

Nervously watching around them, they begin their journey back to Larret Hamlet. Everyone seems uncertain as to what the moment holds, and no one dares to speak.

Because of the encumbered goat cart, the trek back to the hamlet takes twice as long.

Larret Army

It is well into the darkness of night when they arrive among the buildings of Larret.

G, having had much time to think, pulls Jess aside. "We are going to find the walking-dead and deal with them, so they cause no further issues. I want Mi, Tripper, you, and Eren to come with me. I will appoint village caretakers during our absence. Can you tell Mi to meet us at gods-rise, at Reeve House, armed with prayers to deal with walking-dead? Will you be ready as well, Jess?"

Eren, who had been listening, smiles broadly. "I will be ready, Reeve G. This is part of my new job that I get so well paid for. I will get Tripper up and ready as well. She's renting your house, right?"

Giving a broad smile, G adds, "Yes, Tripper is renting my house. She'll be going with us as Village Mage. If she asks, she will receive one Flair per day."

Walking away, and then stopping, G turns to Jess. "As Village Priest, the dead are yours to deal with. You have one now. Thank you." She continues on her walk to Goat's Tavern.

Arriving at the tavern, she opens the door. Looking into the lantern-lit interior of Goat's Tavern, G ponders the wisdom of her decision. Shrugging, she breaks her hesitation.

Larret Army

With several customers in the Tavern, Lorri is very busy, but G walks over to her. She quickly asks Lorri, "Is Ringus in the kitchen?"

With a puzzled expression, Lorri nods. However, she is too busy to ask any questions.

Walking into the kitchen, G finds Old Ringus cleaning a grouse for frying.

Abruptly, Gena says, "I need a second – a Reeve Sergeant. I want it to be you … it should only be for three or four days as I hunt down some walking-dead. I am taking two mages and two priests. I think there is a pack of four or five walking-dead in the area. They already killed Cottar Milsep, down by the Harpen River to the west."

As the memories of the loss of his son are still fresh, Old Ringus, nods and answers, "Whatever you need to do, Reeve G. I will look after Larret and send Lord Ramson notice at the time of your demise. As you know, you will die chasing the walking-dead."

"I can't bring anyone else with me, Ringus. I will have two priests. It will all be okay, and we can put to rest these poor souls."

Ringus viciously chops off the head of another grouse. "Go. I will tend to Larret as needed."

G is beginning to reconsider, even though she knows Ringus was one of Lord Ramson's choices for Reeve. She believes that the time Ringus spent in the service of the King will help him well. Though, G considers that Ringus' recent moodiness may affect his abilities somewhat.

Apprehensively, G leaves Goat's Tavern and returns to Reeve House. There she finds Eren studying at the central table with several tomes and vials.

Summer 32 Bear

With a start, she wakes early, and G moves to start the fire. The fire takes the edge off the cool morning air in Reeve House. She warms some water to wash with, and then cooks a hearty breakfast for her and Eren.

Eren studied late into the night, before cleaning up her items and retiring to her room in Reeve House.

Also, that night, G had cleaned the house and spent time maintaining her weapons and armour for the upcoming trip. She had carefully constructed two packs: one for her and one for Eren.

As she enters the common room, Eren is now ready for the day, wearing her ankle-length red wool dress. "Good morning, G. I see you have morning meal ready for six people. Do you think they will all come?"

As if queued up and ready for this inquiry, there is a knock on the door, and the snort of a boar can be heard from the other side.

Walking over, G opens the portal.

"Good morning, Tripper and Winey. It is good to see you arrive before the gods rise. Did you see Mi or Jess on your way over?" G's studded-leather armour creaks slightly with her movements, but only slightly, as she has oiled and properly tended to the joints. Her longsword, ready for use, imperceptibly swings properly on her left side.

Tripper enters in her orange wool dress and new red boots, while Winey arrives naked yet again.

Winey snorts at G, and he walks over to the bowls that G set out for him. He begins to feed and drink.

As G is about to close the door, a cheery, "good morning!" is heard from the darkness outside.

G responds happily. "Good morning, Mi. I'm glad you're here. At least with one cleric, that means we can put the walking-dead to rest."

Another voice calls out, "Make that two clerics who can put the walking-dead to rest."

G adds, "Gods speed to you as well, Jess. I'm glad you made it. Well, that is everyone I asked to join me: Jess, Mi, Eren, and Tripper. Oh yes, and you, Winey, for tracking. Good, let's eat; I cooked enough for everyone. I hope you prepared packs for a few days, as I don't know how far the walking-dead will have travelled by the time we catch up to them. They are at least a day ahead of us if they moved on right after yesterday's incident. So, we must move faster than they do to catch up. They don't need to sleep, or rest, or eat. Hopefully, they are slower and might get distracted a time or two. Let's eat up, and as soon as the gods rise, let's head out."

One by one, the four others acknowledge the mission, even Winey who snorts twice.

After everyone eats, G cleans up the house, putting away the clean dishes. With everyone prepared and ready to leave, they wait for gods-rise.

As the two day-gods rise, the intrepid group sets out. The trek begins with walking to the point where Cottar Milsep was killed. Because the walking-dead do not have the intelligence or foresight to conceal their tracks, the creatures' tracks are easy enough to find.

Observing the underbrush, tracking is easy as the walking-dead take a direct route, damaging the underbrush as they pass through.

In clear areas, the best the group has is the scent that Winey follows.

The trail is far from straight or consistent, meandering haphazardly westward and north through the woods.

Tripper pipes up during their midday meal break. "Why don't we call ourselves the Black Swans? It sounds great to have an adventuring name. We don't need to form a guild unless we do this more often. But we can be an adventuring group this time. Right?"

He thinks a moment, and then Mi asks. "What if the walking-dead have possessions? Eren will want a share. How will we divide it up?"

Eren, one to jump all over coins and loot, adds, "I think we should keep it simple – fifths evenly. Pool it all and divide it in equal fifths of kind value."

The other four agree to be the Black Swans and to share the loot in equal fifths of kind value.

After their rest, they continue walking on in this scorching day, trudging through the northeast breath of the gods, towards the walking-dead.

It's hard to determine if they are gaining on their prey.

The partial cover in the sphere helps alleviate some of the torturous heat, and the group continues to make good time.

An hour or so before the gods will set G addresses the group. "We should make camp and set up some defences. I will take the first watch. Tripper and Winey take the second watch. Who wants third, then fourth? The fifth person will keep fresh for first watch tomorrow night – if we need them."

Eren pipes in. "I'll take the third watch."

Jess adds, "I'll take the fourth watch as I enjoy watching the gods rise, anyway."

Thus, the night schedule is decided, and the group begins to look for a good place to camp.

Oddly, Winey leads G to a secluded spot, behind a group of raised stones, which is perfect for a night camp. The area is big enough to shelter about eight humans and has a barren area for a small fire pit. The area has three sides walled off completely, and about half of the fourth side is enclosed. The stones rise about nine to ten feet high in an uneven wall, roughly five to ten feet thick. The dark purple stones don't look natural, but their ancient purpose is long lost.

Once the group gathers for the night in the alcove, Tripper sets about lighting a small night fire.

Larret Army

Several times, Winey briefly disappears into the darkness and returns with a few mouthfuls of moss for bedding. Making his nest-like bed, similar as humans do with their bedrolls, Winey settles in for the night.

Everyone rations their food. Most brought enough food for three days, except G, who packed enough for five days for her and Eren.

Being miserly, Eren will probably make her rations last seven or eight days, if needed. Each brought a waterskin with enough water for two days. They all have enough water left for tomorrow.

As G takes her watch, the others rest.

Summer 33 Bear

It has been raining since about two in the morning. The day isn't cold, but the struggle to track in the rain has slowed them drastically. They are now relying entirely on signs of damage to the terrain for their tracking clues. Fortunately, even bulls are gentler and less direct in their choices than these walking-dead. Still able to track their prey, the group continue their drive forward.

The gods are barely breathing, so the outlook for moving the rain away is faint.

G looks at the broken brambles as she stands in the mud. "The fates are cruel. They send us to put to rest four walking-dead. Then, they try to wash away their signs of passage. Now, we find we have almost caught up to the creatures. Is it persistence, stupidity, or cruelty? What do you think, Jess?"

Jess laughs. "Fate, pure and simple fate."

She smiles, and then G laughs as well. "Let's keep moving, as we appear to be catching up. The gods are shining again; the mud will dry in a few hours. These creatures are leaving their marks, which will make them easier to find. Fate, you say Jess. I think if there are gods, the gods are laughing at us. Let's walk."

They continue, and they soon discover that with the rain ending, so has the tracking trail of the walking-dead. There is less than an hour before gods-set.

G makes the decision. "Time to camp. Let's find a spot. Mi, you're first to watch. I will take second watch. The third watch is Tripper and Winey, with fourth being Eren. Jess, you rest tonight."

Again, Winey finds a camping spot with a stream and a natural shelter. The shelter is big enough for six humans and a small campfire. Oh yes, and a boar.

Again, Tripper sets the fire for the camp, as everyone else gets ready for the night.

Winey finds a moss patch close by and gets everyone his or her night's nest bedding.

Summer 34 Bear

Everyone fills their waterskins with fresh water. Today is the last day of rations for most of them. Therefore, they need to cut their intake in half.

Winey, who is still in good condition, has been foraging on his own as he has been travelling.

This morning, before they head out to search for the walking-dead, Mi begins preparing for the day. He forages for berries and other food stock to supplement his rations. After nearly an hour of foraging, he has a day and a half worth of raw rations. He offers to share some with Tripper.

An-hour-and-three-quarters into a bright, warm day with the gods breathing hard east, the Black Swans start tracking the walking-dead again. The tracks in the dried mud are much easier to follow than yesterday, and the Black Swans make good time. It is easy to determine that they are gaining on their targets.

Larret Army

Another full day passes, and still, the Black Swans have not caught the walking-dead. However, the tracking indicates that they are within a few hours of their target. But the gods will set in two hours.

Again, G makes the call. "Okay, some of you are out of food. So, let's forage and see if we can find enough food for tomorrow. I believe we will catch up to the walking-dead tomorrow if we get an early start. We all forage now. While we forage, we look for tonight's shelter. Jess is first to watch tonight, then Mi, then myself, followed by Eren. Tripper, it's you and Winey who are resting tonight."

Tripper finds a shelter where two large trees collapsed, creating V-shaped walls for the group to shelter in. Foraging locates plenty of food for tomorrow and the day after for everyone in the group.

Summer 35 Bear

Eren tells G, "I am not sure how much farther we can go. We have followed the walking-dead for three days now and haven't encountered them." It's watch change, as Eren is coming on watch and G is going off. They are discussing the events.

Larret Army

Abruptly a young Toydon boy walks out of the darkness of the night into the light of the campfire.

G gasps, as she is shocked to see the young boy walk into their camp, hesitating to react as he begins to attack Eren.

At the same time, a Jalfem of about fifty-years-age comes out of the darkness and charges G.

The Toymal and the Jalfem are soon followed by a teenage Jalmal who also begins attacking G, and a nearly century-old Tedmal follows her, attacking Eren.

Horrified, G suddenly reacts with shouts of, "Shit! Everyone, wake up!"

The Toymal clubs Eren's head fiercely with his fist, stunning Eren.

G is viciously struck in the body by the Jalfem who charged her.

Having stunned Eren, the Toymal pulls harshly on Eren's arm, causing her to scream in agonizing pain.

Eren loses consciousness.

G's shout and Eren's scream accomplishes the task of waking the other members of the camp, and they begin to rouse.

The fifty-year-old Jalfem slashes at G's abdomen, raking her clawed fingers along the bowyer's studded-leather armour.

In his frenzy, the Toymal boy rakes his fingers across Eren's prone body.

With a swing of her longsword, G fends off the century-old Tedmal as he lunges at her.

The teenage Jalmal rushes over toward Mi, who is rising from his bedding to deal with the assault.

In frantic desperation and fear, Jess is also rising erratically to get ready to deal with the attack.

The young Toymal grabs onto G's sword arm, briefly raking her armour with his fingers.

Winey, who was in his nest at the back of the V-shaped camp, rushes at the half-century-old Jalfem who is rapidly approaching the boar.

The Jalfem misses her wildly insane attack on Winey.

As Mi tries to turn the walking-dead creatures, the teenage Jalmal strikes at Mi's chest. The attack causes Mi's to fail his call upon the powers of his god, Ikerus.

So, giving up on that avenue, and in a quick decision, Mi tries another tactic.

The Toymal boy fails in another clawing strike at a moving G.

Striking out at the Tedmal with her longsword, G cleaves into the Tedmal's leg. Pulling her sword free, she comes around rapidly with her full force, severing the leg off completely. Thus, removing the first walking-dead from the confrontation.

Winey, in a frenzied swing of his head, tears open the abdomen of the Jalfem who is attacking him.

Seeing Eren fading away quickly, Jess decides it is in their best interest to call upon the gods to heal her wounds. Moving over to Eren, Jess calls upon Lorn to do them the favour of healing her. He closes his eyes and focuses deeply within himself, drawing upon his faith in Lorn with all the belief he can muster at the moment. Holding Eren's hand, he can feel the warm blue-grey power of his faith in Lorn travel through to Eren. Knowing she has been healed, Jess lets go of her hand.

Opening his eyes, he turns to the battle, hoping nothing has turned its attention on him.

Tripper draws the attention of the half-century-old Jalfem.

As Mi shouts out with the power of an orison *"Stop!"*, he points at the teenage Jalfem.

The young girl stops still in her tracks, confused.

Winey, using his tusks again, with a powerful blow rips open the older Jalfem's leg as she scrapes her foot along Winey's abdomen in a feeble kick.

Larret Army

G now turns her attention to the young boy. With her longsword, she slashes open the boy's abdomen, dropping him, taking a second walking-dead out of the combat.

Drawing upon the success of his prayer to Lorn, Jess bolsters his courage and swings his quarterstaff into the teenager's leg.

With her hand-axe, Tripper severs a leg off the teenager.

The half-century-old Jalfem, severely wounded and now alone, tries to slay Winey, who is still unfaltering.

G slashes through the Jalfem's shoulder with her longsword, ending the battle.

With the destruction of four walking-dead – hopefully, only four – the Black Swans, in spite of being took by surprise on such a dark covered night – has only one severely wounded – Eren.

Thankfully, the walking-dead could only come at the camp from one direction, and thankfully, there only seems to have been four of them.

Jess looks the walking-dead over quickly, as Mi watches for more who may be approaching.

Quick, Jess reports to the group. "These are the four that attacked Cottar Milsep. After we give them Right of Passage, we can return home. I'm going to tend to Eren now."

Taking a few deep sighs, G then says, "Okay, Jess, thank you … Mi, tend to the other wounds. I'll take watch for the rest of the night. You two tend to the wounds, and everyone else cleans up camp. Then you rest if you can."

Furtively, Mi takes G aside. "G, I have no skills with first aid or healing; this is best left to Jess. I will tend to the walking-dead, though. That will be my contribution. I can get them ready to finally release their spirits."

G nods in understanding. "Ok Mi, I guess that will work. Get Tripper to help you with the walking-dead, and then clean up the camp. We will stay here today, but we will need water for tomorrow."

Jess strides over to Eren, getting the young woman laid out comfortably so he can make sure that her wounds are tended to properly.

Once again, Jess calls upon Lorn to heal Eren, in hopes of accelerating the healing process. He knows it will be some time before Eren will be okay again, as her head and arm are in dire condition, beyond severely bruised. Any other wounds are additional damages that have to be healed as well.

Again, Jess takes Eren's hand as he closes his eyes. Focusing, he prays his small prayer to Lorn, feeling the blue-grey warmth of Lorn, he smiles. Finished, placing Eren's hands comfortably on her abdomen, Jess leaves Eren and moves on to tend to the others.

Jess finds that Mi has not tended to any of the battle wounds, so he hurries to each combatant to inspect for injury. He begins with the obvious: the warrior who was on watch, G.

Inspecting her for wounds, Jess finds G to have some bruises underneath her scratched armour.

He then moves on to Mi, finding the one wound. He cleans and dresses Mi's injury.

Finishing up with Mi, Jess consults with Tripper and finds no combat contact.

There is one camp fellow left to be tended to. So, Jess, being dutiful, checks out his fellow camp jockey. Winey indeed took damage, and he allows Jess to clean and dress the wounds. Thus, everyone in the camp has been addressed and treated, leaving Jess to breathe easier.

He had noted that one of G's bruises has left G in a bit of a bad way. So, deciding that Lorn would approve, Jess walks over to G. "May I pray for you, G?"

Feeling as she does about the gods, G answers rather sarcastically. "I don't care what you do with your gods, Jess. If you want to pray, they won't answer you. You know that, right?"

Knowing that one day he will convince G otherwise, Jess smiles. Today may be that day. "Okay, thank you."

Jess takes G's hand in his and he closes his eyes. Again, he begins his deep focused and inner prayers to Lorn, knowing in his heart and mind that all he needs is his belief. He also knows that G doesn't need to believe. He concentrates intensely, praying, and he feels the blue-grey warmth of Lorn flow into G.

He releases G's hand and Jess smiles. Opening his eyes, he watches her. He wonders if the recipient ever feels the warmth. But, he can see no sign of a reaction in her eyes, so Jess surmises that they probably don't feel the warmth.

Mi has been busy wrestling the corpses of the walking-dead to a place outside the camp.

Tripper had enlarged the camp fire enough to light a twenty-foot radius area.

The four corpses are not functioning now; two are missing a leg each. The unattached legs are not threats either.

As he looks the corpses over, Mi sighs. Then, he looks at Tripper, who is keeping the fire fed. He says, "You can let the fire die down now. I said a prayer over each of the corpses that will keep them there until tomorrow evening at the least. We can start dealing with them tomorrow … it is so sad to see this happen. When we die and don't receive proper Right of Passage, this is what happens. I noticed that all four have the same tattoo on their neck. I wonder if they are from the same village."

Once again, the camp settles back down to rest, with G and Winey keeping watch.

Jess, Mi, and Tripper return to rest until the gods-rise.

Eren continues to be unconscious until an hour before gods-rise.

…..

There is a piercing scream in the dimness of the camp as Eren emerges from her unconsciousness to a conscious state.

The prayers of Lorn, made by Jess, healed much of the wounds of body, but the prayers do little to heal the mind, this is left to time.

With a flourish, G rushes over to Eren. Kneeling, she holds Eren close. "It's okay Eren; you're safe. Calm down, my friend. Calm," she says in soothing tones.

Meanwhile, the piercing screams by Eren have awakened the rest of their group.

Mi and Jess rush over to Eren.

Seeing Eren's distress, Jess casts the orison *"Calm"* to relax her.

They are rewarded immediately with Eren quieting as she is calming down and relaxing.

Larret Army

With a few minutes passing, and while G rocks Eren in her lap, the orison wears off. However, the orison's effects remain, and Eren, who is becoming aware of her situation, senses that she is safe in camp.

Satisfied, G gives a slight sigh and looks at the rest of her group. "Try and get more rest. I will take care of her."

The others nod and agree, returning to their bedrolls. They all know that they still have a few hard days ahead of them for their return home.

G holds Eren for the rest of the early-morning, soothing her by stroking her hair, while watching and hoping that Winey can fend off anything that might attack, giving G time to respond.

Summer 36 Bear

The gods rise, and so does the camp.

Near exhaustion, G has been awake almost the entire night, after engaging in a battle and travelling the entire previous day. Now, she is kneeling as she still holds a shivering Eren.

Finally, having had enough of this, G looks down at Eren. "Look kitten, you have done worse to others. Dolon has done worse to you. Get over it and get up; let's eat and get on with it

… okay? I need to sleep. We dropped all four walking-dead, and the boys are going to make sure the walking-dead don't do this to anyone else. And, you are going to help them with anything they need … understand? That is what you're paid to do. If you can't do that, then I will stop your pay today … understand, Eren the Unwilling?"

Shakily, Eren sits up and moves, placing her back against the log. "They were so quick and quiet. We didn't even know they were here until they attacked … the pain! … I never felt such pain before. I am sorry, G … I will be okay. I can do my work … I can. I will be fine … G? … thank you. Who saved us? … you again?"

G laughs. "No … it was the pig again. Now freshen up and get the boys moving. Welcome back … we almost lost you that time, my friend. You can thank Jess, Mi, or the pig, not me."

With both of them feeling stiff from being in the same position for so long, they help each other to stand.

Eren puts on her 'Eren the Unwilling' face, and she wobbles over to Jess, kicking his foot that is sticking out from his bedroll. She says, "Hey you, time to stop healing and start praying. Let's get up."

Larret Army

Wandering over to Mi, she kicks his foot to rouse him as well. "Morning for mourning the dead … let's get them to the sphere, Mi."

Eren looks at Tripper – unsure if they are friends or not – she sees that Tripper is looking back at her, smiling. Eren returns the smile and nods.

Turning, Eren walks off into the woods to relieve her morning duties, which are long overdue. Passing by the corpses, her body shivers in fear again, but she manages to contain the fear.

Being the first of the four sleepers to get out of her bedroll, Tripper cleans up her nest and then heads out into the woods, followed shortly by Winey.

Dogged, Mi gets out of bed after Tripper returns, while she organizes her bedroll. He freshens up and then organizes his own nest. Leaving his bed neat for tonight, he too then heads out into the woods.

As he takes his time getting out of bed, Jess is much slower than the others are. Suddenly, like a spring that had been wound up, he goes off quickly to relieve himself in the woods. Soon, he returns to clean his nest, setting it up for the next night.

Jess freshens up before he finds a comfortable spot to sit and pray. He needs to refresh his prayers if he can. After last night's activities, Jess is not sure if Lorn will answer his petitions today. He settles down and focuses in prayer, hoping to spend at least half-an-hour petitioning his god, Lorn.

Mi also looks for a spot to pray. He is also not sure that his god, Ikerus, will listen to his petitions today. He solemnly begins his prayers.

With a measured look around the camp, G so wants to walk over to the corpses and light them on fire – to be done with the whole thing. But she understands that if she were to do that, then the spirits or souls would be lost between realms. She believes that their souls would be lost forever without a realm to belong to. She also believes that to deliberately cause such a thing would be evil – pure evil.

G doesn't believe she is evil at heart, but simply angry right now. So, instead, G walks to her bedding nest and settles in, quickly finding the rest she needs.

Returning solemnly to camp, Tripper diligently tends to the campfire, bringing it to a small cooking fire. Setting up the cooking pot, she begins preparing the morning brew of roots to be eaten.

Winey returns soon after, carrying a rabbit in his mouth and dropping it beside the cook fire.

Looking down at the carcass, Tripper chuckles. "So, you're a warrior now? Or a hunter?"

In answer, Winey snorts twice and gives a pig's chuckle, laying down near Tripper. He hasn't had water for two days now, and it is beginning to wear on him.

It is mid-morning when Eren eventually returns, carrying some roots and berries for eating. Squatting beside Tripper, Eren says, "I had to earn my keep after last night. I think these can feed everyone today."

With great care, Tripper takes the offered food and places them with the rest of the stores for the camp.

After an hour or more of prayer, Mi and Jess eventually come over to the campfire, smiling and ready for today's chores.

As G sleeps, Tripper has food ready for everyone. They do this while Mi and Jess discuss how best to deal with the walking-dead.

While four of the Black Swans are eating, G wearily wakes and wanders over. "We are out of water today. We have to move or look for water. Do any of you four casters have spells or prayers that can create drinkable water?"

Knowingly, Jess smiles. "Of course, any priest can produce drinking water. Mi and I can create some, that way we all have enough for today and tomorrow. I will fill G's, Tripper's, and my skins. Mi can fill his, Eren's, and a container for Winey. Fair enough?"

Happy, Mi beams a broad grin. "I can agree to that, sure."

G sighs contently, and then says, "Thank you, boyos. So, what is the plan for those four? We have to do this, so they don't wander around again."

Mi speaks up as the group's authority. "Well, Jess and I talked about it. We don't want to spend the usual seven days on each corpse for a typical Jalnoric Right of Passage. So, what we think will work is a Blessing Ceremony on each of them, and then a Passing Ceremony on each. It's quick and it's cheating, but, hopefully, it releases the spirits from the bodies and frees the souls, separating the three parts. The bodies and souls will be able to rest. Hopefully, the souls can move on freeing the spirit from the body. Then, we will stop any further wandering by cremating the bodies, just in case the ceremonies fail."

Jess adds, "Yes, I agree. It's the best we can do. The military has a ceremony for quick release, but it requires three clerics, and one must be of Stonewire and one from either Imvor or Ikerus. We are two clerics. I worship Lorn and Mi worships Ikerus, so that isn't an option for us … so, it's your call G. Do we spend the proper time on the Right of Passages? Which means we will be here at least fourteen days; hoping none of the

corpses decide to wander while we deal with them individually?
Or, do we cheat and hope the gods accept our best attempt at
this?"

G answers slowly. "Let's eat while I think ... okay?"

Everyone nods and Winey snorts twice. Well, everyone
nods except the four walking-dead.

We chuckle, thinking, '*Yah! Right!*'

The six Black Swans eat as silently as five humans and a
boar can eat.

Eventually, G gathers everyone together. "Okay, this is the
plan: Eren, you collect fuel for a funeral pyre mound. Tripper
and Winey, you are on foraging and water detail. Jess and Mi,
cast your water orisons. Then I think we will try your Blessing
and Passing Ceremonies. I want to get home as soon as possible.
How long do you think the ceremonies will take? While you're
all doing that, I will do my best to keep an eye on everything. I
am still a bit tired, as I only had a couple of hours sleep in the
last two days. But let me kick walking-dead bones again."

Tripper raises her hand to speak first, as is her usual habit.
"Okay, Winey and I will head north right away."

Mi answers for the two clerics. "I think the ceremonies
will take all morning and a good part of the afternoon. I will take
two of the walking-dead, and Jess can take two ... we both know

the ceremonies. The ceremonies don't usually take more than ten to fifteen minutes each if done right. So first, the Blessing Ceremony, followed by the Passing Ceremony, and then we move onto the next walking-dead. It should take about a half-an-hour each corpse, an hour total for two. I should finish by two this afternoon. Jess, what do you think?"

Jess hesitates before he answers. "I have never done these ceremonies separate, outside of the Right of Passage Ceremony. However, I think Mi is probably right. So yes, we should be done by about two this afternoon. Then, we build a fire and hold the funeral, with the final ceremony as close as possible to a military release ceremony."

With two deep sighs, G gives the two priests the go-ahead. "Let's do this, folks; we want to go home. Eren, gather lots of fuel; we don't want any bones left when we burn the bodies – no wandering fingers or toes. Okay, everyone go to work. You too, Winey."

Using their orisons for water, Mi and Jess fill the waterskins with water and fill the cleaned cooking pot with water for Winey to drink.

Winey snorts twice before he fills his belly with water. After Winey finishes drinking, he and Tripper head northwards into the woods.

Larret Army

Eren has already started a fuel pile in a small cleared area that is nearby.

While they do these things, G sits by the campfire semi-relaxed. She watches everything as she wonders about events and how to improve upon their travels if they have to do something like this again. They have to get home yet. Seven Hells, she is Reeve of Larret. So, she has that to think about as well.

Next on her agenda, upon arriving home, will be a Moot Hall, considering that she already had two cases to deal with before they left.

. . . . .

With a firm voice, Mi says to Jess. "Okay, I will take the teenage Jalmal; you start with the Jalfem. We can do this, Jess, no fear. Remember, this is what we train to do. The gods grant us this ability. Just bless them, and then grant them passing. That's all there is to it ... just as we have done dozens of times before."

As his voice waivers, Jess responds to Mi's encouragement. "I know. But we usually have their families and the community with us as well. Typically, we knew who the dead were. Usually, we take seven days to pass them on – to release the soul to the sphere, and we have the time needed to release the spirit from the body. Here, we are trying to do it all in under an hour, Mi. Can we succeed in the release when we are rushing?

And, they died violently and have been walking-dead for how long?"

Understanding Jess's misgivings, Mi consoles his partner. "The military does this all the time. You don't see thousands of walking-dead warriors, do you? Come on, let's get this done ... we are men of the gods. We believe, and we can release the souls and spirits from the bodies. We! ... you and I."

Mi starts with blessing the teenage Jalmal and then grants him passing.

First, Jess blesses the half-century-old Jalfem and then performs the Passing Ceremony.

Both men feel confident in their results.

"Okay, now the next ones. Are you ready, or do you need a break, Jess?" asks an eager Mi.

"I think we should continue. I will take the old man who lost his leg, and you take the other boy," responds a more confident Jess.

Mi smiles wisely. "Okay, that sounds good to me."

Beginning fresh, Mi takes the action of blessing the boy, followed by the passing of the boy's soul onto the sphere. Hopefully, leaving only the body here.

Jess blesses the century-old Tedmal, taking longer than expected in doing so. Finally finished, Jess looks at the corpse but doesn't feel the light he should. Examining it further, his brows furrow as his eyes narrow. Jess grunts and follows up saying, "That wasn't right; I have to do it again."

With a single firm nod, Mi consoles Jess. "Fair enough, if that's how you feel."

With a fresh start, Jess performs the blessing again, and then he flows into the Passing Ceremony.

Not sure if any of these ceremonies succeeded, the two men step back from the four corpses.

It is now about one in the afternoon as they approach G.

Mi takes on the role as the duo's spokesperson. "We have completed our task. With Eren's help, we will begin building the pyre mound. How are you holding up, G?"

Pausing, G looks up from cleaning and sharpening her longsword. "Sounds good, Mi. I am fine – nothing a little sleep tonight can't cure. Hopefully, we don't have a repeat of last night."

Jess shivers while Mi chuckles. "How about if I take your watch tonight, G," suggests Mi.

Quickly, G replies, "You have it."

Both chuckle.

Mi, Jess, and with help from Eren, the three build a funeral pyre mound.

Larret Army

Early in the afternoon, Tripper wanders into camp singing softly – a tune G hasn't heard her sing since before Jeston died.

Winey walks in proudly beside his companion.

We feel his pride in their efforts today, as the two worked in unison.

Setting down her overflowing pack by the fire, Tripper addresses their group leader. "I found a pond, and Winey found a pool not far from here. So, we have fresh water as long as we need. I think we found enough food for a few days, and there is more out there if we need it. I am going to dump Winey's pot of water and cook midday meal. Hungry, G?"

G looks curiously at this changed Tripper – she is a new Black Swan in G's mind. "Yes. Yes, I am. Let me help. Do you think I should go hunting, or will we be fine for three days?"

Tripper carefully empties her pack. "I think I have enough here for all six of us, for four or five days. There is no need for you to go hunting, and your help will be welcome. How good are your peeling skills, oh mighty bowyer?"

Together they chuckle, as they begin preparing midday meal.

It is about three in the afternoon when G rounds up the three mound builders. "Hey, midday feast is ready, courtesy of

Winey. Come and take a break. Let's eat; we can burn people soon enough. I will even let Jess start the fire … or you, Eren."

"I want to start the fire," replies Eren the Unwilling.

Jess remains silent as the whole crew walks with G to the campfire. In camp they all eat happily, enjoying their feast.

After eating, the building team returns to their work as Tripper returns to her chores.

About an hour later, Jess seeks out G. "We are ready."

She looks around the camp, and then G calls Tripper over. "Help me and Jess get the walking-dead onto the mound. We need to finish this."

Soon, all four bodies are on the mound, and Eren has a torch ready.

G looks it all over and then nods to Mi. "I think all the body parts are accounted for … let's do this."

Bold as a Goran Hawk, Mi turns to Jess, and he says, "Ready old man?"

With a single sigh, Jess then says, "Yes."

Mi slowly and solemnly turns to Eren and says, "Burn em, my friend."

With that, Eren lights the tinder under the base of the pyre, and the funeral fire begins.

Larret Army

With hollow voices, Jess and Mi start their funeral ceremony in military style.

As everyone had hoped, the four bodies start to burn. The non-priests watch vigilantly.

Standing as clost to the fire as comfortable, G has her longsword ready, just in case a body crawls off the mound.

The fire burns for well over four hours, consuming fuel and the walking-dead body parts. Nothing remains but ash.

It is half-past seven in the evening, and everyone is relieved to finally be finished. The adrenalin rush is past. The mental fallout after the rush is consuming everyone, even Winey. They are sitting in camp, each in their own silent thoughts.

Carefully, Tripper tends to the medium sized campfire, while G remains on watch as the day winds down.

G looks around at the group, assigning watches before she goes to sleep for the night, content that everything has been tended to.

We see into the exhausted spirits and dreading souls of the six Black Swans; they are eager to return home.

Larret Army

The day blows in clear and cold, but at least the gods are breathing in their proper general east direction. Perhaps that is a good omen for the day.

The Black Swans check their gear again, ready to travel.

The men, Mi and Jess, just spent half-an-hour praying to Ikerus and Lorn, respectfully, hoping things are good between themselves and their gods.

The group's lone human warrior, G, is feeling more rested, having slept all night.

The group checks on their food supplies before going with Winey to the waterhole and returning with filled waterskins. The Black Swans are ready for the beginning of their journey home. Hopefully, they don't get lost.

With a few shallow sighs in resignation, G is ready to go. The priests have prayed, and hopefully, the dead are now dead. G commands, "Let's walk, Black Swans. We have a long way to go, and I hope the weather stays good."

The walk begins an hour or so after the gods have started their journey across the sphere. The group sets a comfortable pace, the weather cooperates, and a lot of distance is covered over the day. With G navigating, the Black Swans are sure they are not lost and that they are travelling in the correct direction.

After nearly ten hours of walking, they decide to find a camp location and rest for the night.

Minutes later, finding a suitable location, they set up their camp with appropriate watches.

Summer 37 Bear

After another peaceful night for the Black Swans, they are a little more eager to travel.

Both clerics forego prayers so that the Black Swans can get an early start walking. But as the Swans walk, the gods show their displeasure. The gods begin breathing fiercely and raising the heat of the air.

Consequently, the Black Swans are uncomfortable due to the weather, and they have breaking branches falling from the trees overhead to deal with.

Resigning himself to their failure in their duties, Mi shudders, asking forgiveness in silent prayer. But the gods continue to breathe hard all day, and the travellers struggle to walk.

Larret Army

Tired, after more than ten hours of hard walking, G stops their travels. The Black Swans set up a hasty unsheltered camp along the southern bank of the Harpen River.

The Swan's two women, G and Tripper, estimate that the group will be home late tomorrow, sometime after the two day-gods set.

Tripper recognizes the riverbank location they're at from her recent trip to Lord Ramson's Manor.

Still in command, G sets the camp's watch schedule, though most of the group feel it unnecessary.

Tripper agrees with G in setting up the night's watches, informing the group of the poachers and ruffians near at hand.

Summer 38 Bear

The Black Swans are almost home. The sphere's cover may have broken today, but the air is hotter, and with little to no gods-breath, it is even more unbearable than yesterday.

Judging from their current location, G offers the group: "If we are close enough to Larret tonight, then we should keep walking. I want to sleep in a bed as soon as possible, for a change."

Eren chuckles after Tripper says, "I don't know, after sleeping on the bed that you left in your house, I kind of like camping out."

With long faces, Mi and Jess look at Tripper. Mi speaks first, asking, "Do you need a new mattress, Tripper? I can have you a new one in a six-day."

Jess adds, "I can as well."

Winking at G, Tripper laughs and G rolls her eyes. Tripper says, "Sarcasm boys. The mattress is just fine; it's a dream to sleep on, actually."

The team walk until they are nearly three kilometres from Larret Hamlet. It is four hours until the gods set, when, suddenly, an arrow whizzes past them, striking the ground thirty-feet in front of the group.

"Stop there ... yield to the authority of Tearmain," someone shouts to them in Jalnoric.

G rapidly spins around, and with a sly motion, she pulls the slip knot on her pack, releasing the pack and dropping her gear to the ground so that she can be free for combat.

The rest of the Black Swans also react, ready for conflict.

Jess cowers behind the group.

Tripper takes up a position on G's left flank and Eren to G's right side.

Larret Army

Winey flanks Tripper.

Mi boldly walks up beside Jess – ready with prayers.

The group can see nine people rapidly approaching them. Three of the nine people stop, staying about thirty metres from the Black Swans.

The one who shouted leads the group of six who are still approaching.

This six divide into two wings of three each. As they approach, it is easy to determine that there are four men-at-arms and that two others are experienced folks, one of which seems out of place.

Perhaps the one out of place is a priestess as she wields a footman's mace and bears an odd set of symbols.

Maybe she's a warrior-mage?

One of the experienced is in each of the wings.

The six closing in on the Black Swans are surprised as Eren casts a fan-flame on the priestess type and the two men-at-arms by her side. Eren catches all three in her fan of fire.

The two men-at-arm have the misfortune of their gear catching aflame and are now brightly burning as they approach.

One of the men-at-arms immediately stops to combat the fire, trying to put out the flames, while the priestess sees fit to move in and challenge G in melee.

The second man-at-arms determines Eren to be a suitable target. As he continues to burn, he attacks Eren.

While these events are happening, Tripper feels obliged to do likewise and she fans-flames the two men-at-arms and their lead confronting warrior.

All three are caught in the fan of fire, and all three have their gear burst into flames. One of the men-at-arms is scorched so badly that he falls to the ground unconscious. The second man-at-arms stops to put out the flames.

The lead warrior continues approaching the Black Swans to enter combat with G.

The burning Toymal who is combating Eren takes a stab at Eren, and the point of the blade penetrates into Eren's upper leg.

Stepping back, he finds the burning too much, so he pulls back even further and drops his blade so that he can put out the flames.

Determined, G takes the opportunity to use her longsword. She is the first of the three to draw blood between them, as she slices into the lead warrior's forearm.

Seeing an opportunity to cast another spell, Eren blinds the burning Toymal who is struggling to put out his flames.

Larret Army

The one who we assume is their captain, is burning and flailing about with his longsword as he tries to attack G. Howerver, G awkwardly fends him off.

Seeing a situation that needs rendering, Winey rushes across the thirty-meter space at the three stragglers who are standing off in the distance.

Reaching them, Winey takes on the closer of the three – the surprised archer who is now taking Winey on in melee combat. Winey leaps up, severely slashing the man's head.

With her hand-axe, Tripper attacks, expertly slicing through the armour on the leg of the Toymal she is battling. Using her newly practised skills, Tripper has severely damaged the Toymal's armour and leg.

Slowing down, G, calmly takes more time in her efforts. With an improved focus, using her longsword, she slices neatly into the captain's leg. As G's arm receives a strike, she is knocked down soundly by a blow from the priestess' footman's mace.

The Toymal who Tripper has been combating, stabs into Tripper's somewhat unprotected chest with his shortsword.

In the distance, the twenty-something Jalmal man-at-arms who had been recovering from his exhausting forced march is now somewhat rested. He moves forward to replace the unconscious burning Jalmal who Tripper has scorched.

Shakily, G stands back up, while Jess spots the unarmoured Jalmal rushing towards the battle.

Taking the opportunity for a free shot, Jess fires a sling bullet straight into the abdomen of the Jalmal, knocking the wind out of him. He has managed to stun the charging man and briefly slow him down.

The archer stabs Winey's foreleg, drawing blood and leaving a wound that continues to bleed slightly.

Mi continues to hold back, watching for anyone who might seriously need his assistance. He is ready to jump in when the need arises.

Needing a melee weapon, Eren improvises by placing a stone in the cup of her sling. Using this sling as a club, Eren makes contact to the head of the thirtyish-year-old Jalmal.

G is busy with the captain and the priestess. Focusing on who she thinks to be the more obvious threat, she slices into the chest of the burning Jalmal captain, drawing more blood.

Meanwhile, after Eren rings the man-at-arms in the head, he tries to stab Eren with his shortsword, but she catches the blade with her sling and twists so rapidly that the blade breaks.

Larret Army

Mi looks toward Tripper, noticing that the village's mage has been wounded and taken to the ground by her attackers. He rushes over to support Tripper; Mi touches her shoulder as he prays fervently to Ikerus for a quick orison to stabilize Tripper. Noting the light transfer from his finger, Mi readies to move on.

Jess, working up with a fury of battle and leaving behind his innate cowardice, he drives his quarterstaff's end with such force directly into the unarmoured young Jalmal's abdomen. It is such a blow that the man is dead before hitting the ground. Jess quickly moves to aid Mi.

G, seeing an opening in the defences of the burning captain, slices through his leg, dropping him unconscious as he falls to the ground.

Worked up and angry, Winey tears off the archer's leg at the knee, killing the man as he drops to the ground, with the archer's blood draining out from his wound. Winey rushes back toward the main foray.

The priestess, becoming desperate, furiously smashes G's left shoulder with her footman's mace, driving G back with such force that she drops slightly, her eyes glazed over from the pain. No longer able to fight and barely moving, it is all she can do to avoid further strikes.

The heavier set Jalmal man-at-arms, who is attacking Eren, draws a club to replace his now broken shortsword, and he wades back into combat.

The fight is not going well for the short Toymal man-at-arms who is in combat with Jess. In a furious downswing with his quarterstaff, Jess brings the man's shortsword down to the ground, pinning and breaking it.

The man is forced back with no weapon in hand.

The priestess has exhausted herself to the point that she can no longer move and collapses to her knees.

The Toymal who is in melee with Jess, pulls a mallet from his belt and he wades back into the combat, determined to finish this.

Eren is not satisfied with ending the combat so quickly. Seeing the attackers continuing, she lives up to the unwilling name again, striking the thirtyish Jalmal on the leg with her improvised sling-club.

The man loses consciousness from a combination of exhaustion and pain, thus falling to the ground.

Mi, seeing G's state of health, rushes to her aid and prays frantically to Ikerus for aid as he casts a healing orison upon G. With the prayer cast, Mi waits, but with no answer to his prayer, he touches G, nothing – no response.

Larret Army

Mi feels a great disappointment as he groans. This lack of response has happened in the past, but he hasn't determined why Ikerus doesn't always grant his prayers. Is it because something is not said correctly in the prayers? Maybe Mi doesn't believe strong enough, or isn't smart enough, or isn't wise enough, or isn't powerful enough? Or perhaps he just doesn't know the right words? He will have to pilgrimage to the Holy Temple in Mount Oryn to pray and to speak with the Arch-Bishop. But, for now, we have to deal with this.

Winey, still bleeding slightly from the leg wound, continues to be in his battle fury. He engages Eren's Toymal, while three attackers on the ground still burning from the fires ignited by the two mages.

Mi refocuses and prays again for another healing orison for G. This time, as he touches her shoulder, to both of their relief, there is the light and she feels some relief from the pain.

Jess is still in his battle fury as he brings his quarterstaff into the leg of the Jalmal giant he is engaged with.

The young Toymal, seeing that he is engaged by an enraged boar and a female mage, and seeing that most of the opponents are still active and only three of the nine he came with are still conscious, comes to a decision. He drops his weapon, and speaking in Toydon, he says to Eren, "I give myself over. I'm done."

Jess, not hearing the surrender or even caring if one was offered, is still in his fury. Blind with anger, he continues to battle the priestess. He brings his quarterstaff around too fast and too short, striking the ground in front of the priestess, shattering his quarterstaff.

Now, without his staff, Jess steps back and shakes himself out of his fury.

The others are also recovering their senses.

Eren looks at the Toymal as she hears Jess shatter his staff. She smiles, nods, and then she utters, "Remove all weapons and packs. All you should have is your armour and boots."

The Toymal moves to comply, as he is too tired to object and too afraid to argue with the fire mage.

Meanwhile, Mi is attempting to calm Winey. Once he has Winey settled, he notes the bleeding wound and again calls upon Ikerus for aid. Praying for an orison to stop the bleeding, Mi touches the wound.

But Winey goes back into a fury, pulling away, negating the prayer. Winey charges at the priestess.

Eren is watching the surrendering Toymal when she spots movement out of the corner of her eye. Looking over at the movement, she sees a Jalmal man-at-arm get up and start running for the tree line.

With a stone already in the cup of her sling, Eren doesn't hesitate. She winds up and fires the stone, squarely striking the man in the back as she calls out. "Jess, a runaway … headed towards the woods."

Jess pulls free his sling and a bullet. He lets a bullet fly as the man is running and Eren is getting off the second shot. Both miss.

The Jalmal is mere meters from the trees when Jess's second bullet drives deep, breaking bones and killing him.

Eren's third stone flies by the falling man.

While Jess and Eren are shooting down the escaping Jalmal, Winey isn't leaving the priestess in peace. The boar tears into the priestess' leg, drawing her away from the two priests.

The giant Jalmal man-at-arms and the priestess collapse to their knees, exhausted from their forced march to catch the Black Swans and this combat to capture recruits. They are no longer able to continue melee.

Mi is finally able to calm Winey. Holding the boar, he prays to Ikerus again for another heal orison, watching as the light flows between the two, and the bleeding stops. Winey has lost a lot of blood and will need Jess for a long while. But, for now, others need Jess. G has collapsed to the ground, losing consciousness to the world.

The enemy priestess, tired but having recovered enough to speak, looks up and addresses Eren. "You! Mage! I ask for asylum in your care."

Eren slowly walks over and looks down upon the opposing Jalfem. "Why would I? It'll cost you. A lot."

The priestess frowns and spits. Then, she shakily utters. "Name your price."

Eren chuckles in a harsh tone. "You won't like it. You will work for me for ten years at a wage of one duster a day. Then, if you have no debt, you will be free to go. Those are my terms."

We see the malice in Eren's mind and fear for the priestess' future.

The woman growls. She doesn't answer for a few moments and then says, "Five years and one Dyns a day. Then, if debt free, I am free to go."

Eren smiles as she shakes her head. "I should kill you now and save myself a whole lot of trouble. But you have me curious. Okay, here is my final offer: ten years at five dusters a day. After ten years, if you are debt free, you're free to go. Nothing else. Anything else and my pig friend has more to eat."

Larret Army

The woman scowls even more. But she extends her arm and bows.

Eren clasps arms with the priestess. "What is the name of my new employee? And what are your skills?"

"I am Priestess Lenna of Tearmain. Do I at least have space for a shrine to Tearmain?" She says, bold as brass.

Eren looks at Lenna as Eren helps her to her feet. "Place your weapons alongside his. We will talk about the shrine later. I've never heard of Tearmain before … new one to me."

Eren walks over to the first opponent to surrender, who is kneeling and is still recovering from his fatigue. "Name and skills. Ten years and two dusters, and if you are without debt, then you'll be free. But you won't be mine; you will belong to the hamlet of Larret."

The man sighs and stands, trying to decide how to respond. "I am called Maken. I was a woodworker before these gaffers recruited me as a mercenary three seasons ago. I would prefer to be a woodworker again. So, I accept, thank you."

Eren nods approvingly. "Your first job, Maken … we dropped one of your people running away, near the woods. Go and drag him back here. Then, arrange all these bodies nice and neat, so our healer can determine who is alive and who is dead. Get moving now. It will be dark soon."

Mi is watching for anyone else moving on the battlefield and for anyone approaching. So far, nothing unexpected is happening.

Jess discovers that Tripper and G are out like the dead, but they are alive. Winey has a wound that bled severely before the orison was cast to heal him and seal the bleeding.

After arranging Tripper in a comfortable position, Jess tends to G with some basic medical aid. He feels confident in his skills and believes that she will survive.

Looking around, Eren spots a third living assailant who was unaccounted for. Approaching him, Eren says, "Hey you, what is your story? Death, try to run, or surrender?"

The giant looks up at her, and in drawn-out Jalnoric, he says, "I will look to surrender under proper terms."

Eren smiles. "Good, an educated giant. I offer you two dusters a day for ten years unless you can convince me you are worth more. At the end of ten years, you are free if you are debt free."

The giant sighs and stands to his full seven-foot-three-inch height. "My name is Ennder ... for a reason. But I won't go into that now. I am a master jeweller ... a fine smith with good skills. With a degree of capability, I can scribe in Jal. I am a bit of a herald. So, I would say I am worth at least a Dyns. And, I can back it all up with weapons and a shield. So now what do you offer?"

Eren ponders this. With a grim frown, she considers it a little more, finally saying, "I offer this: ten years in any case. If you craft jewellery, then you get ten percent commission on crafted items. Straight up deal. If you lie to me, and you craft shit, then you will be cleaning chamber pots for a duster a day for those ten years. That is my offer."

Ennder extends his arm.

Eren accepts and grimaces from the strength of the grip of the Jalmal.

Jess spends nearly fifteen minutes tending to G before he finally feels that her wounds are set. He then moves on to tend to Tripper's wounds.

Meanwhile, Ennder and Maken are dragging the dead bodies and placing them in a row. They pile all the good weapons neatly in one pile and put the three broken weapons in a heap nearby. Shields are stacked neatly with the aid of Eren.

Winey and Mi keep watch over the whole works, ready to do battle again. They keep an eye on the embattled Priestess of Tearmain, who is near G's unconscious form.

Finally, all the bodies are arranged, weapons gathered, and Jess finishes with Tripper, giving her a smile.

Jess says to Tripper. "Join the others. I have to do something with Winey, and then figure out what to do with G. Talk with Eren about this mess. Maybe make camp?"

Tired, Tripper nods and says, "Yes, making camp is a good idea. We should all eat." Tripper, moving raggedly, approaches Eren.

Seeing Tripper move so poorly, Eren quickly wanders over to her. "Yes, Tripper, you burned those bastards well."

Tripper manages a meek smile. She then says, "You didn't do so bad yourself, Eren. Hey, let's set up a camp while Jess deals with Winey and G. And, let's rest and eat. What do you think?"

Eren ponders this and then nods enthusiastically. "Sit down ... we have a workforce now. Hey, Ennder and Maken, get enough tinder and fuel for a fire for tonight. Also, make a campfire while I set up a camp for us. We are staying here tonight unless you know of any friends of yours who are going to show up?"

Priestess Lenna speaks up. "We are the advance force, scouting for the main force. The main advance groups are a couple of days behind us. We were out recruiting. It'll be quiet for a couple of days until the main Tearmain forces arrive."

Tripper beams back dully. "I doubt that. We are a small hamlet on the coast and of no strategic value. It is too shallow on the coast to be a proper port. So, I don't foresee any forces coming here. But later I will listen to what you have to say about Tearmain's forces. For now, we will set up camp."

Dejected, Lenna lays on the ground, no longer caring about what's next.

Having been offered food at the end of a day's work, Maken and Ennder enthusiastically take up their task. We see their drive to please and carry on after their release from the Tearmain yoke.

Eren begins clearing a camp area next to the Harpen River, away from the corpses. She then looks in on Jess.

As the camp is prepared, Jess cleans and dresses Winey's wounds and stitches his leg wound closed. Now, finding G is stable but weak and still not responding to him, Jess fusses more with good old healing arts. But he eventually comes to a loss as to what else he can do. It's time to call upon his god.

Jess considers his options. He has already called upon Lorn to repair Tripper's severe wounds and was rewarded with Tripper gaining consciousness after the wound closed. Now it is G's turn, but the wounds are broken bones and bruises deep inside, not the kind of injuries that heal or repair easily. Though this will take time, it is all Jess can do for now. Focusing for all he is worth, Jess begins the familiar prayer of heal wounds while holding onto G's unconscious form. Praying to Lorn with the certainty that Lorn's powers can heal at least a small amount of the internal damages, Jess feels the power flow between himself and G, but she doesn't stir.

Jess thinks he has exhausted his full power of prayers for today. He feels he may have enough energy left in him for a few minor orisons. Maybe? Summoning his focus, yet again, he calls upon his belief in Lorn and his faith in G's trust in him. First, one orison. The power flows.

There is a twinge of a response, and hope ignites in Jess.

He tries again. Again, Jess is praying and he intensely focuses. He knows that he is healing her as the power flows between them.

G flutters her eyes, and then she groans and looks at him. She says, "You can let go now, you know. Let me rest a bit. How long have I been out, my friend?"

Jess holds onto her a little longer. Debating further action, he decides to hold back. He releases G's hand and answers her. "About an hour, G. The bodies are settled; we need to know your ideas. Eren took three in surrender. You can talk to her when you're ready. We all made it through okay. We're a little battered, but we made it. You took the worst."

G holds up her hand. "Jess, shut up for now. Later, okay?"

Jess, only nineteen, turns reddish as he blushes. He nods and then quickly stands. He hurries as he walks over to Eren. "G is awake and ready for you when you want."

Eren smiles slightly and nods. With a brisk pace she walks away from the small campfire and over to G. Eren says to G, "Hey, do you want roasted ants, or boiled ants?"

G chuckles, and then winces from the discomfort. "Pickled if you don't mind. So how did it all work out?"

Eren slumps down onto the ground next to G and begins her report. "Well, let's see, I took the personal surrender of two and Larret Hamlet took one. Larret took the ten-year surrender of a woodworker for two dusters per day with freedom conditional on being debt free at the end of the term. I got myself a giant mercenary who fancies himself a jeweller. If he isn't a jeweller, he will be cleaning chamber pots for a duster a day for ten years, freedom conditional on being debt free. The second one I got, I think the Black Swans should talk to as a group. She claims to be a Priestess of a god called Tearmain, and she claims her group was an advance scout pack. They were out recruiting for the main attack force of Tearmain and building their attack force. She says the main force is two days away from here. She surrendered for five dusters a day for ten years, and her freedom is conditional on being debt free. I didn't do too badly. I'm still making a profit on my cottage and as Larret Beadle. If this giant is a jeweller and any good, then I can continue my mage studies again from where I left off after I set up my new study, shop, and laboratory, which I had to abandon in the last village – the village I nearly got roasted in."

G smiles weakly. "Let me think a moment. How many dead? And how much cargo did they have?"

Eren laughs loudly, and then she answers. "Six dead and just the belongings which they were marching with. You're not carrying anything back with you, so someone else needs to carry your forty-pound pack for you. Why?"

"Then we need at least one medium wagon to get it all back. I recognize this spot. There is an ox-bow that I collect resources from not far from here. We must send someone to Larret to get a wagon team. It feels as if a team of bulls are pulling my arm off, so the sooner we can get back and get things straightened out, the better off we will all be." She struggles weakly but does manage to sit up. "Mi, get over here, please."

Mi arrives, and G addresses him and Eren. "Can the two of you go to Larret? It is still three kilometres away, but you will make it before gods-set. We must begin the proper passing ceremonies for the dead, or we will have more walking-dead. We need to put these six to rest properly. I want you to bring the village's medium-sized wagon and horse team. Bring back with you: Nela Milin, Enda Sorel, Pepsid Morile, and Tairy. If you leave now, then you shouldn't have to travel back in too much darkness."

Mi and Eren both stand and bow. Leaving their packs, they start their brisk walk along the Harpen riverbank, headed southeast towards Larret Hamlet.

We sense Mi's resolve and Eren's reluctance to be walking alone and to be leaving the others with the Tearmain fodder.

. . . ..

Arriving in Larret Hamlet, approximately an-hour-and-a-half later, Eren and Mi head straight to the Watch-house.

Entering, they find Enda Sorel sitting at the command desk.

The Jalfem gazes up at the pair with a bewildered look.

Not willing to waste time, Eren addresses her. "Look, we are in a rush. It is nearly half-an-hour until gods-set. We need to have the medium wagon harnessed, plus a team of people ready to travel before gods-set. These are the people I want: you, Nela, Tairy, and Pepsid Morile. So, stand up and let's get moving. You and Nela get the wagon ready to travel. I will get Tairy, and Mi will find Pepsid. Let's move; be ready in half-an-hour."

Enda nods and says, "Yes, Beadle Eren. Nela is in the stable anyway. We will use the good team of horses then?"

Eren nods and curtly answers as she walks out the door. "Yes."

. . . ..

Just over half-an-hour later, the group is ready with these members: Mi, Eren, Enda, Nela, Pepsid, Tairy, and a tag-along who may not be welcome at the destination, G's Uncle Trevour.

Tairy is driving the wagon team as they set out westward along Harpen River, travelling the three kilometres to the grizzly battle scene. Hooded lanterns are lit and mounted on the wagon to light the way, as the two day-gods have set over the western horizon.

. . . ..

Nearly two-and-a-half hours later, the wagon group arrives at the dismal battle scene to find that everyone in camp is sleeping, except for the anxious G and Jess.

G stumbles over to the wagon team and takes the lead of the horses, settling them. Her limp left arm is in a sling.

Seeing Trevour walking into camp, G growls, and she curtly says, "How did he manage to tag along? Can I kill him

253

now and be done with him? Can we say he was a fatality of a battle? Or will someone here rat me out?"

Eren looks at G and then says in a whisper, "If you want to kill him, you have to do it yourself. Considering your arm, I think you might have a tough time of it. Maybe later? Go and get some sleep. I will take watch tonight with Nela, and then Enda and Pepsid can do watch. Tairy can unhitch the wagon team for the night."

Still glaring at Trevour, G shuffles back to the fire. Fuming, she rests for the night but doesn't sleep because of her pain.

Summer 39 Bear

As the two day-gods rise above the eastern horizon, the heat is already causing bloating of the bodies on the loaded wagon. The dead are stacked like cordwood, along with their possessions; they are given no respect today. The eastern breath of the gods is not providing any relief from the heat.

Tairy cracks the horsewhip over the horses and the journey back to Larret Hamlet begins steady and slow.

. . . ..

Larret Army

Arriving back in Larret just after noon, G instructs Tairy to drive the wagon to Mi's Church of Ikerus. From there, the group unloads the bodies into the cooler interior of the building.

Beginning preparations for Right of Passage, Mi acts according to protocol for the race. Not knowing which of the gods any of the deceased followed, Mi decides that the best option is to give them the Right of Passage as based on racial heritage.

For the Jalnoric dead, this will take seven days each.

For the Toydon dead, each will take six days.

On a whim, G decides that if Trevour truly wants to make amends, he will stay and help Mi with the entire lot.

Trevour helps unload the wagon, and he stays to help Mi. Thus, Trevour is starting to change G's view of him, slightly.

After having been away for over six days, G heads home to Reeve House.

Eren returns to her cottage, taking Ender and Lenna with her.

Tripper and Winey go home to the house they rent from G.

Sad, Jess stands there a moment with Maken.

They look at each other, and then Jess asks, "Who did you surrender to?"

Maken answers, confused. "The fire mage, but she said I surrendered to Larret Hamlet."

Jess beams a grin, and then he says, "Okay, follow me. What skills do you have?"

Frowning, Maken follows Jess as they walk toward Reeve House. "My trade is as a woodworker. Those were my skills before being recruited as a mercenary by the Tearmain forces. I would appreciate working as a woodworker again."

Jess nods without answering as they walk through the quiet Larret Hamlet.

We laugh, '*Yah! Right!*'

Knocking on the Reeve House door, Jess waits.

The door opens and a dirty, tired-appearing, snarling G answers, "What?"

Jess backs up, as he's seen G like this once before; just before she took to a melee with the local shepherd over the price of her wool.

Cautiously, he speaks, "I believe this man is directly answerable to you. He is Woodworker Maken, who surrendered to Larret Hamlet on the field of battle. I leave him to you, Reeve G. Have a good day. Gods-grace to you, and great fate." Quickly, Jess escapes, leaving the clueless two to deal with the issue.

G looks at Maken and then steps aside. "Get in; you're letting in the heat."

Maken walks in rapidly, and G hurries as she closes the door.

G just stands for a few moments as she watches Maken's hands, which he holds low in front of him.

We speak to G, telling her to go easy on the refugee.

She walks to the kitchen and pours two mugs of water. Setting one mug on the table, she drinks from the other. She then sits down at the table. Pointing to the seat across the table from her, she calls to Maken. "Take a seat and have a drink, as we need to talk."

Maken, following the order, sits and drinks happily from the mug.

G inquisitively observes the man. "You're a woodworker?" she asks.

Carefully setting down the mug, he replies, "Yes, Reeve. I have several years of journeyman experience. I was on my way to take my master's exam in Mount Oryn when the Tearmain recruiters captured me and branded me into their forces." He exposes his neck showing the three-parallel red tattoo lines on the left side of his neck.

G nods, pointing at the mugs. "Would you like an ale? I have a good light ale."

Maken's eyes light up. "I haven't had ale in two seasons. Yes, please."

G chuckles. "Then fill them both; it's the second keg from the right."

Eagerly walking to the shelf with the kegs, Maken fills both mugs and then retakes his seat. He waits for G to drink before he takes his first sip, enjoying the experience as he savours the taste. Sighing, he then takes a second drink. Maken carefully nurses the ale during their conversation.

G takes the conversational lead. "Ok, we can use a woodworker for the village. You will be doing repairs for a long while. You'll start with Reeve House, and then the outbuildings, and then whatever else needs work. You will work with the mason, as he requires your aid. For tonight, you can stay in the second bedroom of this house. The bed is made. I will decide what to do with you after that. I don't have any more private housing, unless Tripper is willing to give up a room in my house. Or, I could rent you the second bedroom, here, until we find you a place. If you want the room, it is one duster every six days."

Maken looks shocked. "You would rent it to me? This close and in such high class? For such low cost? Yes, of course, I will take the room. Take the rent out of my wages."

G nods. "Okay then. You get paid on every thirty-day mark. So, your next payday is Summer 60 Bear. I will deduct the rent for all your summer's rent on that payday so that you will be paid up until Autumn 1. As for food, you have no coin as we confiscated that by rights of battle. So, you are destitute. But, I can't have you starve to death under my roof. Meals will cost you one duster a day. Fair enough? I will include one ale with each meal."

Maken's eyes are sparkling. "Yes! Yes, of course."

As G watches Maken, she slowly comes to another decision. "To earn extra coin, you can do work for others and charge what you think is fair. But, I want twenty percent of your earnings. You can use my shop. I will show you where it is. Stay out of the house, as it is rented by the hamlet's Mage Tripper. You can use my tools until you can make or afford your own. You must replace any worn or damaged tools. Understood? If you get ten hours a day of hamlet work done, then I don't care about your other time."

Maken, in shock, stutters. "Y... you'll ... Let ... t ... m ... me do that?"

Larret Army

Affirming her words, G nods, and then she says, "Yes, Maken, you fix anything you wear out or damage, and you can use my shop during your off-time to earn extra coin in the hamlet." She extends her arm.

We smile at G's generosity and kindness as they make arrangements.

Before her arm is fully extended, Maken is standing with his arm out, and they clasp. "Deal!" He nearly shouts, grinning from ear-to-ear.

After clasping arms with G, and then sitting back down, Maken drains his ale and earnestly asks, "May I buy another? Just one?"

She nods slowly and G smiles. She then confirms softly. "One duster off your wages, but only one more ale."

Carefully, Maken rises and fills both mugs, and then he sits again. With his eyes gleaming cheerfully, he waits.

G stands and stokes the flames in her stove that she had just started when she was interrupted. She heats up water and has a bath in the storeroom, and then instructs Maken to do likewise.

While Maken is bathing, G cooks the two of them a decent hot meal. As G sets out each of them another ale, a freshly scrubbed Maken enters the common room.

Larret Army

G shows Maken his room and then proceeds to explain to him his full duties as they consume their meal.

Summer 40 Bear

The Black Swans have returned to hamlet life.

Evening arrives on their first full day back, finding the Black Swans gathered in Reeve House with the three new residents of Larret Hamlet. Thus, making for crowded quarters in Reeve House, as this brings eight folks in the common room.

G has supplied each person with a mug of ale. She is chairing this meeting. "We have an issue here – an attack on our group by you three. You, Priestess Lenna, claim your group to be advance scouts recruiting for a force who are fighting for a god called Tearmain. So, I open the floor to you. Then we will ask you some questions. Tell us about this Tearmain and the forces fighting for it," instructs G, sharply.

Lenna stands, boldly looking each Black Swan in the eyes, and then she starts her oratory. "We are recruiting for the forces of Tearmain. Tearmain is a new god, growing in strength each day. He is powerful now. And, in time, he will rule all the gods. He is ruthless towards those who defy him, but he grants great powers to those who aid him. His realm is bright and strong.

Larret Army

You will do well aiding Tearmain now as leaders of his forces. Supply the army with food and fighting personnel, also equipment, and you will be rewarded far beyond what your current Lord ever will."

G stands and smirks. She asks. "Tell me how many we have to supply, so we know how much to send and where?"

Lenna smiles, cheered to hear the proposed support from Larret Hamlet, as Tearmain's generals have promised bonus rewards for any extra supplies of equipment and personnel. "There are two-thousand in the army, 185 to 190 kilometres west from here, headed towards Mount Oryn to battle the Royal Army. I will lead you to them if you send all supplies that you have available."

G peers at each Black Swan. Then, after each of them nods, she picks up her kitchen knife and walks over to Lenna. "I swear to go to these forces of Tearmain. But it will be under the banner of Lord Ramson and King Dolan." She swiftly brings the blade of the knife across Lenna's throat, drawing a fountain of blood from the open wound. G looks at the other two, glaring at them. "Do you desire to join her?"

We feel their intense fear and G's rising anger and determination.

Both men uniformly shake their heads negatively, and Ennder speaks happily. "Thank you. I have been waiting to be free of their yoke. I swear fealty to this hamlet and the five of you, now and forward. I swear to uphold my surrender contract to Mage Eren."

Maken stands, and then kneeling, he calls forth. "I, too, swear fealty to Larret Hamlet as a citizen and contracted agent, swearing to fulfil my commitment to Larret Hamlet, as designated by Reeve G. I break all oaths to Tearmain and its filth."

Chapter
Five

Ever-Knot

Chapter Five:

Ever-Knot

*S*ummer *49 Bear*

The Black Swans gather to board the barge, Ever-Knot.

Mi, Jess, G, and Eren are all going to take up poles. Tripper will be captain and pilot of the barge for the trip northwest to Dartoln Village and Lord Ramson's Manor.

For the last few days, the Black Swans were busy with affairs in the hamlet of Larret. Yesterday, the Tearmain priestess was buried. She was the last of the attacking raiders to be laid to

264

rest. So, it is now time for the group to warn Lord Ramson of this Tearmain issue.

Over these last days, the Right of Passage was conducted for each of the seven dead attackers from Tearmain.

G and Eren conducted a moot hall.

Several worship services were performed by both priests, Jess and Mi.

Both Tripper and Eren were busy with their businesses and farms.

G was busy with the hamlet's daily business and working in her own bowyer business.

All the loose ends are now tied up; everyone can travel again.

We feel the ease of being settled and ready to leave Larret again.

G left Old Ringus as interim Reeve Sergeant again. Her shoulder has healed fairly well. Even though the shoulder is still damaged, it is now less painful for her.

Tripper's and Winey's wounds are healed, thanks to the ministrations of Jess and Lorn.

The five humans and one boar casually walk down the bank to Harpen River's shore ready to board the Ever-Knot. With their packs gathered, everyone is set for a new journey together. Well, almost everyone. We shudder as we feel her nerves twinge.

Eren stops just short of stepping off from the solid ground. She peers out at the river's bright gentle flowing currents of water. Eren is shaking noticeably; she is more pale than usual.

Winey grunts as he curls up and settles himself in the crowded centre of the barge.

G, upon seeing Eren's reaction, looks around for immediate danger. Seeing no threatening danger, she sets her pack in the centre of the barge with Winey and the other items: a barrel of ale and a sack of tubers that she and Tripper had loaded this morning. Strolling over to Eren, who is now turning a slight shade of blue, G asks her, "What's the matter, Eren? Do you need to be paid to board the Ever-Knot?"

Eren stares at the moving water a moment longer, and then she flashes her icy grey eyes up at G. Staring into Gès clear grey eyes, Eren says, "I don't know if I can do it. I might not be able to go. I can't get on the barge, G."

Sensing more than a simple unwillingness, G takes the time to ferret out this problem. "Tell me why. Why this time? Why now?"

Eren starts to back up slowly away from the river, but G takes her gently by the shoulder and stops her.

Eren says, "It's the water. I don't know if I can go out on the water, G. I had an accident when I was young. I was in Jon Lon Hamlet, which is also along a river. I was fishing with a cousin when I was six; she pushed me in. I want to think it was an accident, but I nearly drowned, G. I almost died in that water, and it still haunts me."

G thinks about this. Then, giving Eren a firm friend's hug, she offers. "Okay, you sit in the centre with Winey. The others – the three of us – will pole. It will be slower. If you come along and remain calm, I will pay you one Dyns per day. Deal?"

Eren breaks away from the hug, but none too quickly. She replies, "Two Dyns a day, and I will try it."

G extends her arm to clasp.

For a moment, Eren looks intensely at G, and then she looks at the river for a few moments, considering this.

We watch as her shaking becomes less.

Everyone else, except for Winey who lays calmly watching Eren, is growing impatient.

Finally, Eren firmly clasps arms with G, and stepping forward up to the edge of the bank and barge, she looks at the barge and then the water. Steeling her resolve, Eren closes her bright icy eyes and takes the two steps up onto the barge planks. Opening her eyes, she quickly moves to the centre and flops down, leaning on Winey.

If boars can smile, then yes, Winey just smiled. However, the other Black Swans on the barge deck are not smiling.

G, Jess, and Mi each take up a pole. Setting their poles into the cold, shallow water, they prepare to push the barge free.

Tripper releases the mooring ropes, which are holding the barge in place, attached to trees on shore.

On Summer 49 Bear, a new journey begins for the Black Swans. They must report to Lord Ramson the news of the Army of Tearmain.

Summer 53 Bear

The Ever-Knot creaks and groans as it is moored on Dartoln's dock at the Harpen River's muddy, clay shore. The breaths of the gods are ripping the world of Quantos apart.

It was late last night when the Black Swans arrived at the dock in Dartoln.

They all agree that if they ever have a choice, they will not sail in such breaths of the gods again. They lost some of the barge's sailing gearing. The gearing must be replaced, and some repairs need to be completed before the Ever-Knot can sail again.

Yesterday, upon reaching the dark, cold, noisy shores of Dartoln, the group decided that since it was already after evening meal, they would tend to the Ever-Knot for the night.

G had informed the others it would be a bad time to intrude upon Lord Ramson if they wanted a positive response, and Tripper had agreed.

Over an hour ago, the two day-gods rose brightly, displaying Stonewire's yellow lighting with Imvor's orange-red lighting.

Now, the dishevelled group knocks on the hardwood door of Ramson Manor.

The ever-vigilant servant opens the door, excitedly beaming her rare smile. "Gena, it is a pleasant surprise to see you. We thought you passed away. Please, you and your friends come in … get out of the god's displeasure. Hurry now."

The Black Swans enter quickly. Brushing themselves off, they stand as the servant diligently observes them. "Master Tripper, good to see you again. Lord Ramson was in a pleasant mood for a few days after you left last time. Gena, you being here will spark excitement for a long time to come. Please, all of you come to the great hall."

269

G addresses the girl in a calm tone. "Willa, is Lord Ramson taking calls now? We have a report to deliver to him as soon as he is available."

Willa replies, "I will see if he will see you today. Gena and Tripper, you know where the great hall is. I will go upstairs to hear the Lord's instructions, and I will come back and let you know, Master Gena."

G smiles as Tripper answers. "Good enough. Thank you."

G and Tripper lead the Black Swans along the hallway and into the meeting hall. The Black Swans take seats and wait patiently.

Only a few brief minutes pass before Lord Ramson, huffing and excited, bursts into the room. He observes those gathered, and smiling with excitement, he chuckles gleefully. Lord Ramson says, "Well now, wine and meats are going to be served. My goodness, two of my favourite Larret villagers in the same visit – sorry, three of my favourites. Hello, Winey."

We note Winey greet the Lord with a snort and shimmy of his body.

Lord Ramson hastily takes his seat, saying, "Is this informal or formal?"

G and Tripper both stand and bow.

G answers, "It's a formal matter, Lord Ramson."

Larret Army

Willis frowns as a knock on the door is heard, and then the door opens. Three servants enter, carrying containers with wine, goblets, plates, and cold pickled meats. Setting these supplies on the table, the servants leave, closing the door behind them.

Lord Ramson nods to the Black Swans, and he says, "Lord Ramson acknowledges Larret Hamlet and its' Reeve Gena. Please … help yourselves to drink and meats."

The Black Swans dish themselves a plate of meats and a goblet of wine. With Willis' blessing, Tripper dishes up a plate for Winey.

When all are settled, G starts by saying, "Lord Ramson, we have news to report from the shireward. We are the group who dealt with it, so we have come to report our encounters. First, we formally formed ourselves into the adventure group known as Black Swans. I hear that it was a suggestion of yours to Mage Tripper. Anyway, the Black Swans consist of myself, as Reeve G of Larret Hamlet; Tripper, as Mage Enda Lon of Larret Hamlet; Enda's animal companion, the Boar Winey; Eren the Unwilling, as Beadle Heather Molan of Larret Hamlet; our Village Priest, Jessep Whitestone of Larret Hamlet, simply know as Jess; and Cleric of Ikerus, Mikene Lornet, who is known as Mi."

Larret Army

G continues, "While Jess was on a daily swim in the Harpen River, he was witness to several walking-dead attacking a villager. After reporting the attack to me, I took it upon myself to lead a small group and investigate the attack site. At the location, we found the victim had become a walking-dead. No sign of the other walking-dead was to be found. We took the disabled villager back to his family for proper Right of Passage."

"The Black Swans came together as a new group to seek out and deal with the missing walking-dead. It took us several days of tracking to locate the walking-dead. On one particular night, several walking-dead attacked our camp. We disposed of the walking-dead, giving field Right of Passage and cremating the bodies. Jess confirmed that those were all the walking-dead who assaulted the now dead villager. After disposing of the walking-dead, we then proceeded to return to Larret Hamlet. Nearing the hamlet, we were confronted by a large party intent on acquiring us for their own purposes. We killed six of their members, and three others surrendered to us. We lost none of our own, but two of our members were incapacitated, one of which was me."

"In interviewing those captured assailants, they revealed that a gathering army of over two-thousand was recruited to overthrow the monarchy and rule the kingdom under the governorship of a new god's rule. The army is gathering west of here. The group who attacked us was a raiding party, out seeking to recruit for their army. Unfortunately, the leader of the three we captured died in the interviews while she was giving the information about the treason she was planning. She professed to be a priestess of this new god they call Tearmain."

Lord Ramson listens and intently observes the other Black Swans as well. When G finishes, he earnestly asks, "Did the other two captives confirm everything the priest said?"

G nods, and then she responds. "Yes, they did. They also renounced ties with this god Tearmain. They also swear fealty to King Dolan and to us. The Right of Passage was completed for all the dead before we came here, to ensure no repeat of the walking-dead incident occurs."

Lord Ramson sharply turns to Tripper, and he asks her in a commanding tone. "Do you have anything to add?"

Tripper frowns at being put in an uncomfortable position, but she answers in an even tone and with a cool resolve. "No, Reeve G covered everything."

Lord Ramson sighs deeply. He then says, "There is nothing I can do to aid you. But I would like you to go to Mount Oryn to report this to an officer of the army. Protocol dictates that you report it to at least a captain of the royal army; that is our duty. But being as I did not directly observe these events I can not supply you with a letter to give the army. Good luck with your report."

G looks at her group, and then she asks in earnest, "Black Swans, are we ready for the journey to Mount Oryn?"

They look from one to another, and they all turn to G and nod.

Gradually G turns to Lord Ramson, and she says with firm conviction. "We will do it."

Tripper looks at each in the group, and then she hesitantly says, "I have an issue. We sailed here in the Ever-Knot. I need to leave it here until we return." Facing Lord Ramson, Tripper continues. "Lord Ramson, may I leave the barge docked at Dartoln dock?"

After some thought, Lord Ramson replies, "For one Flair per season, you can leave it docked any time."

Tripper frowns in frustration, as she is on a tight budget.

G speaks up. "We brought the Black Swan's treasury purse. We will use that to pay for one season of docking."

Relieved, Tripper smiles as she peers at the other three.

Mi smiles and nods.

Jess simply says, "Yes."

Eren taps the table and says, "Okay, I agree."

We silently approve too.

Awed by the group's generosity, Tripper adds, "Lord Ramson, in light of this gift from my fellow travellers, I too will gift. As a tithe to you, if you accept, I offer to your kitchen stores, ten gallons of ale and a sack of tubers that are on the Ever-Knot."

Lord Ramson chuckles. "Of course, Tripped one, I accept. Any untainted food is welcome. You folks can pay my servant as you are leaving. I must retire from this meeting now, as I am to hold another court soon, and I must be ready. Safe journey to you. Gods-grace and good fate, my subjects."

As a group, the Black Swans salute Lord Ramson, all shouting in unison: "Gods-grace and good fate."

.....

With the tithes and fees paid, the Black Swans begin their march westward through the woodlands of the Dominnion of Kannoral, on the Quantos' continent of North Amara.

In the beginning, the trek is easy as they are travelling through the settled farmlands of fiefs and glebes.

They travel well on through the day and into the evening before making a night camp.

Larret Army

Summer 54 Bear

During the day of Summer 54 Bear, the Black Swans are walking along safe and happy, when they suddenly encounter a terrifying sight. They discover the skeletons of human babies – dozens of skeletons.

G recounts to the group the tales she heard relating to this area. "This is the northern boundary of the Winterholm. It is a dragon's territory; he demands the tribute of one baby on the first of every spring. Taking the baby, he melts the soft flesh from the body, leaving only the skeleton, which he deposits here, so the locals will not forget. Anyone who enters this territory is never heard from or seen again. If the locals forget or refuse to leave the tithe of one baby, Winterholm seeks out two adults and takes them instead. The territory runs for some distance to the west; it is best to avoid going anywhere south of here."

The group continues westward, avoiding travelling into the well-marked southern area, which is Winterholm.

Summer 55 Bear

Early in the morning, during their walk in the rain, the group encounters the shore of a huge lake that stretches for kilometres into the horizon north of them. The far shore of the lake is unseen.

We shudder at the vast number of lost souls here and our knowledge of the hidden city on the island at the centre of the lake.

The group walks along the southern shore for most of the day.

G determines that their course should take them away from the lake, as the lakeshore is turning north now, and they need to go west.

The Black Swans are a couple of kilometres from the lake by the time they make evening camp.

The rains continue into the night.

We are relieved to be away from the Lost Lake.

Summer 57 Bear

Another two days have passed, and it is nearing evening time. They are looking for an adequate area to make camp when Eren spots in the distance, what appears to be a campfire.

The Black Swans stop, trying to observe the distant fire.

Pointing out the fires, Eren notes, "There probably shouldn't be campfires around here, as we are getting close to farmlands. We should be nearing populated fiefs. I think we are near where the priest said Tearmain's army is. Does one of us want to carefully check that out?"

G looks over the surrounding area. She points out features of broken bushes and tree branches, and areas of trampled grasses. "It's a group, and they've been here for a while … I'll go and check them out. Keep my pack. I'll be right back."

Cautiously, G walks towards the firelight, using trees and bushes for cover to shadow her approach.

Several minutes later, G returns to the others. She tells the Black Swans. "There are about twenty in the camp. They are set up for battle with defensive works around the camp. I looked to the north and south. There is another camp to the south, a short way from here. But I don't see a camp close by to the north. We should go north and see what we encounter."

As quietly as possible, the Black Swans trek northward, looking for a secluded spot to make a fireless camp for the night. Even though there is no breath from the gods, the group doesn't want to have to worry about the scent of smoke giving away their presence. It will be an uncomfortable night because of the cold.

Even we shudder at the uncomfortable conditions the Black Swans are spending the night in.

Larret Army

Walking away from the river, so that they will not be accidentally spotted, the Black Swans traverse the scrubland hills in the day's extreme heat. They eventually spy a town ahead.

Cautiously closing in on the town, using the terrain for concealment as best as they can, the group discovers it is a fortified town with Tearmain's banner flying tall.

Looking at the others, G says, "We may be too late already. Do we keep going?"

Jess answers for everyone. "We keep going until we reach Mount Oryn and we see who rules there."

"I agree," responds Mi and Tripper together.

Eren remains silent.

The team skirt around the town, while they also seek cover and water for another night.

Summer 59 Bear

Following their route toward Mount Oryn, the Black Swans travel through the gullies of a series of badlands along the river.

We are feeling their exhaustion.

They come out the other side of the badlands, discovering yet another town overrun by Tearmain forces.

The Black Swans avoid this Tearmain occupied town, and the group makes a camp in the woodlands that they find to the far west of the fortified settlement.

Tearmain's influence is as far west as Ferrep Fief. How far west do they actually reach? This is what has the Black Swans concerned.

We try to relieve their concerns, to no avail.

Summer 61 Bear

The Black Swans arrive at a large tributary river feeding into the river. In this heat, as they continue walking along the bank, they sweat profusely. They are becoming dehydrated, even though they are drinking plenty of river water.

The group discovers a mining village that isn't flying a Tearmain forces banner.

Tripper says suspiciously, "I don't trust that. The lack of a banner indicates that Tearmain has not taken over this mining town. Because the town is so close to Mount Oryn, Tearmain forces may deliberately not fly their banner. There are two barges docked, and both barges have their crews staying on board. Why don't we board one tonight, hire it out, and leave during the night?"

G looks at the other three. They nod yes. She turns to Winey, and she asks, "What about you?"

The boar grunts twice.

G answers, "That makes it unanimous; we board and hire one of the barges tonight, and we leave during darkness."

.....

Later, after gods-set, the group creeps aboard the smaller barge. Eren is shaking uncontrollably as the Black Swans move about, concealing themselves among the cargo.

G and Tripper sneak to the deck cabin, where they quietly enter. Closing the cabin door softly, G clears her throat and quietly but firmly calls out. "Excuse me? Captain, may we speak with you?"

A gruff voice calls back. "Who in the seven hells is disturbing my sleep?"

G answers him quick. "Begging your pardon, Captain, my coin purse, my friends, and I do. We seek passage across the river."

Someone opens the shutter of a hooded lantern, lighting the cabin's interior. The man says, "Seven Dyns'll get you across. When do you want to cross?"

G answers rapidly and boldly. "Will a Flair get my friends and me across right now?"

The Jalmal on the bunk stands up, and he says, "Yes, it will. Board the barge while I wake my crew, once you pay."

G hands the man ten silver Dyns from the Black Swans coin pouch. She replies, "We are already all aboard. If you could remain on the other side of the river for the day, in case we want to return here, we would appreciate it."

After accepting the silver coins, the captain energetically clasps arms with G. He says, "Agreed, we will wait."

Summer 63 Bear

Having left the barge on the west shore of the tributary two days ago, the six Black Swans are feeling nervous as they observe another small village. The village appears to have no barricades, no fortifications, no regular patrols, and no armed warriors wandering around.

The gods don't breathe as the Black Swans watch the village.

Eren sighs heavily before she says thoughtfully. "I say we walk in and talk to them. I need a real meal and a place to rest."

Tripper flops onto the ground next to the prone boar. She says, "I hate to admit it, but I agree with the unwilling one."

Sitting on a large granite stone rising from the ground, Jess nods and says, "Me too. It would be nice to be comfortable for a few hours before we go further."

G agrees; she nods her head, and then says, "Let's start walking in. The monastery-like building looks like it's the village's focus. Let's go there and find out what we can."

We sigh in relief as they start walking toward the village. Last night we conversed with the lost who are here to discover the local situation.

As the group walk to the apparent monastery, they cross a small footbridge over a deep stream where there is an apple orchard on the east side, and then they enter the monastery grounds.

They are greeted by a Jalfem in her middle years, who grumpily greets them. "Gods-grace, good day, and how may I help you?" she says in clear Jal.

Not often deterred by a grumpy person, G nods, and addresses her. "Gods-grace and good fate, master. We seek safe lodging for a night and then a barge to Mount Oryn. We are weary travellers from the Web. We are from a hamlet called Larret."

Larret Army

The woman wearily sighs, and then she says, "The priests will put you up for the night. There is a barge down at the docks now. If you go down and see the captain, he may agree to give you passage. I am not sure where his next destination is. The fee for a night here is by donation. The evening meal is in four hours. If you follow the road out front, through the village, down to the river, you will find the docks. Last I knew, there was only one barge, and he is loading our apples to take. How many rooms do you need?"

G cheers up measurably. For being grumpy, this Jalfem is extremely helpful, and G notices that she is large with child, which might explain the mood. "Five rooms if you have them. If not, fewer are fine. Will a Flair donation work?"

Obviously exhausted, the woman nods, and she answers, "Yes to five rooms, and a Flair is fair. My name is Allagra. The priests will be at evening meal. Barge Master Nevil will be at the dock."

The Black Swans lazily leave the monastery and begin walking along the only road they find.

The group arrives at an intersection, which runs north south and the direction they just came from. They know the river is south. Walking toward them from the south are two figures: a Toymal and a Jalmal.

Larret Army

The twentyish Jalmal stops the group. The man wears a longsword, studded-leather armour, and has a shield. "Gods-grace and good fate folks. Where would you be from and where are you heading?"

Thinking that this appears to be a village guard, G answers respectfully. "I am Reeve G from Larret Hamlet, heading to Mount Oryn. We are staying the night in the monastery. But right now, we are going down to the river to book passage on any barge at your dock."

The warrior respectfully offers his arm to clasp. "Good meeting you, Reeve G. I am Officer Bartlett of Appledon Village. Please behave during your stay. Captain Troden is docked with the Golden Rose, if you catch him. He is loading barrels of our apple juice. He will be sailing to Mount Oryn."

Smiling gleefully, G respectfully clasping arms at the elbows, warrior style. "Well met, Officer. We'll speak with Captain Troden then. Thank you."

The Black Swans arrive at the dock to find two people overseeing the loading of barrels onto a midsize barge. The Golden Rose is nearly forty-five feet long.

G motions for the rest of her group to wait as she approaches the two people who are managing the loading of the barge.

The Jalmal and Jalfem note G's approach and they stop their efforts to address G.

Reaching the duo, G brashly speaks first. "Gods-grace and good fate, folks. I am Reeve G from Larret Hamlet. I am looking for Captain Troden."

The sixty-year-old Jalfem nods, and in clear Jal, she answers. "How may I be of service, Reeve G."

The mature Jalmal stands by, waiting, patiently observing the discussion and watching the loading of the barge.

As she stops, she continues quickly, G says, "We seek to book passage for six passengers to Mount Oryn."

Troden smiles as she does quick math in her head. "Twelve Dyns, Master G, and we set sail tomorrow at gods-rise. If you agree to book passage, you must pay now."

G offers her arm to clasp, and Captain Troden firmly clasps arms with her.

With speed, G pays the captain and then returns to her waiting companions. "We leave for Mount Oryn in the morning with Captain Troden. It's all booked. Let's get back to the monastery. It should be near mealtime when we return. It'll take about twenty minutes to walk back to the monastery."

Arriving back at the old monastery, they find there is no one in the hall.

G calls out with a loud, "Hello?"

The north door opens, and a young Jalmal comes through. "Greetings. Are you the folks Allagra is expecting?"

G smiles as she nods. "Yes." G retrieves a Flair from her pouch and offers it to the man.

He leads the group to the southernmost of the doors, as he says, "Follow me; the stairs to the second floor and your rooms are through here." He accepts the gold coin. "The meal is ready and will be served in half-an-hour. The priests will gather in the dining room in half-an-hour if you care to join them."

Mi and Jess are grinning.

Finally, more priests.

Mi asks quickly, "Where is your dining room?"

The man smiles and then answers, "Through these doors as well. The door to the north when you come down the stairs through here is the dining room. My name is Elban; I am the servant for the priests."

After showing the Black Swans their individual medium-sized rooms, Elban leaves them be.

Later, in the dining room, the Black Swans find a long dining table, large enough for thity, with six occupants and a small feast.

Larret Army

"Greetings from Appledon. We don't get many guests. Our last guest ended up solving our one-hundred-year-old mystery, and he stayed on. He also ended up marrying our village guard's captain. I'm village elder and monastery leader, Alexo," says the elderly Jalmal who sits at the head of the table and wears a holy symbol of Johndar adorning his chest.

Next to him is the oddest site – a type of humanoid that none of the Black Swans has seen before. This short barrel of a humanoid is a mountain dwarf male who introduces himself in course Jal. "Greetings, I am Crusader of Forgefire, Leonian, Appledon's organizer and quartermaster."

Next to him is one who strikes fear in all five Black Swan's minds and hearts, an Elfmal. He introduces himself in musical tones of Jal. "Greetings, I am Mathias, Cleric of Nosambalee."

The Toymal next to the elf is to speak the briefest so far. In Jal, he only says, "Otis of Stonewire."

The next one around the table is a jovial Jalmal. "Greetings, I am the Druid Thom. I look after the orchards that make Appledon famous and which feed the village. May you enjoy the fruits of our labour tonight."

The last at the table is a noble-dressed young Jalfem. "Gods-grace and good fate, I am Lady Nicholea, liege of this village, fief, and surrounding lands. Welcome to Appledon. Please, tell us who are you?"

The Black Swans introduce themselves, and Tripper introduces Winey as well. They each give a brief account of their journey.

G informs their hosts about the army to the east that is spreading westward.

The evening closes in as they exchange stories. The Black Swans feel some relief as Appledon has been warned of Tearmain's blight.

We feel dread knowing what is about to befall this peaceful, tranquil village that is so far from the protection of the Royal Army.

Soon after, with the Black Swans fed and bathed, they turn in for the night.

Summer 65 Bear

After an arduous journey by barge, sailing on the broad river, at two hours after evening meal the Golden Rose leaves the Black Swans on the bustling East Docks of the Royal City of Mount Oryn, near Palace Hill.

Larret Army

Eren shivered and rasped for most of the journey on the barge. But, by the end of the voyage, she began to come out of her fear of the dark waters. She even started venturing away from the centre of the barge while the vessel was sailing.

Looking for an inn or tavern along the docks, the Black Swans discover the Morris Inn. They soon have rooms booked for the night, along with hot meals and steaming luxurious oiled baths.

Summer 66 Bear

Tripper wakes first, and she meticulously grooms. We watch her, as her grooming is an art form in itself. The gods have yet to rise as Tripper takes Winey down into the tavern, which is just opening for the day. Tripper addresses the staff, to query about the stable courtyard where Winey can do his morning voiding, feeding, and get his fill of water.

After Winey is fed and watered, the two then hurry back inside to join the others who are gathering in the inn's dimly lit tavern.

Tripper thinks that today they will need a dragoman to help them get around the city. She is pondering the hiring of a dragoman when G solemnly joins her in the tavern.

Larret Army

Tripper says with enthusiasm, "We need a dragoman to find anyone or any place. The city is just too much."

G yawns, and then says, "I agree that we need a dragoman, but where do we find one? We are totally new here."

Today, the spirits of these two are at their absolute opposites. The river barge trip and the journey overland from Dartoln Village has finally caught up with both of them.

We laugh heartily at them while wondering if either hears us.

Tripper eagerly suggests, "Let's ask the barmaid."

Even though the barmaid shows no enthusiasm while serving their table, Tripper asks her, "How do we get a dragoman? We are in need."

Tilla now smiles, and she cautiously replies, "I can have one here in an hour for you. What quality do you seek, and what city territory are you looking for?"

Eren is quick to answer her. "A dragoman with knowledge of the Royal Watch and Royal Army – a good one. We can pay a fair wage."

Tilla nods with knowing pride, before answering. "Okay, by the time you are done eating, I should have a dragoman here."

An hour later, Tilla brings an Elffem to the table. Tilla says, "Excuse me, this is Upselan. She will be your dragoman. She is the best in this territory."

For a moment, the group is stunned and shocked into silence. Again, here is another elf. Fear, seated through ages of tales and myths told strike hard repeatedly. But due to recent experiences, the fear settles to a dull ache.

G is the first to deal with her fear, and she hazards to address Upselan. "Gods-grace Upselan. Please excuse us. Where we come from, elves are not a part of society. In fact, elves, where we are from, are known to be human killers. May I ask how you come to be in human society? You are the second elf we have seen as part of society."

Upselan gestures to a vacant chair, asking, "May I?"

Tripper is the next one to recover, and she answers, "Yes, of course, please sit with us."

Gracefully sitting, Upselan starts speaking with subdued animation. "Well, because of your accent and what you say, I am going to assume you are from the east – probably close to the Web. That being the case, you are referring to the Winterholm elves: a very private and solitary band of elves who promote their solitude through fear. My friends, most elves do not kill other races unless they are first threatened. We are as friendly or as aggressive as any race. We react as any human would. I came to Mount Oryn two-hundred and some years ago, to see what I could find. Humans intrigue me, and I have seen three generations of humans' pass. With the changes that I've seen, I am curious to see at least two more generations. You have little to fear from me."

Tripper sighs. "Then, you know Mount Oryn well? We seek a military captain of the Royal Army, or an officer of higher rank, to report to. An army is being formed to the east which is determined to challenge King Dolan's reign."

Upselan chuckles. "Humans and their political struggles are humorous. If you wish to report such, then the best place is a Royal Military Post. If we start now, it should take about four hours to get to the closest one."

…..

Later, arriving at the Palace Hill Royal Military Post Three, the Black Swans are ushered to Captain Maynard's office.

The group wait for over an hour in the receiving area before it is their turn to speak with Captain Maynard.

Receiving their turn in the captain's office, there are only two guest chairs.

G elects to stand with Mi and Jess, while Eren and Tripper sit.

Larret Army

G addresses Captain Maynard. "Gods-grace and good fate, Captain Maynard. I am Reeve G of Larret Hamlet. We come to you with a report from the Web."

The fiftyish-year-old Toymal military captain sighs dejectedly. He states, "What now? Donkeys stampeding through your village's square?"

G is put off by this captain's attitude. However, not wanting to damage the report, G continues politely. "No, Captain Maynard. Many six-days ago, a group of walking-dead attacked one of our villagers. Investigating the attack, we tracked down the walking-dead and destroyed them. On our trek back to Larret Hamlet, a military band who is seeking recruits for an army set upon us. We killed all but two of their nine. Deciding to report this growing army, we came on a journey to warn the King's army. On our journey here, we encountered the enemy army that is forming. It is around two-thousand strong, situated at the headwater of the east branch of the river. The army is spreading its reach slowly westward."

Maynard guffaws. "If there were such an army, I would already know about it. You are wasting my time. Please leave."

Trying one more tactic, Tripper says, "We were sent by Lord Commander Earl Ramson to make this report."

Maynard rolls his eyes and sighs deeply. He says, "I will put this on my list. When I get to it, I will check it out. You did your duty. Consider it reported. Now, away with you, before I lock you up for interfering with my duties."

.....

Frustrated by the captain, the Black Swans have Upselan guide them back to the Morris Inn, where they pay Upselan her dragoman fees.

The team arranges rooms for another night at the Morris Inn.

Summer 67 Bear

After asking several captains for passage across the river, the Black Swans discover the captain of the Heaven's Gate barge.

Captain Holdon agrees to take the team across for a fee of seven Dyns. He is willing to take the Black Swans directly across to the far shore of the river.

.....

It is two hours before gods-set when the eighty-six-year-old Jalmal and his crew drop off the Black Swans on the uncivilized eastern bank of the river's south arm.

Larret Army

Summer 69 Bear

It is pitch black under the clear sphere, and the souls twinkle sharply in their places. The frigid cold is biting into Tripper, as she is getting ready to take her watch, replacing Eren.

Stoking the small camp fire, Eren shivers. They are conserving fuel and keeping the fire small, so as not to draw attention to their presence. Their travel, so far, has been uneventful. There is no need to start drawing attention to them now.

We try to warn the duo, but we are too late.

Suddenly, a medium-sized ragged rock slams into Eren's chest, knocking her back.

Another rock hits the ground near Tripper.

Immediately, Tripper begins waking the other Black Swans, as she feels the impending high-level threat.

Eren spots the threat in the near darkness. She sees three trolls loping, ungainly, and rushing toward camp. The three olive-coloured, thin, eight-foot-tall creatures look haggard and frail. They are hunched forward and running unevenly.

Eren, Tripper, and Winey take up positions to protect the others who are in their bedrolls and are just beginning to rise and gather themselves.

Larret Army

The trolls engage the three defenders.

Eren and Tripper use their standby offence, both shooting out fans of fire. The mages burn all three trolls, just as one of the trolls bites into Eren's leg, nearly biting it clean off.

Eren goes deep into shock, falling back to the ground.

Two of the trolls flee in terror from the flames of the fire mages.

But the third troll goes into a panicked frenzy, clawing at its leg and biting Tripper's arm.

The remaining troll tries grabbing Tripper, as Tripper attempts to fend it off.

Up and about and ready, Mi pulls free three unworked river stones, and he prays over them.

G is also ready, and she moves in to do combat, assaulting the troll as it is struggling to grasp Tripper.

Ready to join the fray, Mi throws one stone after the other at the troll. Two of the stones strike the target with great force.

In its struggles, the troll is ripping away at Tripper's chest and abdomen. Finally, the troll obtains a grip on Tripper's arm.

Now, with a solid grip on Tripper's arm and with Tripper heavily wounded, the troll ignores everyone else. The creature marches towards the river, dragging a reluctant, struggling Tripper.

Larret Army

Winey gouges the leg of the troll before Mi commands the troll to stop.

The troll obeys, and he ceases to move.

Tripper violently swings her hand-axe, slashing open the troll's leg, thus freeing the troll from Mi's command.

In frustration, G also slashes open the troll's leg, causing emerald-green blood to ooze out profusely.

The troll continues its walk toward the river, while the group struggles to keep up and continue the conflict while avoiding obstacles.

Finally, when they are about forty feet from the river, the group finds a clear opportunity to rescue Tripper.

Jess jabs his quarterstaff hard into the arm of the troll, followed by G slicing open the troll's head with her longsword.

Within sight of the river, the troll drops unconscious and releases its grip on Tripper.

Angry, and having gone berserker, G isn't satisfied. She cleaves off the leg of the troll, watching the emerald-green blood seep out.

Rising up, Tripper carries the leg while commanding the rest to drag the troll back to camp.

After some discussion, the group assumes that the river troll is similar to the ocean scrags. They decide to burn every bit of the troll and end its reign of terror. As the group is cutting the troll up, they discover a sack made from animal hides roughly sewn together. Inside the rough sack, they find thirteen rough gems.

While Mi and G are tending to the troll, Jess tends to Tripper's wounds. Even though he has advanced healing skills, he inadvertently causes more bleeding. Reacting quickly, Jess prays for an orison to stop the new bleeding.

With Tripper's bleeding stopped, Jess moves on to help Eren. He prays to Lorn for the healing of Eren's significant wounds.

Once comfortable with the knowledge that Eren is safe, Jess returns to Tripper.

Tripper is in a bad way; she is close to losing consciousness.

Jess prays to Lorn while holding onto Tripper's hand. He feels a strong flow of the blue-grey healing light pass through him to Tripper. But he knows it is only a small bit of what she actually needs. He prays again, and again, he feels the immense power flow as he watches more minor healing effects take place.

Realising how serious Tripper's wounds had been, Jess knows that the process of healing will take days of intense healing skills and prayer, from him and Lorn, to begin to heal both Tripper and Eren.

Praying twice more for each of the wounded victims and seeing only small amounts of healing effects take place, Jess understands the grievousness of their injuries.

G and Mi spend two hours burning the troll, finishing the job before Jess completes his healing work.

G decides that from now on, the group should utilize dual member watches, as they are taking a more dangerous route home – a more direct land route, one without waterways.

Thus, hopefully, they can avoid Tearmain's army.

Summer 71 Bear

The partial sphere cover adds to the eeriness as the group walks along the north shore of Moren Lake.

Jess, with the help of Lorn, has healed the physical wounds of Eren and Tripper. But the physical and emotional scars will remain.

The air doesn't move with more than a slight northeast zephyr as the group walk along the mysterious shore of the incredibly deep lake.

Larret Army

Summer 73 Bear

As they pass by, G looks at the Winterholm elves' north boundary marker that the locals were made to believe was shared with a dragon. G notices that there are more baby skeletons than she first realized. She thinks as the walk, '*No, Upselan is wrong. These elves are killers; this isn't just scare tactics to cause fear so that the elves can remain isolated.*'

Thinking about it, G knows of no recorded instance of anyone who crossed those skeletons and came out alive. She shivers involuntarily. Maybe not all elves are the same?

We agree. '*Yah! Right!*'

Summer 76 Bear

There is not even a zephyr in the air as G looks at the clear night sphere. '*Damn seven hells; we're off track.*' As the two day-gods begin to rise, G recalculates their location.

Disgruntled, G turns to her group. "We have to turn south; we went too far north. Dartoln is southeast from here," she says sarcastically. She has been their navigator, but yesterday's sphere was covered, and in the extreme heat she got careless and lazy. They've paid dearly for her carelessness; getting

off track by a full day. It will be evening before they arrive in
Dartoln.

. . . ..

That evening, when the Black Swans arrive in Dartoln
village, G knocks on the manor house door. It is now an hour
after evening meal.

Opening the manor door, the servant cheerfully
acknowledges the group. "Yes, Lord Ramson will see you now.
Go to the great hall."

The Black Swans enter the great hall and take their now
accustomed seats to wait. Tired and exhausted after days of
travelling, they relax in the dining chairs. Even Winey lays
relaxing on the mat by the fireplace. No one worries about food.
Though, they are all excited when servants bring in the evening
meal with pitchers of ale.

They all eat eagerly.

After an hour, Lord Ramson casually arrives.

"Well, the intrepid travellers have returned. I suppose
you'll get that rattrap barge off my dock now?" Lord Ramson
says with humour to the group.

Smiling, now that she has had some food and rest, G
answers first. "Gods-grace and good fate, Lord Ramson. We will
remove the Ever-Knot, yes. We reported to Captain Maynard of

the Royal Army, but he didn't seem to care much. In fact, he threatened to put us in the goal if we persisted in our report."

Lord Ramson nods. "I assumed that would be your fate. Never mind. Go home. We will serve whichever King is on the throne. They have little care for us out here on the Web. As a reward for your efforts, I offer each of you five Flairs. Tripper, you can carry Winey's coins. But remember, it is Winey's. You may all stay in the manor tonight, and then take your barge home and continue with your real jobs – jobs that I have been paying you for."

We laugh, knowing that Ramson wants to do more for these six, but his reputation disallows it.

Summer 79 Bear

Eren walks around the deck of the Ever-Knot as they glide along on the Harpen River, closing in on Larret Hamlet. "You know, after those trolls, the open water causes me no fear. Thank you, G. You no longer need to pay me for passage on barges. I'm all right."

G looks at Eren as the barge butts up on land. "Those trolls did a job on you. You are walking openly upon the barge and helping pole on open water, and you're turning down free coin? You sure that you're okay?"

The friends disembark from the Ever-Knot to return to their homes. They are safely in Larret Hamlet. It is evening mealtime, and they are ready to return to their village duties.

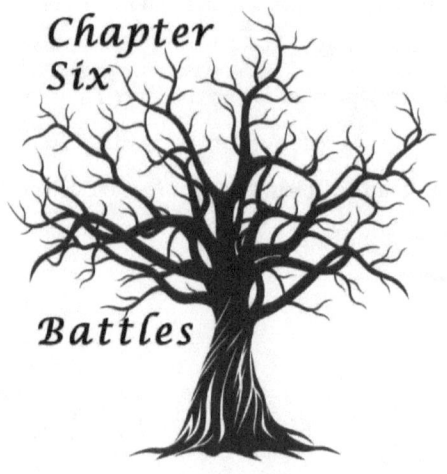

Chapter Six

Battles

Chapter Six:

Battles

*S*ummer 79 Bear

G steps off the Ever-knot onto the shores of Larret Hamlet as the chilly west breath of the gods blow across the landscape. Is this a sign of things to come? Or the end of things?

Eren hurries off the barge. Though she has admitted to no longer being afraid, she's still feeling nervous when it comes to being on the water. She utters, "Finally! Solid ground! I said I am okay with the barge now. I didn't say that I like it."

Larret Army

The Black Swans go to their homes in the hamlet, to return to their lives as they were before the Tearmain attack and the walking-dead, before their dealings with Lord Ramson in Dartoln Village, and before their adventure trip to Mount Oryn.

They have their shared experiences dealing with the trials of all that has happened. Can they just return to life as it was earlier?

Tripper can't! Her father is dead. His death is frozen in her mind, on that horrible morning along the Harpen River on Summer 1. Tripper's magic has grown. She has seen and done things that have forced her out of her shell and out from the protection of her father's shield, causing her to evolve into a new and different person.

G can't return to life as it was either. She carries the weight of Larret Hamlet and Laret Fief squarely upon her shoulders. She is now living in a new residence. She is responsible for the entire population with their lands, containing its infrastructure and possessions. She reluctantly accepted this responsibility from everyone, including her seventeen-year-old self. Her past already has G looking middle-aged. What will the weight of being a reeve and the woodward of the hamlet and fief do to her?

Eren? Maybe she will be able to carry on as before. There have been some changes for her. She is now the bailiff and beadle of Larret Hamlet and Laret Fief, as well as the village herder. She still has her cottage, her goat herd, her fields, and above all else, she still has her magic.

Mi? Except for the adventure where he joined the Black Swans, very little has changed. So, the nineteen-year-old Toymal can return to life as Village Cleric, administering to the hamlet's believers of Ikerus.

Oddly, as a pious priest of the god of war and hunting, Mi has never fully learned the melee arts. This is not because he is a coward, far from that. Mi stands face-to-face and toe-to-toe with any threat. Until recently, Mi never saw a need to learn combat skills. Now he has been participating in some moments of training with G and Jess, training to learn some much-desired melee skills.

Perhaps one of the most mentally and spiritually conflicted Black Swans is Jess, a priest of Lorn, who is willing to heal anyone and everyone. Jess was forced to face his most dire fear – the walking-dead.

Jess was the first of the group to encounter the walking-dead. The walking-dead that Jess faced while swimming alone in the Harpen River, three kilometres upstream, precipitated this whole series of events. Then, he met them again at four in the morning in the darkness of night. It was the same group of walking-dead who attacked the cottar, who then assaulted the Black Swans and almost paralyzed Jess with fear. Jess dealt with the fear that time, enough to help with the threat and the aftermath.

He still has nightmares from all of those encounters. Jess prays fervently to Lorn each morning to take away the visions of the walking-dead attacking him.

Summer 80 Bear

G decides to continue with hamlet duties and some mundane tasks today. She holds the moot hall in the afternoon, dealing with only one case.

Mi also decides that it might be best to return to regular priestly duties. So, in the name of Ikerus, he holds morning services for the villagers. This morning, thirteen regular worshippers from the hamlet attend the service.

Yesterday evening, Jess, struggling with his fears, held services to Lorn with an attendance of fourteen villagers. This morning he holds services again for the same villagers.

Today, Eren does the milking of her nanny goats herself, relieving her hired milkmaid for the day.

Larret Army

Tripper takes stock of her stored supplies in G's small two-story house. She then makes the rounds to the taverns and sells all her perishables. Then, she seeks out the different craftsmen of the hamlet to sell some of her iron and silver ingots which she salvaged from the cargo of the Ever-Knot. Tripper converts as much of the salvaged goods as possible into coins.

The Black Swans now feel as if they can return to a normal life.

G has completed the hamlet census, and Tripper has delivered it to Lord Ramson.

Tripper is now content, as she has a substantial collection of coins, a barge, and a home with the rent paid for one year. She can relax and focus on getting ahead for next year, possibly improving her mage-craft or developing a trade.

Eren has her hamlet duties and her cottage to tend to, keeping her busy.

Mi and Jess return to tending to their respective flock of parishioners, keeping the villagers happy.

G has her duties as reeve to tend to and her craft as bowyer/fletcher keeping her busy, as she has some outstanding orders for arrows and bows.

The sphere covers over that night, and a heavy rain settles in. The air becomes frigid, much as it was on Summer 1 Bear.

Larret Army

Summer 88 Bear

The broken cover in the sphere is slowly blowing northeast when there is a heavy knock on the Reeve House door.

Curious, G quickly rises from her chair at the dining table and briskly walks to the door to see who is knocking.

Herdsman Gerret, who is out of breath, rasps and gasps. "Army ... coming ... from the west." He nearly collapses into the Reeve House.

G quickly helps the youth in to the room to sit at her table. She fetches Gerret a warm mug of black tea to take the edge off the chill from the air coming in from the Web.

Gerret wraps his cold hands around the warm mug as he struggles to regain an even breathing pattern.

After a minute, Eren, a little more impatient than G, asks Gerret, "So, what army is coming?"

Gerret, gasping still, manages to get out: "Horsemen and footmen, armoured and armed, marching this way – forty or more – flying banners of war."

Now it's G who loses patience with Gerret, and she demands: "Did you recognize the banner?"

Larret Army

Gerret, trying hard to speak clearly, says directly, "Three horizontal red lines, parallel to each other."

Simultaneously, G and Eren say, "Tearmain!"

"I have to get a militia of some sort together and meet these people before they get into the hamlet. Eren, you get Nela, Maken, and Daren. Have them round up as many able-bodied people as quickly as possible and have them gather in the hamlet square. We have a deadly army threat approaching! You know as well as I do, from our experience on our trip to Mount Oryn, what Tearmain's army does to settlements. Move it. I'll get Delamor, Lesna, Tarre, and Enda moving. Enda and I will get the armoury open, and we'll start arming folks as they arrive. It's now just an hour before evening meal so most people will be at home. Gerret, you start from over by the Web and work your way inland along the Harpen. Eren's team will start from the Web and work its way inland on the opposite side of Larret from the Harpen. You send Nela with a couple of others to collect people from the outlying areas. I think that we have about an hour to get a militia ready. Right, Gerret?"

Now more collected, Gerret answers, "Probably two hours. I ran, and they are walking. They were more than four kilometres away, to the west."

311

Larret Army

"Let's go quickly. We will aim to be ready with the militia in an hour. I want to meet the Tearmain force a fair distance away from Larret," commands G.

In under an hour, G and her people have a militia of over seventy people armoured and armed. She organizes them in companies according to their skills and how they're equipped.

Ten minutes later, steadfastly marching out of Larret Hamlet, the militia arrives at a ridge twenty minutes away from Larret.

With strict commands, G sets up her troops so that her militia conceals her ranged companies behind her second melee companies.

Then, they all stand and patiently wait.

Tearmain's forces arrive below the ridge about twenty minutes before gods-set. Tearmain's forces consist of one rank of light footmen, one rank of heavy footmen, and one rank of horsemen. The Tearmain army comes to a stop when they spot the Larret militia.

A heavy silence follows. Then, the Tearmain troops start marching forward until they are about fifty metres from Larret's Army.

Suddenly, the footmen and the horsemen break into a charge, shouting and shield bashing.

Larret Army

We wait patiently and anticipate the clash of forces.

As per G's command, the Larret militia remains steadfast and silent.

When the Tearmain forces are ten metres from Larret's Army, G gives the shield command.

Shields are brought into position, forming a wall, which the Tearmain horses ram into in front of the militia.

The Larret spears snap into Tearmain horses and men, dropping some, while Tearmain's charge injures some Larret fighters.

A melee breaks out immediately, and soon there are falling warriors on both sides.

Tearmain's light footmen break to the right, rushing into Larret Army's men-at-arms who are waiting there with shields ready. Bashing into the shield wall, a fierce melee ensues, with the two sides evenly matched.

Tearmain's heavy footmen break to the left, charging into Larret militia's least experienced and least prepared. Even with their shield wall ready, the Larret militia is no match for the Tearmain heavy footmen.

The Tearmain horsemen are rapidly defeated. Three of the riders attempt to quickly ride off.

Larret Army

As they try to escape, G orders the Larret ranged troops to fire upon the riders. Under the heavy barrage of arrows and sling stone fire, all three riders fall.

Following this, G gives orders for half of the main central militia to move to the west, and the other half of the main central militia to traverse to the east to help engage those footmen.

Soon, the Tearmain light footmen are defeated by the combined forces of Larret Army's militias.

Panicked, five Tearmain light footmen run for the woods.

Again, G orders the prepared Larret ranged units to fire upon the fleeing troops. However, three of the light footmen manage to escape into the woods.

The battle to the west is not going so well for the Larret militia. Many of the Larret men-at-arms have fallen.

Unfortunately, few of the Tearmain heavy footmen have even been injured.

Nela has taken the reserve Larret militia to join forces with half of the main central militia, to aid those Larret men-at-arms fighting the heavy footmen of Tearmain.

This battle is terrible. Even with the experienced Larret officers, the Larret militia are challenged by the Tearmain heavy

Larret Army

footmen. It is by sheer weight of Larret numbers that they start to overcome the Tearmain heavy footmen.

As the weight of the battle wears on, the morale falters for several of the Tearmain heavy footmen, and they break off, running away once they see the futility of their assault.

As the Tearmain heavy footmen break off to run, G orders them to be fired upon by the Larret ranged units.

Scores of arrows and sling stones rain upon them as they clear the melee. In the end, with armour deflecting arrows and stones, one of the heavy footmen survives to reach the safety of the woods.

Cleaning up the battlefield, Larret Hamlet finds they lost thirty-nine fighters to the Tearmain forces, which is only half the number that Tearmain troops lost.

Six Tearmain warriors survive and have been captured, as well as half-a-dozen horses and a wealth of booty.

Relieved, G grants the Larret troops all of the loot and the horses. She takes no shares for the Larret officers, Larret Hamlet, or Lord Ramson.

Once the assessment is made and looting is cleared, G orders everyone back to Larret Hamlet to prepare Larret for a possible attack by further forces of Tearmain. They transport the dead and injured back to Larret.

Larret Army

In Larret, G takes the prisoners to the Larret Hamlet goal.

Deliberately keeping the prisoners isolated from one another, G and the rest of the Black Swans thoroughly interrogate the prisoners.

The Black Swans discover that they have one of the sergeants of the heavy footmen.

. . . ..

"You marched on Larret, thinking us an easy target, but you lost your entire force. Six of you survived to be captured. None of your force got away. Are there more troops planning to march here, preparing to attack Larret?" asks G as she feigns her anger.

The Jalmal prisoner is the fourth one that G is interrogating, and she is becoming tired of the task.

"I wouldn't know. I just lead a squad of heavy footmen of Tearmain's lead assault force. We take the villages. The occupation crews follow, and they do the setup," answers the approximately thirty-year-old Jalmal.

"So, you do know how long it takes the occupation force to arrive after you take the settlement. How long?" demands an apparently angrier G.

The man hesitates. "Tomorrow, usually."

Larret Army

Eren and G received a much different answer from the previous three prisoners.

As she appears to calm down, G changes tactics. "Sergeant Alander, I know General Penner doesn't send the occupation force right behind the assault force. So, try telling me again. How far behind you does General Penner plan to send this occupation force?"

Alander, taken aback at being addressed by his name and at having General Penner's name mentioned, freezes up. He begins to panic, looking from one Black Swan member to another. Alander, shivering, is becoming considerably pale. He utters, "I ... don't know. Honest ... I wasn't at the meeting. I had stomach issues before we marched ... how? How do you know?"

G looks at Eren, then at Tripper, and then she looks at Mi and Jess. Turning back to Alander, G says, "In this room are two very powerful mages who defeated a trio of river scraggs. Also, in this room are two very powerful clerics who defeated and put to rest a group of five walking-dead. And, there is me, the warrior who defeated a pair of Tearmain officers: a Tearmain recruiting captain and his Tearmain priest who were working together in combat. So, do you really need to ask how? I ask again – tell us where the camp is and how many troops there are?"

Larret Army

Alander's jaw falls, almost touching his chest; his eyes widen, and if possible, his skin turns even whiter. "Don't ... please. I'll tell you what I can. The stronghold is in the swamp to the southwest. Our stronghold has over one-hundred heavy footmen and horsemen, two gates, and three guard towers. The gate controls are in the two towers, and there are three guardsmen at each tower at all times. The officer's camp is in the centre of the stronghold. The horsemen occupy the eastern side of the compound, and the footmen hold the western side. The cooking area and equipment maintenance section are past the officer's area in the middle, between the horse and footmen. Oh, and there are two sets of walls with a ringing moat that is twenty-foot wide and ten-foot deep. On the backside of the stronghold is the swamp. We have two swamp barges used for fishing and scavenging supplies."

Sighing deeply, G, feeling redeemed, relaxes slightly. She offers Alander a mug of water, and then asks him, "Alander, one more thing. How far away is this stronghold from Larret?"

Alander eagerly accepts the water, as it has been over eight hours since he has had any fluids. He replies to G's question, "It was three days marching for us. Lieutenant Huffers was our guide, and she set the pace. I don't know land distances, so I don't know how far it is. I didn't count my paces."

G makes a quick calculation and nods. Turning to Tripper and Eren, she says, "I assume it is over thirty kilometres. Let's go it alone, as the Black Swans. We can backtrack the assault force's tracks to their stronghold. We will assess the stronghold while the Larret Army gets ready, here, for an attack. A battle is happening with these people one way or another, whether we go to them or they come to us. We are outnumbered, so I want it on our terms. We need whatever advantage we can get."

Turning to Alander, G has a thought. She asks, "Alander, does the assault force send a message back to General Penner when the force is successful and ready for the occupying force?"

Alander drops the mug, as though caught in a trap. He slowly answers, "Yes."

G smiles and then asks, "Does General Penner send a second assault force if he doesn't hear from the first within a certain length of time?"

Alander blinks several times and trembles visibly. He answers softly. "I ... don't know. We never failed before."

G nods. "This is a first, then. I guess we will be finding out. The other prisoners – are any of them officers?" We know, and so does G that no one else has been identified as an officer by the other three. But G is curious as to Alander's tactics under interrogation.

Larret Army

The man is still shaking visibly as he shakes his head and says, "No."

G calls Nela into the room.

"We are done with the prisoners, for now. They should be locked into the large goal cell to stew together. They will reside there until this is over. You and Enda are now Captains in the Larret Army. You will recruit, organize, equip, and train the new Larret Army. We are going into battle against an army called Tearmain's Army. They rape, burn, and pillage settlements. They torture, kill, or put to work those they don't recruit into their army. We are not going to let that happen to Larret Hamlet without a fight. I want every person who is able to travel to be ready for battle when the Black Swans return from our scouting trip of Tearmain's forces. The army must be equipped, packed for the battle march, and prepared to travel for ten days. You are the melee Captain; Enda is the ranged Captain. We, the Black Swan's, are leaving tomorrow morning to scout the enemy's encampment. Dismissed!"

Summer 89 Bear

With the extreme heat and high breaths from the gods blowing east, G ponders if this is an omen for their task. The

Larret Army

Black Swans begin tracking the Tearmain forces trail back towards their original location. It is an easy task as the swath of impressions left by the large group of men and horses are easy to follow.

Thinking sardonically to herself, G hopes that they're headed to the stronghold of General Penner.

Autumn 1 Bear

Standing, hidden in the woods, with the cold south breath of the gods blowing hard on them, G wonders if the overhead sphere cover was enough to conceal the Black Swans as they walked out from the edge of the timberline, exposing the group to any observers on the fortification's towers.

They step back deeper into the woods, knowing they have discovered General Penner's stronghold.

The four-man-tall dark stone wall, with the twenty-foot-wide scummy moat in front, was apparent once the Black Swans cleared the obscuring thick woods. The Black Swans quickly hurried back inside the forest cover, hoping they weren't spotted by guards from any of the seven-men-tall brown and green stained stone towers.

Larret Army

Forlorn, G looks at her companions. "Well, we found it. We're not going to be burning our way in. I'll take a walk along the dead man zone inside the woods to see what I can find. I'll be back. Stay here, so I can find you again."

. . . . .

Later, returning to her companions, G huffs grumpily; her leather boots are squishing. Water is dripping from her studded leather leggings. "Well, I went to the right as far as I could. I even tried to walk out into the swamp. But the land drops off quickly into the water and rapidly gets rather deep. The stonewall extends out into the deep water. The woods have been cleared back from the wall about one-hundred metres for the entire length of the wall. The moat is consistent for its full length, being about twenty feet wide. So, I went to the left, and I found the same thing. I found a couple of observation points in the woods, where I could look through the gates and see between the two walls. There are three thirty-foot-tall stone towers between the walls. There are also inner and outer stonewalls. It appears as if each wall has two sets of gates. But the gates are offset, so there isn't a straight run in. Each wall-gate entrance looks like it has a wooden drop-gate. Next to each inner gate is a fifteen-foot diameter square tower, thirty-feet-tall, made of stone. The guards are pretty much concealed if they duck down, but about a third of their body is exposed when they are standing. While I was observing, I noticed a patrol of five footmen walking in between the inner and outer walls. I heard the whinny of horses coming from inside of the fortification. There are at least six distinct smoke sources inside, as well. Watching each of the different towers for five minutes or so, I saw three guards in each one."

After some thought, Eren says, "We can move forces up to the gates within clouds of fog at night. But that just gets us up to the gates. They can still lock us out before we get inside."

Evily, G smiles. "We have ranged troops. If you can get our ranged troops close enough, and if we are lucky on our first volley, then we can eliminate the tower guards before they can react. Then, we can send in the melee squads to take the ground troops at the gates. Then, we move the bulk of our forces in."

The others nod and Eren smiles. "We should be able to do it. We need a signal system other than shouts, though."

Tripper grunts. "I can use owl hoots."

With cheer, G clasps arms with her companions. "We now have a plan. Let's refine it on our walk back to Larret, and then we can make it work, as long as Penner stays put."

Larret Army

Autumn 3 Bear

The northwest breath of the gods is breaking trees like kindling, and to top it off, during yesterday's rain, G got the Black Swans lost. They walked in an entirely wrong direction.

Today, fighting with the gods-breath they still have no visible gods to sight through sphere cover. G is trying to move the Black Swans towards Larret Hamlet the best she can.

On the plus side, even though yesterday was miserable all day with rain coming down from before noon until midnight, they hashed out a solid plan of attack against the Tearmain stronghold, even with the unknown Tearmain numbers. They know there are supposed to be over two-hundred Tearmain in that stronghold.

Autumn 6 Bear

The light westerly breath of the gods is blowing hot from the Web. The gentle breath of the gods is welcome after all the cold heavy breathing of the gods the last few days.

It is noon, and the Black Swans walk into Larret Hamlet, greeting and then walking past the two sentries on the outskirts of the hamlet.

Larret Army

The hamlet has the look of a military training facility.

This brings G a smile; she is satisfied that her orders have been obeyed.

We assure her how hard Nela and Enda have been working.

The Black Swans search around Larret Hamlet and locate Nela and Enda, informing them about the attack plan on the fortress.

G impresses upon Nela and Enda that no one else is to know any details of the plan, or where the Larret troops will be marching to.

G instructs the two Captains to have their army ready to march two hours before gods-rise on Autumn 8 Bear.

Autumn 8 Bear

In the darkness before gods-rise, the weather is already hot. The sphere is clear, and with the light of the three night-gods, G can see that her army of one-hundred-and-twenty troops is gathered and ready. With more than half the population of Larret's able-bodied adults in the army, G has decided that a third of the troops are to be left to defend Larret, along with the less able-bodied.

Larret Army

Everyone is equipped with weapons and armour according to skills and training. They are organized in companies, per their equipment and skill. The instructions to them are vague; they received just enough commands for what is necessary to get to the launch point, which the Black Swans pre-determined.

With the company's commanders appointed, the march begins before the two day-gods, the yellow Stonewire and orange-red Imvor, rise above the eastern horizon of the Web.

Autumn 10 Bear

The entire march has been in heat. Today it continues to be hot, but not quite as hot due to the gods breathing vigorously westward. Luckily, the gods-breath is blowing the sounds of the marching army away from Tearmain's stronghold of General Penner. The breaths of the gods are more than three times stronger today than they have been the last two days.

By evening mealtime, G has the army setting up their camp about three kilometres directly north from Penner's stronghold.

In took three days for G to march her army about thirty-five kilometres. It's now time to rest them, as they will go into battle before gods-rise tomorrow.

Larret Army

Being the hamlet's Cleric, Mi feels a need to perform a ceremonial service of Ikerus, the god of war, for the Larret troops.

After their evening meal, over one-hundred soldiers stop to attend Mi's service. But Mi's heart isn't in the service, and the soldiers notice this. This is somewhat demoralizing for many who listen.

Mi leaves the ceremonies half-hearted and sad, feeling that he let down Larret Hamlet and the Black Swans. He is not able to rouse his own spirits for this task.

We know and understand his misgivings about this and his concern over the future loss of Larret lives.

At gods-set, following Mi's service, Jess decides to recoup the morale of the troops with a service of his own. The nineteen-years-old Jalmal raises the spirits of the seventy or so people who attend his service, significantly boosting their morale for tomorrow's task.

Jess clasps arms with many of the troops and wishes them Lorn's blessings for tomorrow, offering personal blessings of Lorn to the few who ask.

Larret Army

Autumn 11 Bear

This morning the gods are not co-operating with Larret Army and the Black Swans. The sphere is bright, the air is near freezing, and the gods are breathing moderately east, aiding the travel of sound and smell.

G enquiringly looks at Eren and Tripper, and she whispers, "Are you ready?"

Eren and Tripper nod affirmatively.

So much can go wrong, and only one thing need go wrong for this to utterly fail.

Haggard, G looks up at the night gods. Their positions tell her it is roughly fifteen minutes until the first day-god, Stonewire, breaks the eastern horizon. She nods to Eren. "Okay."

They are standing ten feet back in the woods from the dead-man-zone, which is between them and the stonewall. They're located in the woods at roughly the mid-point between the two gates.

The night-gods give Eren all the light she needs. Focusing at a point, nearly thirty metres into the kill zone, between woods and wall in front of the first gate, she casts her first fog cloud into the darkness of night. Turning, she does likewise in front of the second gate.

Eren then taps Tripper's right shoulder.

Tripper casts her cantrip of double Horned Owl hoots.

Quietly as possible, the Larret ranged troops of slingers, and then the archers, move up inside the two fog clouds.

They are followed by the first companies of melee assault troops.

The ranged troops do as they were instructed; they walk as far forward as possible without exiting the cloud, thus not exposing themselves.

After a count of ninety, G taps Tripper's left shoulder.

Tripper casts another cantrip – a single Horned Owl hoot.

The ranged troop units can only guess at their targets, as they are firing blindly through the fog. They must shoot at targets at the height of thirty feet and a distance of ninety metres ahead of them. All ranged fire is fired blindly at their assigned target, volley after volley, for three sets of volleys.

G counts three slinger volleys and six archer volleys. She then taps Tripper's left elbow.

Tripper casts yet another cantrip – the sound of an eagle screeching twice.

Larret Army

The ranged troops hesitate as they change targets. They now aim to points over the wall, a distance farther and deeper inside.

The Larret gate melee militia troops rush the still open drop-gates.

G tries to observe the tower occupants, watching for survivors, but it is too dark, and the light sources were knocked off the towers. But she does note the drop-gates are still open.

As the ranged troops pin down any support from reaching the gate crews, the Larret militia engages any Tearmain troops near the gates.

The Larret militia finds a small group near each gate, and after a short battle, Larret troops control the inner and outer gates at the west and eastern end of the wall.

G has counted to two-hundred-and-sixty, and she taps Tripper's left shoulder.

Tripper casts the next cantrip – the sound of a single thunderclap.

The full force of Larret's melee troops quietly rushes out of the woods and through the two gates into General Penner's stronghold.

Larret Army

Once all melee troops are past them, the Larret officers, including the Blacks Swans, follow their respective troops through the gates.

Once the officers are through, the last of the melee troops with the ranged companies enter into the stronghold to take control of the gates.

Holding the east gate is Eren and Nela, with group-two slingers and the Second Company Archers.

Holding the west gate is the Black Swans, with group-one slingers and the First Company Archers.

Deeper inside the stronghold, at the first two control points, with Tearmain's troops in full combat, are the initial Larret gate-assault troops. The third, fourth, fifth, and sixth control points are under assault by the main forces of Larret's men-at-arms and the remaining militia from the Larret army.

Tearmain's troops are putting up a strong fight. The troop numbers are at even strength between Larret and Tearmain forces. Tearmain's troops have better equipment and are much better trained, but not many were ready for combat. Many of Tearmain's fighters are not being fully equipped, and because they were somewhat caught off guard, they are momentarily off balance.

Larret Army

G is finding that the information from Sergeant Alander was correct.

The horsemen are separate from the footmen. There are four companies of horsemen and six companies of footmen in the stronghold.

The militia and men-at-arms of Larret have not engaged the officer's quarters yet.

The first Tearmain control points to fall are those near the gates – the points being assaulted by the first Larret militia gate-assault troops.

The winning Larret troops fall back to the gate control points with their captives, to wait for orders as commanded by their officers.

As the battle rages, Enda orders her slingers to volley tower three, instructing the slingers to fire in cycles, in groups of four, using ground rubble as ammo. This is to keep the guards pinned down and unable to observe and report on the battles, as tower three had not been an initial target in Larret army's entry.

After several minutes, the westernmost section of the stronghold is cleared of Tearmain's troops. Soon, this is followed by the surrender of some eastern horsemen troops.

Thus, leaving two raging battles in the stronghold.

The two day-gods have not risen yet.

Larret Army

We eagerly wait for our masters so they can guide the Larret army.

The last of Tearmain's heavy footmen are easily holding out against the men-at-arms of Larret.

The last two companies of Tearmain horsemen are soundly defeating the Larret men-at-arms as the yellow light of Stonewire peeks above the eastern horizon.

Soon, with the light of the gods illuminating the battles, Larret's officers can better assess the fighting.

Nela orders two groups of Larret militia to aid the Larret men-at-arms with the Tearmain horsemen. Nela keeps her last group of men-at-arms back to guard the captured prisoners.

The slingers continue to revolve through their turns, peppering the tower-three guard-post with ground rubble.

Determined, G orders a group of Larret's men-at-arms to go and support the battle against the Tearmain heavy-footmen.

The Black Swans take a company of men-at-arms to engage the officer's quarters.

By this time, General Penner has been advised that he has lost most of his troops and that the invaders hold most of the stronghold.

Larret Army

General Penner and his officers face the Black Swans and their men-at-arms, unaided. More than half of General Penner's officers immediately seek to surrender to the Black Swans.

General Penner approaches G boldly. "Are you in command of this attack?" asking in stilted Jalnoric.

Standing tall, G bows slightly. "I am Commander Gena of the Larret Army and Reeve G of Larret Hamlet. If you are General Penner, you made the mistake of sending troops to assault my home. I now take your stronghold in Lord Ramson's name for the Web Shireward and Earl Ramson. Do you surrender, General Penner?'

"I am indeed General Penner, and I do surrender if you call off your assault on my troops," replies the nearly seventy-year-old Toymal.

G turns to Tripper. "When General Penner gives the signal to his troops to surrender, signal our troops to stand down and accept their surrender." Turning to Penner, she says, "I accept your surrender."

At that moment, a century-old Jalfem warrior, using a shortsword, attacks G.

G avoids the strike, smoothly and professionally drawing her longsword.

They face off against each other, while Penner gives his officers the command to surrender and to give their troops the command to surrender.

One of the officers obeys, and he sounds the trumpet notes of surrender.

Tripper casts a cantrip, causing two thunderclaps that are spaced apart at the count of two.

The angry captain attacks G again a couple more times.

G, seeing that the captain is intent on killing her, asks, "Do you surrender as your general commanded?"

The captain attacks again, drawing blood a second time.

G takes this as her answer. G returns the attack, and using her longsword, the captain's chest is sliced open. Instantly, the captain is killed. All of G's practice and her bits of experience have added up to a moment of clarity in G's ability – an ability that rang out with ease, taking the life of an experienced warrior.

G turns to the other officers, a few with weapons still in hand. "Anyone else not going to surrender?"

All the Tearmain forces in the room surrender.

G, having defended against a seasoned warrior, now has the attention of the Larret men-at-arms, Blacks Swans, and Tearmain officers. The respect in the faces and eyes of all in the area is not lost on G. It doesn't inflate her ego, though, as she notes Tripper is missing, along with four Tearmain officers.

"Eren, did you see Tripper or any of the four Tearmain leave?" asks G hurriedly.

The others look around dumbfounded, and everyone shakes their heads negative. No one saw Tripper nor the four Tearmain leave.

Pointing at two of her men-at-arms, G commands, "You stay with these officers and take their weapons now. The rest of you are to spread out and find Tripper … Winey, take me to Tripper."

Winey snorts twice for G, and the boar immediately starts at a quick pace, sniffing the ground. G, Eren, Mi, and Jess follow Winey on a path directly through the camp. G observes footwear drag marks on the ground at several places along the way.

Arriving at the shore of the swamp, they find a swamp barge is beached.

Winey walks to a spot where the ground is scraped up as if another barge had been beached here. He bellows out to the swamp.

We look out to where Winey is looking and see the object of his concern.

Chapter
Seven

The Swim

Chapter Seven:

The Swim

Autumn 11 Bear

After G notices that Tripper is missing, the Black Swans follow Winey to the shore of the swamp. Peering out into the morning light, Winey bellows out toward the swamp.

Looking out over the dark, despondent waters of the swamp, G and Jess spot a barge gathering speed as it pulls away. The barge is headed away from the stronghold shore.

Upon looking around, G quickly comes to a decision. She commands, "Everyone, let's go after them. Let's use the second barge. Come on now! We have a mission to catch that barge and rescue our friend, despite the pain in the ass she is. We owe it to her and Winey."

Winey snorts twice and runs for the second barge with G; as does Eren, Mi, and Jess.

The four humans quickly unbeach the barge and soon have it moving at full speed, chasing after the errant lead barge.

The two barges race outward from the stronghold, navigating through the trees and mounds of the Dead Swamp.

After some time, the lead barge starts slowing down as a few of its four oarsmen begin to fatigue.

The Black Swans' barge begins to catch up.

Slowly gaining on the enemy, as the Tearmain barge slows, the Black Swans begin to tire as well.

As she watches, G and the Black Swans still gain on the lead barge. Pulling up beside the lead barge, G commands her crew to pass by and then pull in front of the enemy to be able to get aboard.

But Eren tires badly and can no longer push on her oar.

G orders the Black Swans to pull over and to ram into the Tearmain barge.

They can see Tripper bound, gagged, and unconscious on the centre of the deck of the other barge.

Larret Army

As they ram the first barge, G slips and falls to the deck of her barge.

The Tearmain barge, though damaged, keeps up its momentum and pulls ahead again, with its crew pressing on hard.

The Black Swans' team are slow to recover but do get underway again.

Mi casts a *'Dispel Fatigue'* prayer on both G and Eren.

With two fresh crew members and two somewhat rested members, the Black Swans give chase again, slowly regaining the distance on the Tearmain barge.

They travel through the waterways between the trees in the murky waters of the Dead Swamp.

Eventually, catching up with the first barge, G has the Black Swans pull up beside the Tearmain barge. She tries using the grappling iron to hook the first barge.

Catching the barge, G attempts to tie off the two barges. Unfortunately, G slips and falls into the water.

As G was trying to connect with the Tearmain barge, the enemy Elfmal starts repeatedly stabbing Tripper around the head and chest with his shortsword. He leaves the other three crew to frantically oar their barge, but they are nearly exhausted.

G treads water while Mi, Jess, and Eren slow their barge and then after stopping they return to come back for her.

In G's attempt to grab for some support as she was falling into the swamp, she dropped her longsword into the water, thus losing her primary weapon. Gasping for breath in her frustration and anger, G tries to keep floating until the barge comes back for her.

Struggling to climb on board the barge after they return, G swears vehemently at the loss of her longsword.

Once the Black Swans are back together, and after a few minutes recovering, they give chase again, hoping to rescue Tripper.

Winey is in an uproar: bellowing, snorting, and thrashing back and forth on the deck of the barge.

Over half-an-hour later, the Black Swans pull up beside the Tearmain barge. There is blood everywhere on the Tearmain barge deck.

Frantically, G and Winey both jump over to the barge as the Black Swan's barge passes the Tearmain water vessel.

Mi and Jess quit rowing and cast prayers on the crew of the Tearmain barge.

Mi casts his '*Hold Person*' prayer on two humans, while Jess casts his '*Command*' orison, commanding another human to '*Sleep*'.

The Elfmal stops oaring their barge as his fellow crewmembers become immobile. The Tearmain barge goes into a coasting mode, gradually slowing down.

Eren, seeing this, starts guiding the Blacks Swans' barge to match the speed of the Tearmain barge.

An angry Winey goes into a frenzy, and he pushes one of the held humans overboard as the barge continues onward. The female who Winey pushes overboard sinks below the surface of the water.

Mi tries the '*Command*' orison on the elf to '*Sleep*', but the effort fails, and the elf continues to attack G.

The Tearmain elf viscously stabs at G, striking her in the head using his shortsword, causing a wound that slowly trickles blood.

Winey, in his anger, attempts to push another of the immobile humans overboard.

Armed with a dagger – a weapon that she has never trained with – G stabs at the elf in the chest, doing little damage.

The elf, in turn, tries again, stabbing at G's arm that holds her weapon, causing G to drop her dagger.

Trying to quickly attack again, the elf trips, and he drops his shortsword past G. The elf reaches for his spear, which lays near him on the barge deck.

Winey finally manages to push the second Tearmain oarsman off the gradually slowing barge. The woman, due to the weight of her armour, swiftly sinks below the surface.

G strikes out at the Elfmal by hitting him in the chest with her fist, doing little damage to him.

Stooping down, G picks up Tripper's dagger from her belt.

Winey pushes the sleeping Tearmain overboard as the barges are slowly coming to a stop.

The man sinks under the surface as his armour weighs him down.

The elf tries to thrust his spear into G's chest, but he only grazes her.

Angry now, G stabs the elf in the abdomen with Tripper's dagger, drawing a trickle of blood through his armour. As she moves for a better advantage, G slips and falls.

The elf takes full advantage of G's drop and drives his spear into her arm.

Winey is now in an attack frenzy and rushes the elf. Ripping at the elf's legs, Winey horrendously tears the elf's leg off at the thigh.

The elf drops to the barge deck and quickly bleeds out.

The three Tearmain who are overboard have all sunk below the surface of the water and are out of sight.

Eren has the two barges side-by-side, and all three Black Swans cross over to join G and Winey.

Jess confirms that Tripper is deceased; her head and neck have been punctured, and her chest is shattered.

At about the same moment, G and Jess spot one of the Tearmain who Winey pushed overboard surface.

The enemy looks around, and seeing that the two barges are occupied by the Black Swans, she quickly starts swimming away.

G cuts the rope to the second barge, and the four Black Swans start oaring after the woman who is swimming away from them.

With the barge gathering speed, it takes about ten minutes for them to catch up to her.

The woman stops, and after taking a deep breath, she dives under the surface of the water.

Larret Army

The barge has too much momentum to just stop, so it keeps moving forward. The Black Swans begin halting the barge.

All the while, Jess watches the area where the woman went under the water's surface.

As the three Black Swan's stop the barge, and then aim it toward the spot where the woman went below the water's surface, a third barge arrives and starts closing in on them.

The two barges meet at the swimmer's dive spot.

The third barge has two men on it.

We are concerned with this turn of events but don't interfere.

Her voice near breaking, G calls to them. "Hold there. Are you Tearmain, under General Penner?"

An older Jalmal calls back. "Yes. We are the hunters for the stronghold. Is there news?"

With a quick heft of the elf's spear, G is ready for action. "Stand down and surrender. General Penner has surrendered to the Larret Army. You will accompany us back to the stronghold and submit to the rules there."

The two men look at each other and whisper back and forth to each other, and they both nod.

The older Jalmal answers G. "With hopes of your lord's leniency, we agree to peacefully surrender ourselves and our barge with its cargo."

G looks their barge over and can see that it is loaded with animal carcasses. The two men have bows, spears, and other weapons. "Place all your weapons on this barge and be ready to lead back to the stronghold. We wait here for another ten minutes as we are watching for a swimmer."

Fifteen minutes pass and the swimmer is not observed in the area.

We swam with her under the surface. Then, we watch the Black Swans as the swimmer finds safety in a clump of isolated mangrove trees that are far from any safe true solid ground.

Frustrated, G looks at her friends. "We go back now and deal with this mess. There will be walking-dead here in years to come. But it couldn't be helped. We need to address the captured stronghold. Enda and Nela will need us."

This stirs our emotions, as we know about being lost and wish it upon no one.

Looking over at the third barge, G waves to the two lounging men. "Get moving. We go to the stronghold. We will be right behind you."

Larret Army

More than an hour-and-a-half later, nearly two hours after midday meal, the two barges pull up to the shore at Penner's stronghold.

There are five men-at-arms from Larret Army on the beach to greet them.

In a rough beaching of their barge, G gives her commands. "Derrek, go and get Enda and Nela; we require a meeting. Herris and Tem, take these two and put them with the other prisoners. Mina, get a group to help with Tripper; she is to be placed with our deceased. Quickly now, all five of you."

In hectic maneuvers, Jess starts tending to G's injuries by using his healing skills and then prayers to Lorn.

It is later in the midafternoon when they meet with Nela and Enda, who are sitting in General Penner's meeting hall with G, Eren, Mi, and Jess.

"We need to deal with this situation now. How many prisoners do we have?" asks G, in a deadly serious tone.

Nela answers G quickly. "We saved a captain, four lieutenants, seven sergeants, fifteen horsemen, and nine heavy footmen of Penner's army. On our side, sixty-one ranged survived and sixty-three men-at-arms. We lost just over forty of our people to their loss of around seventy."

Intrigued, Jess looks around the table, and then he speaks to the group. "Does anyone object to installing those who surrendered and swear allegiance to Lord Ramson into Larret Army?"

No nays are brought forth.

In her own endeavour to be efficient, Eren takes her turn. "Then I suggest that we put the cavalry under General Enda's command, and the heavy footmen under General Nela's command. And, yes, I said General. We are forming a proper army; we need a proper command form: generals, captains, lieutenants and sergeants. You two figure out the ranks below you. But that's my suggestion. Any nays?"

G looks around at each member of the meeting. Each one shakes their head in agreement.

Not getting any objections, G says, "Since there are no nays, the motion is carried."

With an air of authority, Mi brings up the next subject. "Then we have to broach the next subject – the dead. As noted, there are over one-hundred dead, including our friend Tripper. There are too many dead to do the Right of Passage individually. So, Jess and I will do a form of our own Military Battlefield Right of Passage – our style. This will take five days to perform correctly, and we can't be interrupted. Jess are you ready?"

Larret Army

In nervous tension, Jess nods. "Ready, for sure, as much as the dead and the gods are. While we are doing Right of Passage, I suggest G and Eren have a chat with General Penner to find out as much as possible about the Tearmain army plans."

As she realizes her new rank gives her a field command position in an army, Nela stands and salutes the gathered Larret villagers, who are now the military leaders. "I salute my superiors. As new general of the militia, I would like to go and tend to my troops and swear in the old Tearmain heavy footmen as a new company of Larret heavy footmen. Thank you for your faith in me. I will appoint my captains, lieutenants, and sergeants over the next two days."

Not to be outdone, Enda also stands, salutes each sitting member in the room, and clasps arms with everyone, including Nela. She says, "Thank you for your trust in me. We will protect the Web Shireward from this Tearmain army. That is what we will do, or die trying."

The two generals leave to tend to their new responsibilities for the upcoming days.

Satisfied, G looks at her remaining three friends. "WE will hold a private service for Tripper at gods-rise tomorrow, and then Eren and I will have a chat with General Penner. Be safe my friends, and let's keep the walking-dead to a minimum.

Already, there are going to be at the least three walking-dead. Let's not add to that."

We want to inform them that they only left two, but we refrain.

The four friends part ways to tend to their new duties.

Later in the evening, G, the Army Commanding General, needs to decide many things and plan the army's next actions for their future.

Eren needs to consider the Black Swan's own future and the safety of Larret Hamlet against the Tearmain army.

Mi and Jess have their work cut out for them until the evening of Autumn 16 Bear.

Before gods-set, G searches for Enda, finding her in the common square with the troops. Taking Enda aside privately, G says, "I want you to send five strong and quick warriors back to Larret with the message that we have defeated the General of Tearmain's local army. We are taking our Larret Army to Dartoln Village, along with the prisoners and their General, for Lord Ramson to determine their fate. Have the messengers ride horses and have them leave at gods-rise tomorrow."

In a crisp salute, Enda replies, "Yes, Commander G, it will be done."

Chapter
Eight

Penner's
Battle

Chapter Eight:

Penner's Battle

*A*utumn 12 *Bear*

Morning arrives, heralded by the trumpets of the military's morning roll call.

Morning chow is ready for the men and women of Larret Army – which is now a full army – consisting of fifteen-cavalry, a company of heavy footmen, two companies of slingers, two companies of bowmen, and six companies of men-at-arms. They are all organized, clean, armed, and armoured.

Larret Army

Each stronghold tower is manned with three archers and two men-at-arms. The army's tradesmen have added a groundside control for the drop-gates. At all times now, there are three slingers and three men-at-arms at each gate and at each gate control.

General Nela assigned one lieutenant for every two companies, as did General Enda. Then, after consulting the lieutenants, they chose their sergeants for each company's group of ten. Plus, they assigned an additional sergeant to assist each lieutenant. Enda chose an additional lieutenant and two sergeants to serve her directly. While Nela chose a lieutenant and three sergeants for her direct command. Then the Captains were selected for each pair of lieutenants and for the companies they lead. Thus, the formal Larret Army of the Web Shireward is formed, in the year of Bear, 1st Cycle, II Succession of King Dolan IV, under the Commanding General Reeve Gena of Larret Hamlet for Lord Commander Ramson, Earl of the Web Shireward.

As the last mourning note sounds from the trumpet, the four Black Swans stand together, ready to say goodbye to their deceased friend, Tripper.

Larret Army

The lead holy man, Mi, looks forlorn at Jess, as he says to his friend. "You go ahead. You do the service; she liked you better."

Jess performs a half-hour, mournful, long farewell service for Tripper, and then the pallbearers carefully add Tripper's corpse to the pier, which will burn with the rest of the one-hundred-and-seven dead.

Mourning her friend, G rapidly wipes her eyes dry, and then she coarsely clasps arms with Jess and Mi. Trying to calm herself and her friends, G says in a hoarse voice, "Thank you. She will rest fine. If we had someone who could raise the dead that would have been preferred."

Shaking his head, Mi, near tears himself, calms G. "I am sorry, but with the damages they did, a raise dead prayer wouldn't have worked, G … only a full resurrection will work now. Jess kept one of Tripper's fingers just in case we incur the favour of a cleric … or a mage able to do so. Burning her and doing last rights won't harm that process … we believe."

Feeling somewhat consoled, G nods solemnly, and then she replies with a heavy heart. "Then, I have business in the officer's hall now. Eren, let's go and deal with General Penner."

Larret Army

The two adventuring companions depart from the site of the dead, and they wander toward the officer's hall, walking in to see what comes from dealing with General Penner.

Quietly commanding, G sits with Eren at the rough-hewn table. They look across the table at their nervous captive, General Penner.

G taps the crude table idly as she ponders her line of questioning. She thinks deeply to herself, *'How do you legally question or interrogate a General of an enemy army? How do you deal with them, or treat them? Penner would have no qualms in using torture or murder. But this is the Web Shireward under the command of Lord Ramson, who I answer to. I am the Larret Army Commanding General, Full Commander, and Eren is Second in Command. Eren wants to cut Penner's tongue out, one little piece at a time, whether he talks or not.'* Silently, G questions whether there is some evilness in Eren.

"General Penner, we are taking you to our Lord Ramson, Earl of the Web Shireward. It is for Lord Ramson to determine your fate. But, we have questions for you first. If you answer us, then you might live to see the trip to Lord Ramson."

Penner shrugs and states in a matter-of-fact tone, "By your laws, you can not harm me, as I am a high-ranking officer of the opposing army. You must see to it that I make it alive, unharmed, to your superior."

353

Larret Army

With an evil smile, Eren says, "For all our superior knows, you were wounded in battle and died from bloodfires afterwards. So, don't get too comfortable, Penner. We know what you do to those you question. I'm not above the same tactics."

"Bluffs ... you're both too soft." Penner says, following this with a smile.

Bursting out in anger, G rapidly draws her dagger, grabs Penner's hand and slaps it on the table. Then, G drives the point of her dagger through his hand into the table. "Now that I have your attention, and I think you get my point that we're not playing here, you answer my questions. You can see that I don't make threats; I take action."

Chuckling sardonically, Eren reaches over and pulls free the dagger.

Penner reaches for his bleeding hand, realizing that the bone just below his middle finger is severed. His facial and body expression is a mixture of shock and pain.

Looking smug, Eren states matter-of-factly, "My turn next time, G. I owe him for Tripper."

In shocked pain, General Penner cradles his injured hand. He restrains himself from crying out.

Ready to move forward, G begins her questions. "You are leading a portion of Tearmain's Army, right?"

Slow and brief, Penner nods, answering, "Yes."

"You are the overlord for this region, correct?" asks Eren.

General Penner hesitates, and then he swallows and hesitates again. Finally, after blinking, he answers. "No. Grand-General Selanad is Overlord General for Eastern Kannoral. I'm assigned as his Second. I have the southern half of the east."

Slowly, G takes her backpack off the floor and pulls out parchment, a vial of ink, and two metal tipped quills, which she places in front of Eren. "Make notes for Lord Ramson, please." She continues. "General Penner, you are general for the south of the eastern half of Kannoral. Overlord General Selanad oversees the entire east. Who oversees the northern half?"

Rapidly, Penner turns away, and then looking back into G's eyes, locking stares with her, he answers in a icy voice. "General Istol control's the northeastern portion of Kannoral."

Ice cold as well, G keeps her eyes locked with Penner's eyes, and sarcastically she asks, "Who the seven hells is Tearmain?"

Hesitating, considering how to answer, Penner squints, furrowing his brow, and he says, "You don't know the god Tearmain? He is a powerful god who is bringing the humans of North Amara the blessings from his realm, from the east over the Web. You should learn the powers of Tearmain. You think that you are powerful, wise, and strong now. With blessing from Tearmain, you would be undefeatable."

With genuine confidence, G smiles at Penner, and then she responds, "We defeated you, didn't we? You lost."

With confidence, Penner smiles too, and then he says, "I'm still alive. I'm not defeated yet."

Wanting to move on, Eren taps the table to get attention. She says, "Tell me about Tearmain."

Thinking these are heathens, Penner shrugs and then flinches as he jolts his wounded hand. Penner tells them. "Tearmain is a god from a realm across the Web. He is the most powerful entity there. He rules the entire realm with wisdom and power, granting priests' blessings as required, and as he favours. He will do the same here, as well. He is gathering followers in Dendar and Mount Oryn. Tearmain is ousting the nobility and replacing them with Tearmain priests to rule by his wisdom of force. If you stop following a dead system of rulers, you can be one of the new ruling class ... or, you can perish when Istol and Selanad come to take up their seats in Dartoln."

Shocked and frustrated, G and Eren gasp and look at each other.

Turning back to Penner, G rapidly asks, "When are they taking Dartoln?"

Seeing the loss of confidence in the two, Penner laughs, and he replies, "You can't stop them. Selanad is a Shestan god, and Istol is a remarkable warrior. Istol will ask for Ramson's surrender on Autumn 25th. Grand-general Selanad will follow Istol on Autumn 40 … when the powers align to bring Tearmain to Mount Oryn from his plane of existence. You don't stand a chance of resisting."

In a flash, G reaches out and grabs Penner's uninjured hand. Almost before G has the hand on the table, Eren drives the point of G's dagger into Penner's hand, shattering the bones of two fingers. Pulling the dagger free, Eren gives the dagger back to G. "Maybe bloodfires will be too easy. I so want to end his smug mug now."

Screeching in great pain, Penner lets out an inhuman howl.

Frowning inhumanly, G curtly answers Eren, saying, "Eren, let's go to the other room."

The two enter the second office as Penner nurses his two wounded hands with their broken bones. As G and Eren exit the room, two men-at-arms come to watch over Penner.

In the next office, Eren starts by saying, "We have to get the army to Dartoln quickly – as fast as possible. Hopefully, we can get the upper hand with the surprise of Istol and Selanad."

Larret Army

Truly angry now, G nods in frustration. Pacing the room, she eventually answers, "We can't discuss this with anyone. First, we need to let Mi and Jess finish their work. Then, we march the troops to Dartoln. The troops need to train as hard as possible for now. We must gather enough supplies for ten days gear for each member of the army. We need to tell Nela and Enda today."

We doubt the success of their hopes and plans.

Chapter Nine

Fight for Dartoln

Chapter Nine:

Fight for Dartoln

*A*utumn 15 Bear

The struggles with General Penner's small army and the horrendous loss of Tripper are still fresh in the minds of the Black Swans and us.

Upon waking this morning, there is the news that General Penner and three of his officers have escaped with the aid of some of their horsemen. The group escaped by fleeing on horseback to who knows where.

Larret Army

But from the interrogations, they learned that two armies are converging on Dartoln Village and Earl Ramson's manor. These armies are determined to take the Web Shireward away from Lord Ramson in the name of their god, Tearmain.

Of the two armies, there is the army of General Istol arriving from the southwest, and a second army of the Shestan demigod, General Selenad, coming from the northwest.

In desperate consideration with Eren, G has determined that the Black Swans need to warn Earl Ramson, and they need to move the Larret Army to his aide. So, the Larret Army and the Black Swans have been getting supplies ready for a forced march.

In desperation, G is hoping that the weather holds out for the quick march of her roughly four hundred troops.

The Black Swans have decided that they will recruit more troops through conscription during their march to Dartoln as well.

The information they gained from their interrogations of Penner and his officers indicate that one army, the smaller one, holds a thousand troops, while the more massive army of General Selenad runs with over two thousand warriors.

Larret Army

Autumn 16 Bear

The Larret army begins its long march from Penner's fortification. They are heading toward Dartoln Village to bolster Lord Ramson's forces and to warn him of the two large approaching armies.

There is little hope of Dartoln's success, but some loss in defeat is better than what waits for those surviving after Tearmain takes hold of the Web Shireward.

Autumn 19 Bear

It has been a forty-three-kilometre forced march, and it is evening mealtime when the Larret Army arrives in the south fields of Dartoln Village. The army moves to set up camp in the north of the commons of the village under the guidance of General Gena.

There are no signs or evidence of an opposing invading army.

We sigh, knowing that the Larret Army made it here in time to aid Ramson's village.

Larret Army

The Black Swans give orders to their army to set up defensive works for a semi-permanent position. This will be their standing point against the Tearmain forces.

Now exhausted, G and the rest of the Black Swans venture toward Lord Ramson's manor.

Arriving at the bustling manor, G briskly knocks on the door and waits patiently.

The young page, Willa, opens the door quickly. With excitement, the page motions them in and says, "Master Gena, quickly to the great hall. Lord Ramson is waiting, and he is furious."

Too tired to give a rebuttal, G leads the way into the great hall, taking a seat close to a fuming Ramson, who eyes the Black Swans from beneath thick brows. "What is the meaning of bringing an army to my village, Reeve G?" Loudly queries Ramson.

Offering a bow from her seat, G then answers him. "Please excuse the uninvited army. It is here for your defence, Lord Ramson. A god named Tearmain has aims on taking the Web Shireward away from you. He is sending two armies to do this. They are currently marching toward here. The smaller army numbers one-thousand, while the larger army numbers are two-thousand. How many forces do you have to stand against them? … fifty? … sixty?"

Lord Ramson hesitates and then answers as he settles somewhat. "Twenty-eight. I'll send riders tonight for my vassals to form up. Thank you, G. How many do you bring?"

With sidelong glances, she looks at her companions. G then says to Ramson. "We bring roughly five-hundred, of which most are battle-hardened against a general's forces. Included in the mix are some conscripts who we gathered on the way here. You might have two or three days to assemble a force to add to ours."

Lord Ramson shivers, but he asks, "Will both forces arrive together?"

Eren pipes in. "We don't know. But I doubt it. One is from the north, and one is from the south."

Slowly, G stands and motions to her companions. "We must prepare our force for the night. Lord Ramson, you have things to get ready. We can talk more tomorrow."

We are amazed at the command G has taken in life now, and she's only seventeen.

Larret Army

Autumn 24 Bear

It is near evening meal when a messenger arrives at G's tent. Saluting her, he waits for her to acknowledge him.

Looking over at the messenger, G asks, "What is it?"

The young Jalmal clears his throat, and then he says, "General, a scout has arrived and has informed us that the first army has been spotted. They are clear of the treeline on the south end of Dartoln fief."

Solemn, G nods asking, "How many?"

The messenger replies, "Roughly eight hundred. Half are on horseback, and the other half are archers on foot. They are setting up fortifications in the southwest now."

Quickly strapping on her sword, G stands. Donning her cloak, she says, "Tell the others to get the troops ready. We march on the Tearmain troops today while they are tired and working. I'm going to see Ramson."

The messenger smartly salutes and they both exit the tent, with G going to the manor house for an audience with Lord Ramson.

.....

Ramson's newly formed army of eight hundred, which he conscripted from his vassals in the last few days, march out to confront Tearmain's army of eight-hundred in the southwest fields.

Lord Ramson's army arrives at the encampment an hour before gods-set. Ramson arrays his two companies of medium horsemen on the outer wings of his light horsemen line. His archers are set in ranks with the heavy-footmen in front protecting them, and the one-hundred hobilar at the end are ready for their orders.

The Larret Army stands back, ready in reserve, waiting for their commands from Lord Ramson and the Black Swans to sweep into any weak area.

Tearmain's forces, for their part, have hastily created a defensive work of a ten-foot-wide by a five-foot-deep ditch with the dirt piled behind it and a palisade of sharpened wooden pikes forming a six-foot high wall on top of the dirt, in less than eight hours.

Archers are now lined up in front of the wall with ranks of both short-bow and light crossbow archers. The archers are formed into several fire teams.

Also, prepared for charging into battle, are medium cavalry and light horsemen lined up in front of the ditch with their lances at the ready.

Larret Army

The day-gods, Stonewire and Imvor, are dipping onto the western horizon.

The two armies wait.

The two day-gods are now below the tops of the trees behind the Tearmain's forces of General Istol, looking into the eyes of Ramson's army. Lord Ramson signals for his drummer to beat the staccato tune to signify the charge of the light horsemen.

Instantly, as the beat of the drums gives the signal, the men on horses charge forward from the centre of Lord Ramson's line – ninety riders in total. Then, the beat of the drum changes with Lord Ramson's next order, and a more orderly charge of the thirty-nine medium horsemen on the outer wings begins.

As Ramson's horsemen reach halfway across the field, Istol gives the order for her horsemen to charge and for her archers to fire upon the charging horsemen of Lord Ramson.

Over forty light-horsemen start out in a half-hearted light charge to give the archers free field of fire.

Istol's crossbowmen fire first, raining death upon the lead horsemen of Lord Ramson.

Then, Istol's shortbow archers fire; raining more death upon Lord Ramson's forces.

Finally, the two sets of light horsemen crash heavily into each other, dropping men from their horses and dropping horses from under men.

There is more crossbow fire from Istol's side, followed by more men on horses crashing into each other, and then more arrows.

The central field becomes a mass of chaos.

Lord Ramson's medium horsemen break through Istol's line first, followed by the light horsemen of Lord Ramson.

The illegitimate god's light horsemen are followed by medium horsemen of Istol's, and they break through Lord Ramson's horse line.

The horsemen from both armies are now charging the footmen of the opposing forces.

Two reserved companies of Lord Ramson's light horsemen, which were held back, now engage the light horsemen and medium horsemen of Istol's army.

Ramson has the heavy-footmen with the slingers and archers move forward to engage Istol's crossbow and archers.

Lord Ramson has several of his light-footmen move up to engage the horsemen that are now off their horses, and Ramson's other companies of light-footmen move up to take the two gates of the palisades.

Larret Army

Istol, seeing this, has her archers and crossbow focus on the footmen, trying to slow them down and thinning them out, while Ramson's approaching slingers and archers thin out Istol's ranged firepower.

After several minutes, Istol sees the futility in her men's fight, and she sounds the retreat to get her people inside the fortification. So far, they've kept Ramson's warriors out of the fortifications.

In just over half-an-hour, most of the fire squads are inside the walls, except one. And, all but two companies of Istol's horsemen are inside, when Istol orders the gates dropped.

Three companies of Ramson's hobilar are pushing hard for entry through the two heavy open wooden barricade-type gates.

In the struggle, one company of Ramson's hobilar, and one company of medium horsemen squeeze inside with Istol's forces before the gates swing down and shut.

A killing spree goes unabated on behalf of both sides for an hour or so.

Istol's forces fire steadily upon Ramson's troops that are outside the fortification, while the companies of hobilar from Ramson's army siege the two gates.

Larret Army

At the gates, after several minutes of both sides firing on each other, the two are thinning out, and the hobilar units force open both gates with great loss to their numbers.

Now, with the troops of Ramson able to enter inside, the companies hold formations, retaining enough cohesiveness to hold combat strength, fighting on.

Lord Ramson's hobilar and footmen pour into the fortification, engaging Istol's archers and crossbowmen, while Ramson's horsemen, both light and medium, follow in after the hobilar and engage Istol's horsemen.

This crowds the interior of the compound, but Istol orders the fire squads to keep firing at the companies who have entered, despite the collateral damage to their own troops.

In fifteen minutes, more than half of Ramson remaining forces are inside the compound, and less than half of Istol's original forces are standing alive and in combat condition. The battle rages on with archers and crossbowmen who, despite Istol's orders, drop their missile weapons forsaking them instead for melee weapons, thus engaging Ramson's forces head-on.

Soon, small isolated groups of battle rage on and companies become smaller.

Larret Army

First one, and then another of Istol's companies surrender, dropping their weapons and kneeling, having lost their heart for this battle.

Less than a quarter of Istol's troops are in any condition to fight, leaving only three companies still fighting.

Istol takes command of a company of crossbowmen that she had hidden. Escaping unseen, Istol and her company go through a break in the back wall of the fortification and emerge into the woods of the Shireward.

We watch her sneak away cowardly with the protection of twenty crossbowmen.

The last three companies of Istol's army realize they are defeated, and they lay down their weapons, asking surrender.

Most of Istol's company's leaders are dead or missing; their troop's morale is lost.

With the battle over, Lord Ramson has the warriors and camp followers of Istol's army organized and then moved into a concentration camp near Dartoln.

Lord Ramson has two companies of his footmen and one company of slingers in charge of guarding the 125 surviving Istol troops.

Larret Army

The Shireward Lord has only lost 231 of his own troops, plus a large number of horses which he is more than able to replace with Istol's captured horses.

With the battle over, Lord Ramson leaves the Istol troops to stew in captured tents in their small concentration camp confinement. He takes the three surviving Tearmain sergeants and the one company lieutenant to the Black Swans for interrogation.

Relieved to have survived this battle, Lord Ramson leaves the Istol troops with the option that in the morning, they can hire on with Ramson's troops – with pay, or they can spend the upcoming battle in the internment concentration camp and hope that Tearmain wins. Because, if the Tearmain army that is coming loses, those in the internment centre will be tried for treason. In the end, those who fight along with Ramson will be treated as any proper soldier, with no hard feelings.

That night, the Black Swans take the four officers aside to the Black Swan's Larret army camp. In the darkness of night, as Ramson's villagers loot and pillage the battlefield, the Blacks Swans deal with the officers of Istol's army.

…..

As G sighs, she considers the man before her. She says, "Okay, Lieutenant Bertal, you are telling me that Istol wasn't among any of the living, wounded, or dead bodies that we showed you after the battle? And you state with absolute certainty that you would recognize your General Istol, even by lantern light. And you are saying she is definitely not here?"

"Absolutely, General G, she is not here, and neither is an entire company of my crossbow archers." He says with firm conviction.

Eren chuckles, and then she says, "Your general is a coward and ran from battle, leaving you to answer for the deeds of the army. How do you feel about that? Personally, if my general fled the battlefield leaving me holding the leadership banner, I'd be furious. Especially if I didn't get to make the command decisions. And you say the tall Jalmal you called Argos was second in command? He is the dead fellow with the four arrow wounds?"

Again, Bertal answers firmly. "Yes, Argos was her second. He died in the retreat going inside. I am damn furious, as I know I will go to trial to answer for decisions that I didn't make, for an army that I was forced into by conscription … they forced me off my farm two years ago. I haven't seen my life-companion or three children in two years. Istol told me directly that if I won this for her, I could go home and see them … fat cow's chance of that now."

372

G moves to stand in front of Bertal, and she says, "Lord Ramson needs experienced officers. If you want to be responsible for your decisions, join Lord Ramson, and lead your troops in your name. I can't make any promises as to the outcome in this. If we win, and I live, and you live, then you have my word that I'll put my word in for you to go find your family. I hope they are still alive, and that you can find them. But don't hold your breath for that, Bertal. We've seen the Tearmain realm they've claimed, and not many families still live intact. There is a lot of carnage and murder going on. If you want to promote Tearmain and allow the carnage and murder to continue, then deny me. If you want to stop its spread, join me. That is all I can offer you. No promises. No flowers, nothing but pay if we win, and your freedom to go find your family, hoping they are still alive. Can I have your oath?"

Bertal sits looking stern at G. His eyes betray his anger. G wonders who the anger is directed at.

We see the frustration and confusion in his spirit and mind.

Slowly, Bertal extends his arm. "Let me lead my troops against the vermin who took me from my family. If we can win, we'll do it together. If you leave the battlefield before we win, I'll hunt you down myself."

Larret Army

In firm determination, G extends her arm to clasp as she smiles. She then says, "That goes both ways, Lieutenant Bertal of Lord Ramson's First Crossbow Division. Now tell me about Istol, and what you know of General Selenad."

Releasing the warrior's firm clasp, Bertal answers, "I thought Istol was a sound, strong leader with strong plans. I didn't know how much of a coward she is. Obviously, she already had plans for if things went bad – she took a company of crossbowmen and disappeared that easily. Selenad, I've never heard of."

. . . . .

As they are talking with Sergeant Chad, G is elated that they finally found someone who has heard of Selenad. The other two sergeants knew nothing of Selenad and very little about Istol. Both sergeants had been conscripted into the army of Istol by recruitment teams and were forced to serve with promises of freedom when Tearmain's army secured the Web Shireward. Both turned over to the service of Lord Ramson easily; ready to chase down Tearmain's ilk from now until the Seven Hells open up.

Looking at her notes in the rough Jal script that she is learning to scribe, G rereads the notes.

"So, Selenad isn't human? Selenad is a male Shestan demigod who has come to Kannoral to serve this god Tearmain and to rule Kannoral for Tearmain? … are you serious? Or are you pulling my legging to see what will roll out?" asks G.

Chad nods eagerly. The sixteen-year-old had been forced to serve Istol two seasons ago. He had been taken from his apprenticeship as a litigant in Yenal Village, where he lived down south. Istol killed Chad's master and told Chad that he would be a new lawmaker when he won the war in the Web Shireward with Istol. "Seriously, it's all Istol would talk about at her Tearmain services, which I attended in the evenings. She insisted that if I wanted to be a litigant in the new realm, I should attend the services to Tearmain. They were scary, and she was crazy. Lots of chickens and dogs were killed. There were even human sacrifices. Even babies were sacrificed on several occasions. But I never actually participated. I sat in the back and watched the hokey-pokey take place. They're a mean lot. Tearmain's whole thing is cruelty. Selenad excels at cruelty, and so does Istol. You don't anger her; she doesn't forget or forgive. Selenad is all that; ten times worse. They are kittens compared to Tearmain though. Avoid angering him."

G and Eren look at each other, stunned, but grateful that the man is providing them with a gold mine of information.

Clearing his throat, Jess asks, "Do you think you can cross any of them?"

Without hesitation, Chad answers, "No way! I won't cross them."

G asks, "Will you serve with us?"

Chad turns paler than fresh snow, and he replies, "Not in your lifetime. I'd go to the Seven Hells first – voluntarily."

G asks a stronger question. "Do you know how big Selenad's army is?"

Chad nods. "In the last report Istol received, she said Selenad's forces number over two-thousand. She said they would arrive here on the thirty-eighth."

"Thank you, Chad. We will have to honour your decision, allowing you to go voluntarily to the Seven Hells. You will be interned until this is over and then tried for treason and punished accordingly," says G.

"So be it, I accept that fate," says Chad solemnly.

We admire his fear and conviction when faced with the choices set before him. But we are sad at the loss of such a promising person.

. . . ..

Slamming the table, G addresses Ramson again, saying, "We have to fortify and fight a defensive fight against Selenad.

Larret Army

He has the numbers over us and probably has more seasoned troops. But they will be tired from their march. We can harry them initially to weaken them. But we should not over expose ourselves. We have to keep strong and defend ourselves within a fortified position, as tightly as possible. But not so tight that they can overwhelm us. That is our thoughts on this, Lord Ramson. Their leader is supposed to be some kind of a demigod, so we need to spread out in two or three camps so he can't focus all his effort in one spot. We'll take our Larret troops in one camp. We have about three hundred left. Divide your troops into two camps of about roughly equal size, one-hundred metres apart so we can support each other with missile fire, but not so close as to be an easy focus for a concentrated attack."

Ramson thinks about this a moment. Then he answers, "We'll set you up to the north of the manor house and use the manor house as the main anchor fortification. The third fortification will be south of the manor house. We'll place them in a triangle with one-hundred-fifty feet between the walls. Also, we dig canals around each, and we dig another deeper bigger canal around the whole works from the river from the north and around back the river on the south. We can dam the canal anywhere along it to create a water-wall that will flood the ground and sop the area. How long do we have to do all of this?"

Eren answers, "If the information is right, we have about thirteen days at best. You have the villagers and troops to put to work. Start the canal's north end and have three teams on fortifications. We'll get our troops building and digging for the Larret structures."

"We're agreed then. Let's get the two engineers working on setting this up, while the masons, carpenters, foresters, and foremen get work teams set up," says Ramson, now resigned to destroying his village and the home he's lived in for his entire life – the birthplace for him and Gena.

Chapter Ten

Death of a Hero

Chapter Ten:

Death of a Hero

Autumn 40 Bear

Selenad stands in front of his troops outside of Dartoln village, surveying his target. It looks easy. He outnumbers them three to two if his scouts are right. These are yokel farmers of no real martial skills. The two day-gods will set in an hour.

He looks back at his Shestan scout. "You're sure? They're hiding behind wooden walls and water-filled ditches, cowering like females and pups?"

Larret Army

"Yes, master," says the bold scout, his scars attesting to his bravery in hunting and combat.

"Okay, get me the dog-men and the humans. We'll send them up first," says Selenad, not worried about testing the strength of the resolve of these humans and their leaders on his human forces and his few gnolls.

The human light-horsemen soon cross the open causeway first, unchallenged, followed by the two companies of heavy footmen, and then the two companies of the slower heavy gnolls.

As the light-horsemen rapidly approach the entry to Dartoln keep, they are rained upon by scores of crossbow quarrels and war arrows. Thus, savagely killing all the horsemen.

Undaunted, the two companies of heavy footmen press forward. Some actually entering the keep's courtyard before dying from the ranged fire.

The first company of gnolls actually make it into the keep's compound to engage Ramson's light footmen, but they fail to cause any fatalities before perishing under the blows from Ramson's footmen.

The second company of gnolls turn and run away before entering the range of fire from bows or crossbows, returning to the outside of the defensive works of Dartoln.

Larret Army

Ramson has one company of his light footmen roundup the enemy's surviving horses to use later, even as food if need be. They are also to remove the dead enemy, laying them in piles at the causeway's entry as a warning. The footmen strip all treasures and useful items from the dead bodies and kill any enemy still breathing. They are not taking any prisoners, especially not the wounded.

Selenad immediately has the scout killed who gave him the incorrect information.

Selenad begins setting up four distinct siege camps around the Dartoln settlement, as this is going to be a long and protracted siege, and it will take some planning.

…..

Sitting back, G turns to Eren. "So, we're sure that they split into four camps around us, and they are making some semi-permanent fortified structures?"

Eren frowns, creasing her forehead and pursing her lips. She squints slightly. "I said so – right! So, they attacked the keep with a light force and almost lost their entire attack force while we lost no one. We gained a few horses which Ramson's keep can butcher for food supplies if need be. It's a siege, G."

Jess peers out the windows of the fortification into the darkness of night. Looking at the fires in the distance, he says,

Larret Army

"There must be two-thousand of them out there, to our one-thousand. They have giants, gnolls, goblins, and scraggs, too. We are lost without the help of the gods. Plus, they say that they have the direct help of two gods. We need the aid of at least three gods, and our priests can only petition two. I'll pray tonight and so will the others. Let's hope we're heard, and we are answered."

Eren laughs. "Fat chance of that, but I'll hope, too."

Calm, G looks around. "I'll keep training and organize troops, as that's actually how we're going to survive this. Gods, if they exist, are laughing at us and won't help one bit. It's all up to us to win this. We have to be smarter and tougher than those creatures, and hope they don't have reinforcements arriving."

…..

Selenad looks at his lines of troops – 2,097 strong. His troop lines are ready. His giants have their boulder sacks loaded, and the scraggs and goblin-flamers are prepared. But best of all – his pride of Shestan – are his Shestan warriors. He exhausted his entire human resources yesterday on the test raid. He can smell their green putrid rotting bodies from here. The gods are very friendly, breathing east and blowing the stench from the jumbled piles eastward into the human fortifications. Even still, Selenad can smell the death from here, at the front and centre of his troops, to the west of the fortifications.

He turns to his mountain giant lieutenant, and Selenad nods.

The giant blows a single blast from his giant ram's horn.

Eight more mountain giants and two hill giants walk up closer to the moat that surrounds the human's defences, to points closer to the fortification buildings, yet keeping out of easy range of any bowmen.

Giants, being as smart as the average man, know they are susceptible to arrows from bow fire. But they also know that they throw their boulders much farther than archers can fire. So, being at least six-hundred-feet away, the giants, with boulders in hand, are ready, waiting for their next signal. Each giant has an arsenal of five twenty-pound boulders.

Selenad reviews the fortifications, and he can see the observers scurrying about on the structures' tops. He nods once more to the giant, Lieutenant Tron.

The lieutenant blows his horn, two brief notes.

It is now ten minutes after Stonewire and Imvor have risen over the eastern horizon of the Web, and each of the ten forward giants begins hurling their boulders. They each throw all five of their boulders. Then the giants casually return to their place in the line of troops at a thousand feet from the closest point to the moat.

The ten giants reload their sacks with five more large twenty-pound boulders from their own personal piles of seventy boulders each.

…..

G looks out through the breach in the fortification wall. There are huge rents in the timbers, with one gaping hole. The interior is exposed out to the sphere and the Shes army.

G turns to the workers and tells the village foreman. "Repair these the best you can; they'll be back with more. The other two keeps took bombardments as well. We had one breach, but when we signalled Ramson, he signalled back that he has four breaches. Zanday signalled he has two, with a result of several deaths. We were the lucky ones with one breach and no injuries. If we don't fix these, we may not be so lucky next time. Use whatever material you can find."

…..

With a broad smile, Selenad watches the humans scurry to repair the damage from a few meagre boulders hurled by his giants. He'll repeat it again tonight before gods-set. Thinking to himself, *Let them waste their time. Soon they will be out of resources for repairing my bombardment assault, and then we will be starving them.*

384

Larret Army

When they start fighting each other, and when their defences are wrecked,
we'll move my goblin flamers in on their wooden defences at night. Two
bombardments a day – one each morning and night, for five days – that will
do the trick.'

A show of forces each time will rattle the Dartoln people
into a state of anxiety. We have time; Tearmain assured him a
place on the council if he showed patience.

Autumn 42 Bear

The evening is nearing as the fourth round of
bombardments rain in from Selenad's giants. The
bombardments are taking a toll on the fortifications and on the
spirits of the defenders.

Already today, the repair crews are only haphazardly doing
their work, and these boulders are proving that.

Exasperated, G looks at Eren and utters, "It's been two
days now of bombardments, with their forces lined up with
drummers beating a death knell each time. We must take out
their leadership. That's all that will resolve this in our favour. We
head in tonight, under cover of darkness. Agreed?"

Three other humans and a boar signal that they agree.

. . ...

Larret Army

Later, during the dark of night, they make sure that no attackers are watching as they slip over the edge of the moat. The attackers appear overconfident, feeling sure that the defenders won't risk leaving their fortification.

The Black Swan use the cover of a ruined building to climb out of the moat. The five of them watch the enemy across the thousand feet of no man's land.

G turns to Eren, and she says, "You're prepared? You can do this?"

Confident, Eren nods. "Just keep touching me, and we'll be fine. You won't see shit until I dispel the fog. I'll pace off nine-hundred-fifty-feet, headed for that pile of tree debris. Let's hope I'm accurate ... or we're done for. Okay? Here goes."

Eren swallows hard, knowing the price they'll pay if they're suspected or spotted. It is the dark of night, and they're walking into the enemy camp as a group, hopefully into an obscure, less populated area. So much can go wrong. She must count three hundred and eighty paces, as she walks in a straight line, hopefully in the right direction.

Standing up, moving to line herself up, Eren firmly whispers, "I'm ready." She takes a deep breath to calm herself, and then she casts the fog cloud. Waiting until she is sure all three of the others are holding onto her, Eren then starts walking. She counts each pace, focusing on moving the cloud along with them, and listening for any alarm they might set off.

'... *Three-hundred-eighty.*' Eren counts mentally. She stops and swallows.

Her friends let go, and Eren hears weapons being drawn. Eren thinks, *'We're damned if I'm wrong.'*

She quickly dispels the cloud, silently preparing to cast her second cloud if necessary.

They cringe in fear and despair, frightened, finding that they are eighty feet from the closest wood debris pile. Quietly, the group rushes forward with hopes of not being discovered.

All five make it to the wood debris without setting off any alarms.

Giving a slim smile in the darkness, G and the others are now protected by a tall pile of tree trunks stacked haphazardly – these are the only things between them and the enemy army. They have heavy sphere cover, and the gods are breathing eastward, back towards the Swan's own people, which is helpful. They'll use the enemy's campfires and torches to help them see as they move around.

While trying to observe the enemy each day, G didn't see even one human. So, she knows they'll stick out if they're seen.

They have rubbed themselves down with bacon grease to mask their scent. Hopefully, this doesn't give them away.

Looking around the edges of the debris pile, Eren and G try to observe a route to the sizeable black-hide command tent that is nearby. They need a route that won't get them slaughtered. But the span between them and their destination is filled with Shestan warriors and two giants. In fact, all around the tent are wandering Shestan.

Ducking back around to their side of the woodpile to talk, G looks at each of the others, and then settles on Eren. Speaking softly and quietly, she says, "Unwilling guide, can you use your fog cloud again? Then, you all follow me? Are you all willing to follow me through all those Shes and giants to our assumed inevitable deaths?"

There is about a minute of silence. It's Winey who breaks the silence as he nudges Eren's arm with his snout and snorts twice – his 'yes'.

Jess stifles a laugh, and he says, "Yes."

Mi places his hand on G's shoulder and says, "We're here, may as well go knocking."

Eren sighs. "Just don't trip us up. We lost Tripper because of that. In fact, I say let's follow the pig. He can smell the way in, where we can't see."

Winey snorts twice for another yes.

All the others raise their eyebrows in question.

Then G answers for them all. "Okay, Winey, get us in the big black tent."

Winey snorts twice, again answering the group.

Looking apologetically at each other, they all sigh. With all eyes turning to Eren the Unwilling, in the shadows of darkness, she merely smiles and casts another of her fog cloud, perhaps her last.

Everyone in the group makes contact with Winey, and they all stand to follow the boar as quietly as the practised adventurers can.

Winey leads them on a winding path until they enter total darkness, and then Winey stops.

Eren dispels her fog cloud, and they find themselves standing inside an opulent field tent. Sitting on a large carved oak seat is an extremely large male Shestan who is watching them. Laying on his lap is a shining glowing longsword with a jewelled hilt. On either side of this Shesmal, stands an equally menacing Shesmal.

The fearsome appearing Shesmal stands and takes a menacing step forward. "Good evening, you've arrived to surrender … how nice of you. Who are you?" growls the Shesmal in a guttural Jalnoric.

Eren immediately casts a summon swarm, bringing the swarm of insects into focus in front of her and around the Shesmal. Eren looks confused as the flying insects start to swarm, and then disperse.

The Shesmal and his two companions laugh heartily, as if they are settling in for entertainment.

Winey and G take defensive positions in front of Eren, Jess, and Mi.

The Shesmal quietly informs them. "I am known as Selanad. You will submit to me, have no doubt about that. Your magic does not work on me. Nor can you fight me. You can try, and you will fail, as your puny army will fail. Give up and surrender, and I will go easier on your people. I will not bombard them tomorrow if you surrender now."

G and Winey charge simultaneously, as Mi and Jess attack the side guards.

With this distraction, Eren casts her light prayer into the eyes of Selanad, succeeding in blinding Selanad.

Mi's prayer binds his intended Shesmal solidly in position to the right of the seat.

Larret Army

While Jess *'Commands'* his Shesmal, on the left of the chair, to *'Sleep'*, causing the male Shestan to slump to the ground in slumber.

Winey wildly slashes at Selanad's leg, catching the Shesmal as G's longsword tears at the cloth of Selanad's chest garments.

Selenad swings his glowing longsword, opening up Winey's foreleg, followed by Winey tearing again at Selanad's leg.

Selanad immediately strikes Winey's abdomen with the longsword, knocking Winey off his feet. As Winey is regaining his footing, Selanad drives the longsword into Winey's knee, shattering it.

Selanad follows through with a slash to Winey's rear leg.

Eren thrusts at Selanad's leg with her quarterstaff, grazing it.

Mi casts *'hold person'* directly upon Selanad, and yet the Shesmal keeps attacking Winey, slicing cleanly through Winey's foreleg, as Winey is tearing off Selanad's leg.

This messy combination of movements results in gushing blood from both.

G follows up by severing Selanad's arm, removing Selanad from battle.

The Shestan hero drops to the ground twitching and growling, blinking from the blinding lights in his eyes.

G slices open Selenad's chest with a final swing of her longsword, killing the creature, finally.

Picking up the glowing longsword, G heads to the Shesmal who has been commanded to sleep and is now trying groggily to stand.

Jess thrusts at the rising Shesmal with his quarterstaff, trying to incapacitate the creature, but Jess misses.

The Shesmal is standing when Mi casts another command prayer saying forcefully, *"Stop."*

With a flurry of motion, Jess hurries over to Winey, touching the prone boar's leg. The priest prays quickly, casting the strongest healing he can muster.

The profuse bleeding slows and then stops. Whether the prayer stopped the bleeding or the pig ran out of blood is hard to tell.

Then, Winey snorts and nudges Jess.

Jess breathes again and begins praying over the boar again, holding the severed leg back in its proper place.

Determined to finish this battle, G slashes open the abdomen of the Shesmal who has been commanded to stop.

The creature starts to react, as Eren misses with a strike from her quarterstaff.

"I surrender!" calls the Shesmal.

Larret Army

G moves to take the surrender. "Hand over your weapons, all of them, and kneel before us, confirming we are your superiors and have defeated you."

The Shesmal lifts his longsword in defiance. Growling, he says, "I will never give up my weapons. You may take my surrender, but not my weapons."

Jess continues to heal Winey, while G swings at the offending defiant Shes, missing only slightly as a warning.

Eren, though, is tired and not wanting to play games. She strikes outward with her quarterstaff, driving it into the creature's chest, killing him.

The creature falls to the ground, followed by G using the glowing longsword to remove his head. She then removes the head of their leader, Selenad.

Moving to the third Shesmal, G debates … life or death? Looking into his eyes, she sees his animosity. His burning black hatred is so deep that there will be no dealing with him. With one quick swing of the new longsword, his head falls from his body.

G strings the three heads together by tying their long hair in a knot. Then she looks at the other Black Swans, wondering what will have the most impact.

Finally, deciding what will have the highest influence, she says, "Just Eren and I will go out. I'll carry all three heads and claim to be the new leader."

The others agree.

With Eren to her left, G boldly walks out the front flap of the tent. Holding the three heads high for all to see by the light of the fires nearby, she shouts, "I am god. You will follow me, or you too will die."

There is a commotion of hurried soldiers taking up arms, as giants, Shes warriors, as well as scraggs and goblins, hurry to react.

G points to Tron, the mountain giant who she had been observing is Selanad's lieutenant. "You are now the army's leader. Do you understand me?"

Hesitantly, Tron walks forward, shaking the camp with his heavy footsteps. He kneels on one knee, and in rough Jal, he answers, "I understand."

G hands him the three heads. "Good, carry these back to Shestan while leading this entire army. You and all of Shestan are never to send an army to this Dominnion ever again, or your next leaders will die as well. Understood? Your army is to leave at first light. Do not come back, or you will be next to die."

Tron bows his head and then salutes. "Understood, human god. We will leave at first light, taking these heads back with us."

Autumn 43 Bear

G and the rest of the Black Swans stand on top of the Dartoln Keep with Lord Ramson.

Winey, in the infirmary, is going to live. With one missing leg and one shattered knee, Winey won't be walking well or fighting much anymore.

Holding the magical longsword, G examines it with its one inscription etched into the blade: a single crescent shape. The blade glows with a dim blue, even in the light of the day-gods.

Keeping his word, Tron, at half-an-hour after gods-rise, has the Shestan army marching northwest, away from Dartoln where their three heroes were defeated by four humans and a boar. So, with their new leadership, as directed by the victors, the Shestan army is leaving.

The god Tearmain is not going to be happy.

For now, the Web and the Web Shireward are still governed and lead by their original leader. Lord Ramson is rebuilding and planning on constructing a fortified stone-keep structure closer to the river. Hopefully, it'll be ready for the next army attack. Also, Lord Ramson is garrisoning a large standing army in the old and new fortifications.

Autumn 56 Bear

"Lord Ramson, I am Lieutenant Rosmos of the King's Ranger scouts. We came as soon as we could. The King sends word: the upstart god Tearmain was killed by the group Fryers Chozen on Autumn 40 Bear. It seems you survived an attack by his minion army. Do you need the support of King Dolan?" says the twenty-five-year-old Jalmal.

Ramson looks at G, who is sitting next to him at the table. "What do you think, General Gena?"

G laughs. "I think that after defeating a Shes god and his Shes warrior and giant army, we might be offering the King our aid – not asking for his aid. Lord Ramson, do you agree?"

"I do, Gena … I do agree." Turning to Rosmos, Ramson answers. "Some coins to pay my army and for the new fortifications would be appreciated. But we have our own manpower and local resources … does the King need aid?"

Rosmos shakes his head and replies, "No, but the King will send coins as a tribute for your continued support. Also, he

Larret Army

warns that followers of Tearmain are still trying to overthrow the Dominnion and that they still have control of Dendar. Perhaps send aid to retake Dendar?"

G motions for attention. "Tell us about this Tearmain."

Rosmos shrugs. "From what we have gathered, Tearmain was a demigod from another realm who overstepped his power by coming to North Amara and attempting to overthrow the Dominnion. He began as a hero on another continent. He gained worshippers, and then he became king, soon ruling many nations. Then, he rose to godhood, eventually ruling his own plane. But his greed for control and power outgrew him. Fryers Chozen went to his realm, and it was there that Tearmain was slain. The ruling gods banished his soul to the Seven Hells for one-thousand human generations. He won't be bothering us anytime soon. It's his followers here that are now the issue."

G looks at Winey, Eren, Jess, and Mi, and they all smile.

This ends the first book of the '*Lost Souls*,' series: '*Larret Army: Rising Souls.*'

May the words stay with you!

Larret Army

Inevitable Unicorn Press

Rusty's Den

Box 3323

High Prairie, Alberta

T0G 1E0

780-523-5835

cs@inupress.ca

Knowing that you enjoy reading, check out the various serial series published by
Inevitable Unicorn Press
The link to follow is www.inupress.ca
Some of our short-story serial series are
Bard & Dragoman, Dragoman Bloodgrue, **Eren's Challenge,**

Lanis, Markus, **and Star Grean.**

Our fantasy, sci-fi/fantasy, and science fiction serial series of short stories are a quick 10 to 20 minutes read, perfect for your coffee break, lunch, or before bed.
Each set of three episodes is only $0.99, less than the cost of a magazine or the price of a newspaper.

i

Larret Army

The author is

Kenneth Shumaker,

a High Prairie, Alberta, Canada local

on www.inupress.ca
or www.kennethshumaker.ca websites

Kenneth is the lead moderator for the local High Prairie writer's
critique group:

Fellowship of the Scribblers

Larret Army

The Author: Kenneth Shumaker

Kenneth is a writer who also builds, maintains, and repairs computers when he is not developing and managing blogs and web pages. Kenneth tends towards writing in the fantasy, sci-fi/fantasy, or science fiction genres, and he writes non-fiction. In 1982, Kenneth won an award as *'Best New Poet of the Year'* from the American Poetry Society. Kenneth is the lead moderator and the administrator of the local High Prairie writing group, Fellowship of the Scribblers.

Currently, Kenneth is working on a new fantasy novel titled 'Dendar', due to launch in October 2019. He can usually be found at his computer desk writing or working on web development.

Larret Army

Kenneth Shumaker's contact information:

Websites:

www.inupress.ca or
www.kennethshumaker.ca

E-mail address:

inupress@inupress.ca

Postal address:

Kenneth Shumaker
Rusty's Den
P.O. Box 3323
High Prairie, Alberta, Canada
T0G 1E0